Praise for Book

ASHES

"Ashes is a soul-stirring story of sin and redemption, of temptations of the flesh and self-recrimination—both an artful interrogation of clerical sex abuse and a pitch-perfect portrayal of a morally challenged priest that recalls for me the "whiskey priest" in Graham Greene's The Power and the Glory. Masterfully written, it's all the more haunting for the way Anthony Mancini brings the ancient landscape of Sicily to life, with all its demons and angels."
— *Paul Moses, author of The Saint and the Sultan: The Crusades, Islam and Francis of Assisi's Mission of Peace.*

MÉNEGE

"A fast moving, double-cross thriller...absorbing, humorous and raunchy novel." —*Publishers Weekly*

"Deucedly clever" — *Los Angeles Times*

"Entertaining and original" —*Atlanta Journal Constitution*

MIRACLE OF PELHAM BAY PARK

"This book has a profundity far beyond its length."
—*Madeleine L'Engle*

"...martyrdom of a vulnerable child at the hands of a swarm of (mainly clerical) tormentors." —*Kirkus Reviews*

THE GODMOTHER

"Godmother is authentic and fascinating" —*Nicholas Pileggi*

"Mancini's depictions of Italian peasant and immigrant life ring true." —*Publishers Weekly*

TALONS

"...No disappointments! All stops pulled out on schedule."
—*Kirkus Reviews*

"A gripping tale...Exciting and suspenseful...Talons will grab you and hold you to the very end."—*Associated Press*

"A fantastic yarn...original and fun...difficult to put down."
—*Beaumont Express*

ASHES

A Novel

by

Anthony Mancini

Also by Anthony Mancini

Menage
The Miracle of Pelham Bay Park
Talons
Godmother
The Yellow Gardenia
Minnie Santangelo's Mortal Sin
Minnie Santangelo & the Evil Eye

ANTHONY MANCINI

ASHES

Tolmitch Press
New York

ASHES

FIRST EDITION

Published by Tolmitch Press
New York
http://www.tolmitchebooks.com

Trade Paperback ISBN: 978-1-63760-525-7
EBook: 978-1-63760-526-4

Printed in the United States of America

Book jacket designed by Gail Shube

Tolmitch Press
New York

Ashes to ashes, dust to dust

—Book of Common Prayer

PART ONE — EROS

ONE

Anton Weiss made the sign of the cross with one hand and battened down his ancient black felt fedora with the other as he and his fellow passengers were jostled by the corkscrew turns the cranky old Fiat made on the Via Pirandello. The religious gesture had been inspired by the sight of the fire-god Etna belching tongues of flame and gusts of steam into the garishly blue Sicilian sky. Well, the old priest mused, he hardly had expected such a pyrotechnic reception to the town of Taormina, looming above as a wonderland nestled upon a spur at the foot of Mount Taurus. But he appreciated the spectacle. Here he was, a native of the North, where the winter sun was a gray ghost, now drenched in the colorful palette of Sicily. Though the worldly clergyman had lived long in Italy this was his first visit to Sicily. And the kaleidoscopic glories of Italia never failed to astonish him.

The green-colored automobile continued up the steep

road named for the absurdist Sicilian writer. It would lead, he hoped, to a bit of rest and pleasure in his waning years. How long would he stay? he wondered, sitting under the canvas canopy in the back seat of the car as it bumped along the cobbles. He was unsure, leaving the decision in the lap of the gods, a phrase that struck a discordant note in the mind of a monotheist. He could not help but wonder what panpipe had summoned him here.

But here he was.

The old priest was accompanied by the driver and four other passengers bound for hotels and *pensione* at the lofty destination. His companions included a young American couple, apparently on honeymoon, who clutched each other's hands in the front seat next to the driver and stole adoring glances at one another. What must it be like, the celibate mused, to feel this electric current of eroticism sparking back and forth between two persons who had already achieved physical union? He chose a life that barred him from this experience, but he was free to mull the question. Though it was nearly December the lovebirds took account of the region's famously salubrious climate to don summer clothing of straw and linen and were rewarded by a mild day. The driver, a sensible native, wore a cotton duster and a wool peaked cap.

He shared the back seat with two English gentlemen, apparently on holiday together, who bore signs of a faded youth entrenched in such battlements of age that no arsenal of oils, creams and coverups could defend. Yet this couple seemed to soldier on, clinging to their youthful style of dress — rakish

Panamas. florid ascots and saddle shoes — to the illusion of an eternal boyhood. In contrast, Father Weiss wore the Roman collar under a gray gabardine jacket, the picture of a colorless cleric, a common blackbird beside a pair of peacocks. Not that priests shunned gaudy costumes, heaven knew, but they usually confined them to the altar, not the street. Father Weiss was far from a homely man, with his full crop of white hair, piercing blue eyes and regal posture. His teeth had rotted over the years but this deficiency was amended by gleaming dentures, provided at Vatican expense. No, the priest had been handsome in his day, for all the good it did him. The man sitting closer to him, who seemed a touch younger than his companion, now and then flashed Father Weiss a small smile, causing the priest to blush. The smiles seemed to him less friendly than forward, more wicked than beneficent, as if the smiler had divined a secret known only to the two of them. Father Weiss glanced at his wristwatch, an idle act designed to change the mental subject.

The driver honked the horn and swerved to avoid hitting a suddenly looming herd of goats, their whiskered faces reminding the priest of a tapestry of leering satyrs. The tinkling of their bells faded as the animals turned the corner. The driver muttered a medley of oaths under his breath as the sound of the bells continued to fade. Italian curses, the priest noted, had musical quality in his ears, tripping off the tongue like a Brunelli scherzo. The driver turned from the road to seek the priest's eyes, seeking absolution for the vulgarities. The driver had drowsy brown eyes and tufts of gray hair peeking out from the sides of his cap.

The Fiat spat and sputtered over the hairpin turns on the jasmine-perfumed road. Certainly the colors of the clothing worn by the two dandified passengers were no match for the wildflowers adorning the roadside, dazzling the eye even in late autumn. The bright yellow carpets of cape sorrel, the great swaths of borage, blue as a Nordic night, the purple anemones and yellow marigolds combined to form a splendid spectacle for visitors jostling up the hairpin turns. The sight of the flowers did much to boost the Jesuit's mood. And orange groves flanked the road, adding fragrance to the experience as they drew closer to town.

Taormina! — the magnet for European and American dilettantes, debauchees, artistes and writers for over two centuries. What appeal did it exert on a retired clergyman born in the Gothic city of Lübeck, trained and ordained in the Society of Jesus? He had worked in several outposts of the universal church before landing a job at Vatican Radio in Rome, where he spent the war years. Taormina: What brought him in his retirement to this fleshpot? He wanted, among other things, to write his memoirs and this fertile cocoon of writers seemed a good place to try. Father Weiss had read more than the breviary and liturgical documents in his sixty-nine years of life. He gorged on books like a carpenter ant on a stand of wood. And in so doing he paid no attention to *the Index Librorum Prohibitorum* which, as most priests knew, was designed primarily to keep schoolchildren from pleasuring themselves and inquisitors gainfully employed. So he had learned that

Nietzsche had written *Thus Spake Zarathustra* here, Goethe had penned part of his *Italian Journey* and Laxness had completed his first novel, *The Great Weaver from Kashmir*. The ghosts of literary luminaries — Wilde, Lawrence, de Maupassant and a host of others — haunted the town's vertiginous stone streets. Lawrence, it was said, modeled Lady Chatterley after an English expatriate living here. And it is an open secret known to acolytes of the back-fence chatter of certain epicene salons that many writers and artists have ventured here seeking not the inspiration of the nine Muses but rather the example of Zeus and Ganymede. The sojourner's face reddened again as he recalled reading somewhere that one artful cynic had dubbed Taormina a "synonym for Sodom."

The car shuddered to a stop at the Porta Messina, northern entrance to the old town. Here the passengers had to disembark — autos could go no farther on the main street — and await the porters to haul their impedimenta to their destinations. In the blink of an eye a swarm of locals descended on the newcomers to offer their services. But the priest hauled his suitcase to the table of a nearby sidewalk cafe to await the arrival of the sacristan of the Church of *Sant'Antonio* to escort him to his lodgings. Meanwhile he ordered in his fluent Italian a *doppio* and *crostini* and a copy of the *Giornale di Sicilia* to read while he waited. He again checked his wristwatch, this time with a purpose; he had arrived about fifteen minutes earlier than planned.

The sun splashed gold dust on the cobbles of the plaza. He lit a cigarette and coughed after one puff. The priest had bronchitis; his doctor had advised him more than once to quit tobacco but he lacked the willpower. Bah, his vocation had denied him enough earthly pleasures; his vows didn't include quitting smoking. The waiter brought his toast and coffee and the newspaper. He read the journal's date: *Venerdì, 25 Novembre, 1949.*

He filled his lungs with cigarette smoke and sipped the double espresso. Ah, the Italians knew how to brew coffee. The Turks made mud and the Americans made colored water. Sicilians especially had the gift, adding notes of Arabia and Greece to the cup. He spread marmalade, made from the ubiquitous local oranges, on the toast and took a bite. He hadn't realized how hungry he was. He had taken nothing to eat since embarking on the ferry from Reggio. No tentacled monsters inhabited the straits that day, no mythic battles raged. The waters were calm on the short voyage to sulfurous Sicily. The lapping waves, stirred by the rudder and cleaved by the prow, the honk of the foghorn and carping of gulls were the only sounds heard as the sea monsters slept under their rocks. And the scenery on the train ride from Messina to Naxos so captivated him that he paid no mind to the shouts of food vendors who moved from car to car, the train whistles drowning their cries. The bluff hills festooned with prickly pear, the lemon groves and eucalyptus trees all vied for his attention and erased thoughts of hunger. And soon the locomotive puffed and sweated into the station in Naxos, a rocky seaside gem cradled in a half-moon bay where seafaring Greeks founded their first colony in Sicily more than seven hundred years before the birth of Christ.

Reveries of classic beauty no longer eclipsed his hunger. So now he gobbled down the toast and ordered another.

The cafe stood on a high point with a sweeping view of the red-tiled roofs in the valley below and the blue, diamond-studded sea. He let his gaze linger on the view for a while. Nature's gifts lay everywhere. The Campari umbrella shaded his fair skin from the strong sunlight. He fished reading glasses from his breast pocket and scanned the headlines, not nearly as shrill in the years since the war ended. The drum-beats of war and persecution had been supplanted by the coo-ing of doves and the hammering of nails as the world rebuilt. He skimmed over a story about Chancellor Adenauer of West Germany vowing to erase the vestiges of Nazism, demilita-rize the nation and work for European peace and prosperity. He arched an eyebrow. He could be forgiven for his skepti-cism. While he had been sheltered from most of the Third Reich's barbarisms by living the war years in neutral Vatican City and by his identity as a German, he might not have fared so well outside the cradling arms of Mother Church. In much of Europe, the swastika had supplanted the cross. Would he have had the courage to suffer the same martyrdom as the clergy in his hometown of Lübeck where in 1943 three Cath-olic chaplains, one Lutheran pastor and eighteen Catholic lay-persons were guillotined by Hitler's henchmen for opposing the unholy regime? He did not linger on the question. It was best not to add conjectural shortcomings to existing ones. The guillotine, both symbol and reality of terror. Best not to linger.

He took another drag on the cigarette and coughed again.

The priest turned the page. There was a general strike in France. The war was over but of course strife was still part of life. Not interested. His eyes moved to the right: Foreign Minister Sforza was quoted in Rome expressing optimism about the upcoming meeting in Paris to discuss forming a European Union of regional powers. Highly unlikely, the reader thought. If Calabrians couldn't avoid blood feuds with Sicilians and Walloons squabbled with Flemings, how could the French, Italians and Benelux nations ever see eye to eye? His tutors at the Provost of the Sacred Heart had schooled him in the fine art of skepticism and much of his life had bolstered his conviction that humanity had a squalid side. A Jesuit is not a Franciscan, after all. And he was by nature an intellectual ruminant.

The late morning was growing warm and so he removed his Roman collar and stuffed it into his pocket. He checked his wristwatch. Where was that sacristan? Tobacco smoke invaded his lungs. He finished the toast and coffee. Where was that sacristan?

A local man approached. He was about thirty, dressed peasant style: soft peaked cap, dirty, banded white shirt, corduroy coat, flared trousers. Countrified clothes, out of style. He had curly black hair and the irises of his gray eyes gleamed like sea-washed pebbles in the sun. His lascivious lips parted to reveal a string of pearls for teeth, teeth that gripped an old clay pipe. He smiled knowingly at Anton Weiss. The pebble-eyes shone with amusement.

"I have post card," the man said in accented English, his foghorn voice conveying something more than the simplicity of the words. "Lovely picture. Von Gloeden photo. You hear of him, eh? You hear of him for sure. Only twenty-five cent each."

Before the priest could answer, the amused vendor splayed samples on the cafe table: a collection of photos of nude and semi-nude young Sicilian boys, attired in tiaras of oleander leaves and togas, surrounded by Doric columns and amphorae. Lithe boys, with bronze naked bodies and suggestive expressions. The images flashed in Father Weiss's mind and he momentarily was transfixed.

Then he recoiled.

"Take them away," he demanded, his voice laced with horror. "What makes you think...?"

The dark, amused, lascivious peasant shrugged his shoulders, smirked and sauntered off to find another customer.

Father Weiss took a moment to regain his composure. His breathing was labored. After a second or two, he remembered something: he had removed the clerical collar. He quickly fastened it on, like a shield. He took out a handkerchief and mopped his brow. He was lost in thought when he he felt a tap on his shoulder.

"Padre Weiss?" came a raspy voice.

It was the sacristan of *Sant 'Antonio*. The old priest stubbed out the cigarette and paid the check, leaving a five-lira tip

TWO

Ignazio Bello, ineptly named for he was no beauty, led the way to the Church of Saint Anthony the Abbot, carting the priest's luggage fastened to the swayed back of an old donkey who stank to high heaven. "Don't worry," the sacristan assured the priest in Sicilian, a dialect that was rather foreign to Father Weiss, though he could make out a word or two, enough to understand these simple directions. "It's not far off."

The sacristan was a graying middle-aged man with a perpetually lolling tongue and bent back. He fit the mold of sacristans in Italy, drawn from the ranks of peasants with meager mental gifts but pious leanings. The vocation lent them a stature in the community that they otherwise would not enjoy. And besides, he ate meat once a week instead of chicory soup and lentils and had Marsala and nougats whenever he pleased. Ignazio turned and flashed the German priest a gap-toothed smile. The priest's eyes alighted on the the sacristan's curved back as he led the way, a back that matched the donkey's deformity. Father Weiss sensed a primeval kinship between man and beast.

They passed through the weathered stone archway leading to the Corso Umberto, the town's main artery from which veins of alleys lead up and down the hills that make up the Mountain of the Bull, Tauromenium in the old lingo. The two men and the donkey trundled along, passing balconied houses of stucco and stone, tiled outdoor stairways, crumbling Roman walls and cisterns, lively cafes and bustling shops, decaying palaces, baroque churches built over the pentimenti of Greek temples and dedicated to a pantheon of saints, including Pancras, Catherine, Joseph, Michael, Augustine and many others, causing the traveler to reflect that if one followed the practice of signing the cross when passing a religious building the right hand would soon grow numb. Of course, he further reflected, this was true all over Italy. The priest, sacristan and donkey moved on, passing an alley not even a yard wide called Vicolo Stretto, "Narrow Alley," which, the old priest thought, many well-fed prelates of his acquaintance could not fit though. A random notion caused him to chuckle. What did Christ say of camels and eyes of needles?

They came to another archway shouldering a medieval clocktower at the entrance of the checkerboard-tiled main square, Piazza IX Aprile, commanding a panoramic view of the volcano, cascading red-tiled roofs, gardens and sparkling

Ionian Sea. Farther along they arrived at the Piazza Duomo where there stood the Cathedral of Saint Nicholas and a baroque stone fountain.

Ignazio stopped and said, "The beast will drink."

As the donkey slaked her thirst from water flowing from the mouth of a stone creature with the head of a horse and the body of a sea serpent, Father Weiss studied the fountain; it had four such beasts at the corners of the supporting basin and the central basin was surmounted by a small unimposing female centaur wearing a crown and carrying a scepter.

The donkey brayed and shook her head, indicating she was finished drinking. The sacristan gestured to the priest. "Will you drink?"

Father Weiss declined. The sacristan shrugged and took a drink. The pilgrimage resumed.

Soon they approached another stone portal, the Porta Catania marking the southern edge of town. A few paces beyond that place the sacristan stopped before an old stone building with a sloped roof and a small craggy campanile.

"See, we are here already," said the man with lolling tongue. The malodorous donkey hawed as if heralding their arrival. They seemed like soulmates of different species.

Father Weiss thought that the sacristan's use of the word "already" after their journey through town reflected the typical Sicilian relationship toward time and space. The Church of Saint Anthony the Abbot occupied a squat building small enough for a Puritan meeting house rather than a Roman Catholic church, especially in Italy where even small villages often boasted imposing cathedrals or basilicas with soaring spires and graceful bell towers. What marked it still as a Sicilian Catholic church was its polyglot mix of Gothic, baroque and Byzantine styles built of compressed rocks recovered from the ruins of earlier conflicts. The building could stand as a monument to the long, checkered history of this whole blessed and cursed island.

The telepathic jackass brayed again, seemingly in amused agreement. The hybrid stank like an old wet carpet. The sacristan produced a toothless inane grin.

Ignazio led the animal and the priest to a three-story house behind the church; the house was fronted by a small cortile, shaded by lemon trees and surrounded by flowering shrubs. It was constructed of blocks of pitted white travertine yellowed by time. A fountain fitted with stone nymphs gurgled in the center of the courtyard. A television antenna was affixed to the red tile roof.

Father Weiss found the setting agreeable. "I will live here?" he asked.

Ignazio, red tongue lolling, nodded and pointed to a round black Moorish aperture on the ground floor. "Your apartment is there." The door was open and Father Weiss could not see inside but it appeared cool and cozy. "You'll want to rest," the sacristan said. Then he hauled the luggage on his bent back into the house. The priest followed.

His eyes surveyed the room. It was spare and clean. There was a window on one side and a low ceiling, the better to keep it warm at night and cool in the daytime. The room contained a feather mattress on a metal bedstead, a bedside table on which stood a small lamp, a caned wooden chair and a dining table covered with a floral-print oilcloth and a brazier for extra warmth. The copper brazier was three feet wide and mounted on four lion's feet. The room had one plush red couch that shed feathers. It lacked modern appliances other than an electric hot plate to brew coffee. A small mirror hung from a nail over a wash basin with running water. At the rear of the room stood another door that, the priest assumed, led to a bathroom. Quite monastic. A real change for the priest, whose apartments in the Vatican and other posts were rather less Spartan. No pictures nor other adornments except for a crucifix lined the walls. He sighed. He would spruce it up, he thought, with his books and other belongings and he would gather wildflowers, which grew in abundance in the area. And he consoled himself with the idea that the room's austerity would fit his plans to write and meditate.

Ignazio dumped the guest's luggage on the tiled floor. "Here we are," he said. "Pastor Attilio expects you for supper at nine. They live in the apartments upstairs."

The old priest looked quizzical. "They . . . ?"

"He and the housekeeper, Concetta." The sacristan ducked his tousled head.

Father Weiss instantly caught the scent: small town priests in Italy often had few scruples about circumventing the vow of celibacy. After all, this was an ancient society and the celibacy rule had been in force for only about a thousand years.

"You take siesta now," said the sacristan.

"Yes. Thank you."

The sacristan shoveled coals into the bed of the brazier and lit them with a long match.

"I will come to fetch you. Pleasant dreams." The sacristan shuffled out.

Father Weiss took off his coat and collar and lay on the bed. The mattress springs sang under his weight. After many years in the southern climes of Italy the North German priest had adopted the practice of a midday nap after a languorous lunch. It was healthful and productive of good work. But this time sleep would not come. First of all, he had eaten no lunch. And for some reason he was too overwrought. Then he spied a small cupboard near the sink. Following an instinct, he went over to investigate and was pleased to find inside the cupboard some glass tumblers and a half bottle of Marsala. He poured a glassful and went back to sit on the bed. Wine was mistress to sleep, he thought as he took a small sip. It felt warm and sweet on his tongue and palate. He swallowed a larger draught and lay down, setting the glass on the side table.

How does one block a stream of unwanted thoughts and images? The very attempt served to boost their potency and persistence. Consciousness on a tinny carousel run by a leering vendor of postcards. He drank more wine. Would not prayer drown out the strains of this cheap calliope? He tried: *Domine non sum dignus*...Finally he fell asleep but the worm still crawled in his vitals.

Some hours later he awoke to a symphony of noise: the chatter of crickets accompanied by the bleat of bagpipes in the valley and the babble of the fountain in the courtyard. At first he did not remember where he was. The dawning of full consciousness soon restored his memory: Taormina! The prospect of spending time here refueled his enthusiasm. He looked forward to the procession of days ahead without any duties or worries. He would read his breviary, say a mass or two if he liked, but otherwise fill his time as he saw fit. What a luxury! He had saved a nice bundle from the inheritance that his sister had held in escrow for him as a slight circumvention of his vow of poverty and the pastor agreed to charge him just twenty thousand lira a week for rent with full *pensione*, a bargain. Had he opted to stay at the Excelsior he would have had to spend more than triple the price. Cigarettes were cheap enough and he would even have enough money to attend the cinema now and then, with plenty left over for other purchases, whatever they might be. Sightseeing surely was on the agenda.

He rose and stretched. He consulted his wristwatch, which lay on the side table. It was six p.m., giving him plenty of time to prepare for supper with the pastor and his, ahem, housekeeper. It was already pitch-black outside and the room was growing chilly. He looked round, found some charcoal in a trough by the window and refilled the brazier. Then he washed up and put on a fresh suit of clothes.

Afterward he lit a cigarette, coughed twice and decided to unpack and put his things in order. But he was too jittery to finish the task and decided to kill time by strolling the town. He had all the time in the world, didn't he? At least he had the unknown length of time that the Lord in His wisdom had allotted. He put on a wool sweater, gabardine jacket and ventured out.

The Corso lay only a few paces from his doorstep. The night was fragrant with the sour scents of prickly pear and pipe smoke and the streets boisterous with raised voices, as usual in Italy after sunset. The narrow alleys thronged with craggy villagers in berets and soft caps, plump matrons wearing colorful shawls and shopkeepers sitting on folding chairs in doorways. From the lintels hung the ubiquitous horn symbol to ward off the malocchio, the evil eye. The men, gathered in conspiratorial clutches of three or four, smoked malodorous stogies or cigarettes and the women chattered like magpies. They all nodded and greeted him in deference to the clerical collar, still visible under the sweater. They also looked bemused by his foreign appearance and because they already knew most of the priests in the many churches of Taormina.

Finally he reached again Piazza IX Aprile, incorrectly named for the date in 1860 when Garibaldi landed at Marsala to launch his conquest of Sicily. Father Weiss's noble face formed a wry smile. As a student of history the priest knew that the liberator's landing did not take place till a month later. But this did not matter to the town fathers on an island where myth always outranked reality.

This, the main town square, was filled with locals, tourists, bumpkins, con artists, and juveniles on the make, all illuminated by electric laterns strung over the cafes and restaurants

Urchins played football on the tiles. Two baroque churches and the medieval clock tower oversaw a Boschian garden of earthly delights that reeked of life, lust and larceny. Caricature painters, souvenir sellers and God-knows-what-else tugged at visitors' sleeves. A man with the figure of a scarecrow and wearing a folksy Sicilian hat with a dangling red pom-pom played mandolin and sang melancholy local songs. Mount Etna fumed in the distance.

He found himself in front of a tourism office under the gaze of an odd-looking man who was dressed entirely in white from his jacket to his shoes. He was of uncertain age, had ash blond hair and an ethereal manner. He said to the priest, "May I be of service?" and handed him a card: "Angelo Michele — Guide." The man smiled, baring dazzling white teeth.

"No thank you," said the old priest.

The smile did not fade. "Keep the card," the man said. "In case you change your mind." And he slipped away, wraithlike.

Father Weiss slipped the card into his pocket and looked around, selecting an outdoor cafe. He chose a shaded place under a palm tree and near a steep row of stone steps, sat down and ordered a grappa. Would he need a tour guide? He had always chosen the Princes of Serendip as his sightseeing guides; they never let him down. His life as a priest was so regulated that he preferred to free-lance as a vacationer.

A honeyed voice interrupted the priest's thoughts.

"May I join you, Padre?"

Father Weiss looked up and saw one of the English gentlemen who had shared his taxi from the train station, the younger man. He was wearing a brown homburg and a flowery ascot.

"By all means," he replied in fluent English.

The man, who appeared about fifty years old, used a cane with a silver lion's head, more from affectation than need. He leaned it against the table as he sat down, then sighed in relief. "I could use a drink," he said. "Been walking for hours. May I offer you one?"

"Please, let me…" said the priest, summoning the waiter.

"Well, thank you. What are you drinking?"

"Grappa."

The man grimaced. "I'll have a sherry, if you please."

Father Weiss ordered a Marsala as a substitute, knowing that the cafe would not stock sherry.

The man took up his cane and leaned on it, peering at Father Weiss inquisitively. "Let me introduce myself," he said, offering his hand. "Reginald Bliss. My friend and I vacation here every winter."

The priest shook his companion's slightly moist hand. "Indeed? I am Anton Weiss."

"You are German." It was not a question but a statement of fact.

"And you are English."

"Hah! How did you guess? Your first time in Taormina?"

"Yes."

"Ah, lucky you." He looked at his table mate with the pinpointed irises of an alley cat. "You have delights in store."

The priest shrugged. "I don't know about that. I am here to write and to rest."

Reginald Bliss looked curious. The waiter set down a glass of Marsala before him. He took a sip. "What are you writing?"

"Memoirs, I suppose. Or a diary. I'm not sure." The priest's eyes strayed to the fiery antics of the volcano.

The Englishman said, "A retrospective, eh?"

You might call it that."

"You are a priest."

Father Weiss nodded.

"Lutheran?"

"Roman Catholic."

"Ah," the Briton said with a knowing air although what he thought he knew was a mystery to the priest. "I am Church of England, of course. Though I must confess I am not a regular churchgoer." He tittered. He reached into his vest pocket and pulled out a gold cigarette case. "Smoke?" he offered.

"Thank you," Father Weiss said as he took a cigarette from the case. The mandolin player's ethereal falsetto rang in his ears.

The Englishman lit the priest's cigarette before lighting his own. The lighter was also gold and, Father Weiss noted, embossed with an amoretto. As he lit his own cigarette the Englishman's hawkish features were limned and the priest noticed that cosmetic touches had been applied to his face.

"May I ask your profession?" said the priest.

Reginald Bliss straightened his spine. "I am an actor."

"How interesting. A stage actor?"

"Yes, mostly. Though I have appeared in a few films."

"Might I have seen you in one?"

The man took a puff and shrugged. "I doubt it. Have you seen 'Seven Sinners' with Edmund Lowe and Constance Cummings? I played a medical doctor in that one."

The priest shook his head. "I'm afraid not."

"Hah. I suppose the title alone might have put you off. It came out over ten years ago. And the film wasn't widely distributed." Mr. Bliss looked regretful. "I'm no Gregory Peck or Alan Ladd. Hah!" Cigarette smoke formed arabesques around his face and head. A slight breeze came from the sea.

"I have no idea who they are either," the priest admitted.

"My, my, you have led a sheltered life. They are two absolutely gorgeous men." He grimaced. "Though Ladd is a trifle small."

The Jesuit blushed, and quickly changed the subject. "Where is your friend, may I ask?"

The Englishman waved his hand dismissively. "Oh, he's still sleeping. Not as young as he used to be," he added with an impish grin. "He's getting so long in the tooth he could play Dracula without makeup."

The remark sailed right over the priest's head. "Beg pardon."

"Never mind, my dear," said the Englishman. "So mature and yet so innocent. Can you really be so angelic?"

The question was impertinent, Father Weiss thought, draining his glass of grappa.

"Have another," his companion said, signaling the waiter.

The priest made a negative gesture. "I mustn't."

"And why not? You are in Taormina, for heaven's sake. Did you take a vow of abstinence?"

"But..."

"Please allow me to reciprocate."

"Just one more, then."

They nursed their drinks quietly for a while. The tourist kept stealing glances at the priest. "You know, "he said, "had it not been for the clerical collar I might have taken you for an actor too. You are quite a beautiful man. Your ordination must have broken many hearts."

Father Weiss's face turned bright red. He stammered a few denials, then added, "One would rather have a beautiful soul."

The Englishman mused over this reply, then said, "And don't you?"

Father Weiss was momentarily speechless. Then he said, "I am not in a position to confess to you."

"You think me forward, eh? Well, you're right."

"Oh, I admire your candor. I suppose it is a virtue."

The Englishman stamped his cane on the ground. "Hah! One of my few virtues." A pause in conversation followed. Then the tourist said, "I wonder how you can preserve such an air of innocence after having heard, I would guess, hundreds of confessions in your career. What a strange experience that must be! To hear the dark secrets of so many souls."

"Please," said Father Weiss. "I can't discuss this."

"I know: I'm a naughty boy. Would you like to hear my confession?"

The priest looked mortified. "Absolutely not!"

Now Mr. Bliss wore a wicked smile. "I would be happy to hear yours?"

Pigeons strutted near their feet, scavenging for crumbs. The volcano continued to grumble, as if to match the priest's seething impatience with the tenor of the conversation. He rose from the chair. "Thanks for the drink," he said in a curt tone. "I must be going."

The Englishman remained seated. "Ah. I have offended you."

"Not at all," he replied with a lack of conviction.

"I would like to be your friend."

Father Weiss said nothing, gave his flamboyant companion a cavalier nod before turning on his heel to depart. And he hurried away over the checkerboard tiles of the main square of Taormina, whose habitants he now imagined as a parade of satyrs and fauns in bacchanal, a place where past and present merged.

THREE

"Please to be seated," Father Attilio said in rather good German, with an obsequious bow.

Father Weiss looked sheepish. "Many thanks, Padre," he said. "Sorry I'm late."

His host poured homemade wine from a carafe. "Ten or fifteen minutes in these Saracenic parts is not considered late, Reverend Father. I was just a trifle worried when Ignazio couldn't find you." He had switched to classic Italian with no trace of dialect, indicating that his origins might have lain elsewhere than rural Sicily.

Father Weiss settled into a plush chair at the dining table. He said, "I took a stroll to the town square to get my bearings and I fear I lost track of time. And please call me Anton." He paused and added, "So you speak German?"

"I studied it in grade school and seminary," the pastor said, his round face exuding self-satisfaction at the notice of his ability. "Then I got a chance to practice when the Wehr-macht was here."

The Jesuit's face darkened at the mention of Hitler's army. "Your accent is flawless," he said. As he spoke he took measure of his host and their surroundings. The pastor was a pear-shaped man, a generation younger that his guest. He had sea-blue eyes, a sallow complexion and sparsely thatched dark hair. In these homely surroundings he wore a crisp white shirt and black pants and no obvious signs of his voca-tion. The room they occupied was spacious and white-washed, serving as a combination dining room, kitchen and living room. Firewood spat and crackled in a corner fireplace. A sign of affluence: On a marble counter sat an American ta-ble model television set. A painting of Madonna and Child hung on the pitted sandstone wall.

"Yes, time is a cheap commodity in Taormina," Father Attilio observed, "and easily squandered. For some, this trait constitutes its charm."

A woman appeared bearing a tray of appetizers: salted fava beans, salami, green grapes and an array of cheeses and olives. Father Weiss began to understand the pastor's rotun-dity. She set the tray down on at the trestle table before the two men.

"May I introduce my housekeeper, Concetta?"

"Hello," the visitor replied, honoring the charade.

Concetta made a small curtsy but there was little servility in her deportment and certainly none in the hammered steel of her black eyes. Her appearance indeed defied the stereo type he had formed in his imagination before meeting her. This was no mustached peasant widow in crape with balloon breasts and varicose veins. No, she was younger than expected, around thirty-five he guessed, and quite pretty. Her features were of the Greek type, strongly chiseled and sensuous. Her chestnut hair hung loose and straight in contrast to the local custom of braiding hair tightly or sweeping it back into a bun. Her figure was youthful, supple and apparently unconstrained by armature undergarments. Father Weiss had the impious thought that the pastor had done rather well for himself.

She took a seat at the table and speared a morsel of cheese with her fork.

"Please help yourself, Father," she said to their guest, her bright eyes flashing with a mix of cunning and amusement.

Father Attilio cocked his head and said, "So, you worked in the Vatican. That must have been interesting."

"I suppose it was," Father Weiss replied. "I wrote scripts for Vatican Radio."

At this nugget of information the housekeeper's saucer eyes widened.

"I assume you met the Holy Father," the pastor said. "What do you think of him?"

Hmm, thought the guest. No beating around the bush. He said, "I find him admirable, though slightly cool personally."

"Pacelli is an aristocrat," the pastor said in a prideful tone. "There is no more aloof breed than a Roman aristocrat.

They ruled the world when the Saxons still walked on their knuckles." He blushed, having forgotten to take into account his guest's Germanic origins. "I meant no disrespect, Father."

"None taken. I happen to agree with you."

Concetta made bold to ask, "Did you also know Mother Pascalina?"

Father Weiss was surprised that she knew the name of the Bavarian nun who served as Pope Pius's housekeeper. Ah, he thought, this Grecian matron, this Hestia — goddess of the hearth — was not to be underestimated. He told her that he had seen Mother Pascalina Lehnert about the Vatican grounds once or twice but that he was not really acquainted with her. Left unsaid was the question of whether she served in the same capacity as Concetta for Father Attilio, which she most certainly did not, considering the asceticism of Pius XII.

The pastor said, his eyes alight, "Did you ever meet Il Duce?"

"A few times. Just for a handshake," he said with no enthusiasm, recalling with distaste the dictator's fleshy moist grip. "The pope considered him no more than a pagan brute, a heretic like Hitler."

The pastor looked stricken. "But the Lateran treaties, the threat from the Communists and Jews!"

Father Weiss caught the sour scent of Fascism, concluding that his host was an apostle of Bishop Lavitrano of Palermo, the shape-shifter who prayed for the defeat of the American army in '43 and then drank champagne with General Patton. He saw no sense in alienating his landlord. No good ever came of digging up old skeletons, especially in Sicily where the bones of a dozen nations, from Carthaginians to Normans and Angevins, lay scattered beneath the volcanic soil. He scouted for a quick change of subject.

Concetta provided the exit: "We suffered much in this region during the Battle of Sicily," she said, her eyes fixed glumly on the flagstone floor. "In my birth village of Fiumefreddo, the streets were littered with corpses. German corpses, Italian corpses, British corpses, American corpses, piled one upon the other like sandbags. Who cares where they came from? The dead are citizens in common of the nation of the dead." She lifted her gaze and looked Father Weiss squarely in the eye, then turned toward the pastor and said with a hint of mischief, "We greeted the Allies as liberators. Because that's what they were. Liberators. But no army can liberate Sicily from eternal misery for this fate is ordained by God."

"Please, Concetta," the pastor interjected.

She ignored him. "Who caused Mount Etna to erase Mascali from the map in 1928? No invading army did that."

"God has his reasons," said the pastor.

"He reveals little, your God. He plays his game close to the vest."

"Please, Concetta," the pastor repeated. "Our guest will think you sacrilegious."

"Is the truth sacrilege?" she countered.

Father Weiss was frozen with astonishment: What a remarkable woman. It was easy to see who wore the pants in this menage.

Father Attilio said meekly: "The pasta pot is boiling."

Concetta rose and wiped her hands on her apron. She said to the pastor, "Sure, I'll fetch supper. Don't get your nose out of joint."

An hour or so later Father Weiss made his way downstairs to his room. Looking up at the window on the pastor's balcony where a light still burned, he said to himself, "They make an odd couple to say the least."

Sounds of voices and activity from the nearby Corso evoked the memory of his conversation with the English actor. That experience on top of the supper with the pastor and his housekeeper made for an unorthodox introduction to this timeless community, he thought. Or was it really unusual? He supposed upon reflection that few experiences were unorthodox here in the primeval vortex that is Sicily, a place that has sucked into its core over the millennia all experiences, races, sins and virtues, wars, earthquakes and volcanic eruptions, famine, drought and marauding dogs. He entered his apartment and readied himself for bed.

Father Weiss lit a final cigarette before laying his head on the pillow. Concetta had prepared a good supper, pasta with garlic and oil followed by a simple fish soup with crusty bread. The wine was coarse but heady and he felt the satiety of the flesh that accompanied such an evening. He smoked and coughed and let his mind wander in an erratic journey to the past, present and future. And finally the nomadic thinker landed on a question: what in God's name was he really do ing here?

He stubbed out the cigarette and fell into an uneasy sleep where, as usual, he wrestled with the Devil.

FOUR

The sojourner was wakened by singing voices in the court-yard outside his apartment. The sound was silvery and nasal — female, he assumed. He tumbled out of bed and peeked through a mail slot in the front door. There they were, three women — one middle-aged and two young — sitting at the edge of the babbling fountain adorned with nymphs and sa-tyrs, singing as they performed chores. The middle-aged woman used a wooden spindle to form thread from flax; one of the girls measured the thread and the other girl cut it to the length indicated.

And they sang:

> *Ciuri, Cirri*
> *Ciuri di tuttu l'anno*
> *L'amuri ca mi dasti ti lu tordu*
> *Ciuri di rosi russi a lu sbucciari*
> *Amara a cui li tó parole crisi*
> *L'omini siti tutti munsignari*

Jù non ti vogghiu no!

Ti nni pò iri

Though the lyrics sung in the local dialect puzzled him, Father Weiss still was charmed by the song and the tableau of the women at work, surrounded by flowers and fountain spray. Had he a gift for painting he would have fetched brushes, oils and easel. But, alas, he lacked all craft, except for philosophy and self-recrimination.

He washed up and got dressed.

Soon Ignazio of the lolling tongue and bent back was at his door.

"You take breakfast in the garden, Father?"

"A capital idea! I'll be right with you."

As he passed, the women bowed in his direction. He bid them good morning and praised their singing, causing them to titter behind their hands. Then they returned to their tasks.

The priest sat down to breakfast at a wrought iron table with a mosaic top on which were laid olive oil, flat bread with garlic and rosemary, orange slices and a steaming pot of coffee. The setting was edenic, lush and fragrant with eucalyptus, geraniums and laurel. He could still hear the splashing of the fountain. Taormina truly seemed to blend paradise with the nether regions.

"Can I get you anything else?" the sacristan said, pouring coffee.

Father Weiss dunked a piece of flat bread in olive oil. He asked the sacristan, "What does ciuri mean?"

"It's Sicilian for flowers."

Anyhow, our farm was destroyed in '28. We ran for our lives." His tone was philosophical, conveying no note of grievance.

"Mount Etna, yes?"

"Every now and then Vulcan blows his top." He shrugged again. "We do something to make him mad."

The priest silently observed how in these parts even a church worker resorted to pagan symbols before invoking the will of the Christian God. Father Weiss momentarily was distracted by the sight of a white goose waddling over the garden flagstones. Then he returned to questioning the sacristan. "What is your native village?"

"Fiumefreddo," he replied.

"Oh, the same as Concetta."

"She is my baby sister," he said. "The pastor hired us both when our parents could no longer afford to feed us. Concetta was sixteen years old. We survived on *trammuna* — what you call prickly pears. We gathered snails and mushrooms. Life is hard on this three-cornered island."

"Concetta is a remarkable woman," the priest declared in a tone of admiration.

"This is well-known. My sister is a *strega*, a disciple of Diana in the old religion before Christ came. It is not sinful, is it? We could not become Christians before Christ came. And so we have taken some of the old ways." The speaker's fleshy tongue lolled.

Father Weiss was aware of the rustic belief in a form of witchcraft that held sway among some benighted Italians. But he didn't expect it would prevail here in Taormina. a place of some sophistication and many Christian churches. And he surely did not expect it to reign in the household of a parish church. He clucked his tongue. "*Stregoneria* is heretical," he said. Second-guessing himself, the priest inwardly observed that Catholicism had more than its share of superstitions. Yes.

Ignazio formed the usual shrug; it made him resemble an owl. "This means what?" he asked.

"It is against the teachings of Holy Mother Church."

Ignazio frowned and shut his eyes, mulling this over. Then he said, "*Beh,* I know nothing about these things. But I do know that my sister has powers. She inherited them from our mother and our grandmothers on both sides. Big powers."

"For example?"

"She can foretell the future. She predicted that Paolina, the baker's wife, would give birth to twins and she did — twin boys."

"A stroke of luck."

Ignazio bestowed on the priest a condescending smile. "Well, she also can cure illness. One of the twins had yellow disease and she cured it."

"Jaundice?"

"Yes, that's what the doctors called it. My sister advised the nursing mother to eat no corn or durum wheat. And the yellow color went away."

The priest was not convinced. "Jaundice is most often a temporary condition," Father Weiss said, showing his Germanic pragmatism as much as his Catholic piety. He poured himself another espresso. "But leave off. I don't want you to have to confess to heresy."

A bunch of magpies wheeled and cawed in the sky above the garden trees, as if mocking their conversation. Or were they mocking the skeptical priest?

Ignazio, with an Epictetan aura of acceptance, drained his cup and started to leave. "I must get to work. We need holy oils for a baptism this afternoon and I must collect the clean vestments from Concetta. I hope she removed the tallow stain from the gold chasuble."

"Maybe she could just cast a spell to do the job," the priest said, immediately regretting his wicked sarcasm. He thought that perhaps many pathways led to the Divinity and an open mind — even in a clergyman — was a holy virtue. This attitude had led many Jesuits to achieve success as scientists. He then made up his mind that he would take the nearest opportunity to speak at length with Concetta about her talents and maybe expand his understanding of how pre-Christian practices and dogma fit into the theological cosmology and maybe even enriched Catholicism.

"Before you go," he said to the sacristan, "could you tell me when the next mass is scheduled?"

Ignazio shook his head. "We have only one mass at Saint Anthony's on Saturday. At eight a.m. You missed it. But there's a ten o'clock mass in the Duomo. You can make that."

"Thanks," the priest said, mopping his mouth on a napkin and rising from the chair. "I'd better get a move on."

Ignazio cleared off the breakfast things and the priest went back to the apartment to gather up his prayer book, notebook and a few other things. When he arrived he found the place spotlessly clean. He assumed that Concetta had been there. German hausfraus have the reputation as fastidious housekeepers but Father Weiss would soon realize that they couldn't hold a candle to Sicilian women for whom cleanliness and tidiness were a mark of pride far transcending godliness. If you committed a sin of word or deed you could enter the confession box and wipe the slate clean. But the village snoops would never give absolution for an unswept balcony.

As he closed the door behind him the realization waylaid Father Weiss that he had eaten breakfast and would not be able to take Holy Communion. Then he thought to himself, ah well, when in Sicily do as the Sicilians do. And he briskly walked to the Duomo, feeling sprightly as an old dancer. Before entering the cathedral he decided to remove the clerical collar so that he would not scandalize worshippers by not taking the Holy Host.

An hour later he emerged from the darkness of the church to the glare of a halcyon sun washing over the piazza. He heard the wingbeats of pigeons roosting in the belfry of the building. He walked down a narrow stone street toward the main square, passing competing butcher shops displaying garlands of sausages and pink-fleshed hogs split obscenely down the middle from neck to rectum. He passed a tailor's shop designated as such by a swatch of cloth hung over the lintel. He noticed in front of the shop listed for sale an olive drab motor bike, probably left by an American paratrooper during the war. He passed quartets of old men in newsboy caps smoking stubby cheroots and playing *scopa*, the card game ubiquitous in Italian villages. And he passed the toothless old women in widow's weeds who sat on cane chairs in the doorway of every other house. Each wore black stockings that reached just below the knee and each comprised a Greek Chorus of One, mouthing dithyrambs on the human drama of the cobbled streets. Overhead, ivy dangled from balconies aflame with red and pink geraniums in terra cotta pots. And in every alley the wind whipped multi-colored banners of hanging wash, the true guidons of Italy.

The old priest stopped at a souvenir shop to buy a guidebook. He sat on a nearby wooden bench and riffled the pages, looking for a way to fill the next hour or two. He soon decided to visit the Church of Saint Pancras, Taormina's patron saint. It was just outside Porta Messina and the fresco there portraying the martyred bishop's torture and death by stoning in the primeval days of Christianity was famous for its artistry. The remains of a Greek temple on the same site also attracted the visitor.

As he climbed the blue stones of the walkway there came to his ears the sound of a drum followed by a brass band and the clash of a cymbal, which, after many years in Italy, he instantly recognized as the start of a funeral procession. Along with other tourists and villagers he stopped in his tracks and bowed his head in respect. It was not blasphemous to admit that he rather enjoyed such occasions, drawing pleasure from the staccato solemnity of the music and the paradoxical way time seemed to freeze in this melodious marker of death. He soon recalled the composition as Enrico Petrella's Ione, a geographically fitting tribute to the mythical nymph who inhabited the Ionian Sea. The stamp of many feet accompanied the dirge.

The procession had begun at the foot of the baroque steps of Saint Pancras and snaked its way down the narrow streets. After the band came white-robed and hooded members of the local burial guild, the same costume favored by members of the American racist marauders branding themselves the Ku Klux Klan though, as far as Father Weiss knew, there was no relationship between the two groups. The leader hoisted a large cross barnacled with precious gems. The priest in surplice and black cassock was flanked by two altar boys swinging gold-plated incense burners. The incense caused the Jesuit to cough and spit bile into his handkerchief. Mourners holding tapers both led and followed pall bearers shouldering the casket. Locals and shopkeepers filled the balconies and doorways to witness the spectacle and whisper to each other, "Who is the good soul?" while crossing themselves. But the identity of the deceased person mattered less to the casual observer than the solemnity of the ritual, the beauty of the parade and the import of the moment. Rogue or saint, the deceased was exiting a world where hunger and calamity ruled and going to another world. Better or worse? Who knew? Father Weiss figured that many Sicilians, given their history of poverty, war and natural disasters, would say that it couldn't be any worse. The strains of music drowned out the keening of the widow. Even the mongrels lounging on the door saddles stifled their barks, keeping a respectful silence.

And the fire-god Etna brooded in the distance.

The procession was headed past the Messina Gate and on toward the Field of Saints, the Italian idiom for cemetery. There the Good Soul, as Meridionals referred to even rascals who passed beyond the veil, would be interred or entombed, depending on social status and the final resting place adorned with red candle holders and a photo of the deceased.

Postponing his visit to Saint Pancras for another day, Father Weiss followed the procession down to the gate and then made a detour to visit the famous Greco-Roman Theater. He pictured this as an ideal place to sit in the ancient bleachers with notebook in hand, gaze at the sea and mountains and wait for the Daughters of Memory to guide his pen.

He soon arrived at Lu Teatro Greco, as the locals called it, disdaining the Roman side of the place's pedigree from when the blood of gladiators stained the sands. Better to envision the actors, singers and musicians of the enlightened Greek uses of the place, the priest thought. There were but few people around — a scattering of tourists, an old woman harvesting chicory and wildflowers. Father Weiss elected to follow Goethe's example and sit in the top row of the ruined amphitheater where he had a commanding view of the site against the desired backdrop of countryside, sea and volcano.

The mildness of the winter sun lent a mellowness to the surroundings. He felt serene and remembered how D.H. Lawrence once described this land as a place where the past was so much stronger than the present, that it made one feel — and the priest whispered the words to himself: "remote like the immortals. looking back at the world from their other world." Was that what the old priest was doing now as he expected that he was nearing entry to the other world? Or did he fear being barred from the gates by an archangel with a flaming sword? As these thoughts flooded his mind, he took his pen and notebook and scribbled them down. Then another image hijacked his attention, the image of Homer's one-eyed cannibal in this very region flinging tempered lava rocks at Odysseus and his sailors. They had blinded him and rowed away to safety over the same blue Ionian waters, framed by the columns and brick arches that now filled his field of vision. As he sat there and dashed off random notes and ideas, some twenty-three-hundred years dissolved before his eyes to reveal the ancient world, much like a photograph might appear coated with silver atoms of light.

Hours passed and he filled five pages of his notebook. The westering sun cast elongated shadows on the theater stage and the aging priest found himself alone and feeling hungry. He was about to leave and get something to eat when he saw him: a boy of about fifteen or sixteen, striding into the amphitheater with an air of nobility and beauty that belied his peasant costume. A floppy soft cap was perched on a mass of amber-colored ringlets of long hair that strayed over his nape and ears. His light eyes and fair complexion marked him as a member of the Norman type that persisted in parts of Southern Italy but his insouciant gait and manner, if frozen into immobility, would have recalled the Greek marbles and ivories portraying Apollo or some other mythic creature brought to life by a lovesick sculptor's kiss. It would not have surprised the observer if the boy was indeed a shepherd like his beardless legendary model since his clothing — homespun shirt and fleece vest, corduroy knickers and soft boots — showed a rustic background. Draped on his classic form, however, these simple garments might well have been made of silk and velvet. He was, in a word, beautiful — and his beauty sparked both admiration and self-recrimination in the soul of Father Anton Weiss.

The boy sat down in the middle of the semi-circular audience section facing the mountains and removed from his knapsack a chunk of bread, wedge of pecorino studded with peppercorns and a flask of wine or water; the priest could not tell which. He began to eat and drink, reminding Father Weiss of his own gnawing hunger. And the old visitor quickly though reluctantly left the amphitheater to satisfy one earthly appetite in place of another. Before his departure, however, the boy had caught Father Weiss's eye and smiled.

Concetta set before the priest a bowl of homemade sheep's milk ricotta, the warm curds placed atop slices of yellow *bastone* bread garnished with poppy seeds. As she served him, her tongue was still but her eyes were eloquent —

though the language they spoke was foreign to him. She poured into his tumbler the strong black wine that the local volcanic soil produced. She added to the table's bounty a chicory and tomato salad and he ate heartily under the branding iron of her steady gaze.

"You enjoy?" she said.

"Oh yes, thank you." The wine warmed his innards.

"You should eat more. You're skinny like a stray cat."

"Yes, I've been losing weight lately."

She placed her hands on her fleshy hips. Her raven hair was swept to one side and held fast by a clamshell barrette. "And Taormina, Reverend? How do you like it so far?"

He shrugged. "I'm here only one day. But of course it's easy to see that it's beautiful and interesting."

"Yes, beautiful," she echoed, maintaining her inscrutable gaze. "But it is a mixed beauty. The skies are soft but the earth is hard. There are elegant squares with donkey dung on the cobbles. It is the beauty of a seductress with a dagger hidden in her bosom."

Father Weiss studied her with admiration. "You have a gift for expression."

She took the compliment in stride. "Eat," she urged him.

"They tell me you have many gifts," he added before obeying her command by chewing a morsel of ricotta.

"Who tells you?"

"Your brother."

"He also told you we were related, eh? Well. maybe so. Maybe I have gifts, bestowed by my maternal ancestors and the Lord above. I am the second daughter of my parents, named Concetta according to custom after my maternal grandmother. She had the power to cure the evil eye."

"Did she bequeath you the same power?"

"Some say she did." She hunched her shoulders. "I don't know."

Father Weiss returned to a familiar theme, saying, "Such superstitions are against church teaching, you realize."

Her expression conveyed that this consideration was beneath discussion. Inwardly, Father Weiss tended to agree so he dropped the subject.

She then told the story of a wheat farmer who was cursed by a crone with the *malocchio* after he was accused of violating her teenage granddaughter. "Three years ago," she said, "he was struck by lightning and killed. Maybe God works this way."

"Maybe," he conceded as he relished the freshness of the meal she had prepared.

She looked at him intently. She said, "We pray to our patron saints for sun and rain to grow the crops and for breezes to blow the chaff from the grain. We pray for good things to happen. When we invoke the Evil Eye, we pray for punishment of the wicked. What is the difference?"

"What if you punish the good?"

"That is the Devil's work, Father. You ought to know that."

"Are there no bad *stregas*?"

"Sure there are," she said, looking at him to see if he had

all his brains. "They work for the bad angels who rebelled against God."

Father Weiss grunted, marveling at how the local beliefs still mirrored the pantheism of the ancient Phoenicians, Greeks and Romans. And why should this surprise anyone who has viewed the plaster saints and marble demigods arrayed in our churches and public squares? If there were no magic in Roman Catholicism the religion would crumble to dust. The village strega was giving the German Jesuit a theology lesson.

And — near what he supposed were the end of his days — he took it to heart.

She brought him coffee and oranges and sat down opposite him. "You are troubled," she said. "Why did you come here?"

The statement and question visibly unnerved him and he did not contradict her. He wondered, did she have a special talent for intuition or did he wear his discontent so patently on his sleeve that it would be obvious to any observer. He was here for a reckoning. At this stage of his life the holy sacraments seemed no longer to suffice. And he had to answer for himself the crucial question: Why had he strayed from the footpath of the garden of earthly delights in the service of a chimeric divinity? And was it too late to change matters? He could not deny it: a conflict raged within him. He looked up and searched the tawny face of the beautiful witch for a possible answer. He found none.

"Drink your coffee," she said simply.

All the while Father Atillio snored before the television set showing an American cowboy movie.

FIVE

Father Weiss woke to the sound of church bells tolling the Ave Maria. After parting the cobwebs of sleep, he remembered it was Sunday and he had promised Father Attilio he would celebrate nine o'clock mass. He hurriedly washed and dressed and made his way to the sacristy where the vestments had been laid out for him, presumably by Concetta. The vestments were purple, befitting the first day of Advent. He looked for Ignazio, who was scheduled to serve as acolyte, and found him fussing around the altar, changing the roses and anemones in the vases and lighting votive candles.

They traded salutations. Then the priest asked, "Why don't you change the water as well as the flowers?"

Ignazio gave him a look of profound pity for his stupidity. "Ah, my reverend," he said, lighting the white and purple tapers, "water is scarce in these parts. I have to climb a mountain to reach the springs."

"Doesn't the community provide water?" asked the recent resident of Rome, where water was as abundant as the air we breathe.

"Sometimes yes, sometimes no. There are many shortages."

Typical of this beautiful and benighted place, the priest thought. Flowers abounded but water, essential for life, was scarce.

"It's getting late," the sacristan said. "I will put on my surplice."

The service drew few worshippers — of course a few old women in black clothing, one pregnant matron with two fidgety boys in tow. The only adult male was a superannuated villager, his status as widower signaled by the black cloth button fixed to his lapel. Father Weiss noticed this item as the man took communion and the sacristan later explained the meaning.

"It's an old custom here," Ignazio said as he helped the priest remove his vestments. "Not all widowers do this. For men it is optional, especially if they want to take a second wife. But may the saints protect the widow who doesn't wear black."

Ignazio took a whiskbroom and began dusting the priest's shoes. Father Weiss asked, "Why did so few people show up for mass?"

"*Beh*," he said, uttering the gnomic sound Italians favored to express stoicism. "They prefer the Duomo, which has better statues. Or San Pancrazio, the most beautiful church in town and named for the patron saint of Taormina. Those who live close by or have a special bond to Saint Anthony, they come here."

Father Weiss had breakfast before heading again to the Greco-Roman theater with his notebook. This time he also took cheese, bread and a liter of wine in a net bag the housekeeper provided. He had told her that he would not be home for lunch.

"And siesta?" she asked crossly.

"I won't take one today."

"You Germans are a little off," she said, forming a circle with her forefinger on the side of her head.

He smiled in amusement and headed to town, having stripped off his Roman collar. On his way he passed the fountain and the trio of women weaving and working and singing their nasal songs.

On the way to the Messina Gate he stopped at the tobacco shop to buy cigarettes. He wheezed as he climbed the steep Corso but the addiction was stronger than the affliction so he lit his first *Gitanes* of the day and took a long drag. The downslope wind from Castelmola formed arabesques of the expelled smoke. It was the first day of December and the first time since he had arrived that the priest felt a hint of winter in the air. As he smoked he coughed, spitting yellow phlegm into his handkerchief. The ascendant sun cast his bent shadow against the buildings whose ochre walls were choked with crawling lichen. One of the buildings, he noticed, bore the Taormina coat of arms, a rather ugly representation of a crowned queen, half woman, half horse, naked from the waist up and holding a scepter in one hand and a globe in the other, all against a sky-blue background. He recalled that the same figure adorned the fountain in the Piazza del Duomo. He passed a small curio shop and on impulse went inside to have a look around.

Some minutes later he emerged with a spur-of-the-moment purchase, a beechwood cane with a brass gargoyle handle and brass tip, his first concession to old age. He was perfectly capable of walking without one, especially after many years of life in hilly Rome. He realized with a twinge of guilt that the purchase sprang more from a sartorial than physical motive. But he gave himself absolution for this venial sin of vanity. And the act of placing the tip of the stick on the mottled cobblestones lent a strut to his step.

As he reached the entrance to the amphitheater he quashed the cigarette butt underfoot and gazed at the snow-mantled mountain rising incongruously above waving palm trees and he observed to himself that Etna also had a bad smoking habit. Today the ancient theater was filled with tourists. Father Weiss sat again in the upper rows, took out his pen and notebook and again began to write. This time, for some reason, his imagination took a detour to his boyhood, a sort of pilgrimage. The memories flooded back.

The two boys simultaneously cast their fishing lines into the brackish surface of the River Trave. Canopies of beech and walnut trees crowding the banks shaded the companions from the September sun and the idyll of the moment erased from their minds any misgivings about skipping school that day; winter came too soon in the Baltic regions and they wanted to drain the season to the dregs. Fallen leaves and walnut hulls already littered the grass, where squirrels raced around and bobbed their little heads like nervous thieves.

The lads hoped to catch some speckled trout, though not deciding what they would do with the fish if they were fortunate enough to land one or two. Carrying them home for the dinner table would let the cat out of the bag, as they say, and both boys then would feel the paddle from their mothers or far worse from their stern Hanseatic fathers. Paternal disdain stung worse than maternal whippings. But catching fish was not the true aim of their stolen holiday. It was companionship.

For Anton and Helmut were uncommonly fond of each other. Let us call a spade a spade: they were in love or at least Anton loved Helmut. At their tender age of fifteen neither boy would have described their feelings for each other in these precise terms. The inchoate stirrings that moved them to heights of emotional rapture had no such common name, no such counterpart in the lore and experience of their bourgeois existences of dancing classes and Latin lessons. To them the feelings seemed unnamable and unique, a feeling brand new not only to them but in the annals of recorded time. All young Anton Weiss knew was that each morning when he woke his first thoughts were of the sloe-eyed Helmut Feld and the moment he would see him again. He pictured his friend as a Persian prince, though he wore a sailor cap instead of a turban. In physical type they were polar opposites; Anton was tall for his age, blonde and gangly while Helmut, though German to his core, looked like an exile from the south, small and dark with wavy black hair and and the chiseled features of a Roman marble. Somewhere on a bough of the Nordic family tree a Spaniard or Italian must have budded, not a surprising outcome for the long lineage of seafaring merchants. The boys' mutual attraction was for now what the olden Greeks called *Agape*, a selfless outgoing love. *Eros*, the little imp, still lay hidden in the weeds.

"We are missing French class, you know," Anton reminded Helmut, who sat back languorously, biting on a blade of grass and looking as if he had not a care in the world. Anton added: "Father Beckman threatened a quiz for tomorrow."

"Pooh," said Helmut, "I know French like the back of my hand. I have spoken it from childhood. My nanny came from French Martinique. Black as coal she was, but what a bottom!" Helmut made a big show of saying naughty things in his friend's presence. But Anton knew it sprang mostly from vainglory and an attempt to make him blush. "Don't you have some marzipan in your satchel? Give me some."

"Sure," said Anton, eager to please his friend. Anton's father owned a marzipan factory, producing many varieties of a sweet for which the town was famous. He handed over an almond-flavored confection in the shape of a Bosc pear. Helmut popped it into his bow-shaped mouth as he idly grinned at the river.

Anton saw himself struggling tomorrow over his test paper under the vaulted Gothic windows of Sacred Heart school as the bony and bald Father Beck paraded up and down the aisles tapping his hickory pointer ominously on the desks. "But do you know the text?" he asked Helmut. "Dumas' prose is difficult. At least I find it so."

Helmut, insouciant as ever, pronounced, "Anton, you worry too much. Take a breather and enjoy the sights." He gazed across the river at the port crammed with steamers and schooners bound for for the Baltic and North seas. A few of the vessels belonged to his father, a timber trader. "Speaking of enjoying the sights," said Helmut with a devilish grin, "I caught a glimpse of the parlor maid's underpants yesterday as she dusted the upper shelves in the library."

There he goes again, Anton thought. Still he blushed. "Nonsense," he snapped.

Quiet reigned for a while. He searched the water line for the bobbers. Not a nibble. "I quite like the story," Anton said.

"What story."

"You know, The Three Musketeers."

Helmut chewed the blade of grass. "It's all right, I suppose," he replied. "I like the swordplay and all."

"I like the notes of chivalry" said Anton, dreamy-eyed. "The camaraderie among the men. The 'Three Inseparables' and d'Artagnan."

Anton's eyes were drawn to a white water lily floating out toward the sea. His romantic nature attached a cryptic though magnetic symbolism to the flower's appearance on the river. His older sister, Gabi, always teased him about his tendency to make a lyric poem over every passing wraith of emotion, to idolize Brahms and Goethe, whose works she was certain he was too young to fully comprehend. He even mixed his religious fervor with sentimental colors as he favored the novels of Clemens Brentano, who gave the world such heated tales as The Life of the Holy Virgin Mary and Dolorous Passion of Our Lord Jesus Christ. Brentano's Italian lineage and Roman Catholicism also boosted the attraction for the boy. Catholics like Anton and Helmut were scarce in Lübeck ever since the Reformation swept over Northern Europe. The glorious and elaborate medieval Lübeck Cathedral, its twin spires visible from the riverbank, became a bastion of Lutheranism.

"I have to take a leak," Helmut announced, rising and walking over to a nearby beech tree to relieve himself. As he fished his member from the folds of his velvet pantaloons, his companion's face turned crimson and he made certain to look away. He could sense that Helmut wore a mocking smile as he pissed, that he was fully aware of his companion's unease in such situations. Why did he torment him? Why indeed was he tormented? He knew that most boys took such matters casually, that nudity and immodesty were most often sources of sport and horseplay. But Anton's nature for some mysterious reason would not allow him the same attitudes.

Despite himself — he stole a furtive glance as Helmut formed a yellow stream against the tree. And, despite himself, the sight of the one-eyed monster fomented a stir in his own loins. He quickly felt deeply alarmed and ashamed of his reaction. He wanted nothing more than to love Helmut with a purity that fostered no shame and had no distasteful subterranean side such as afflicted him at the moment. But he was young and ignorant and could neither define nor quell these odd feelings. And a voice inside him said that one emotion could not exist without the other.

It was then, looking back, that he later realized that the seed was planted for the ultimate decision to place the prospect of physical love on the sacrificial altar. It was then that a dab of lime was added to his inchoate resolve to become a celibate priest.

Father Weiss lay down his pen and reached for his bundle of food. As he nibbled a bit of cheese and swallowed a swig of wine, he tried to compose himself. The memories he had just recorded still unsettled him. The sun over the amphitheater had risen now to the zenith and along with the wine drew pearls of sweat to his forehead. He noticed that the place was getting crowded and becoming no longer suited to writing or quiet contemplation. He resolved that as soon as he finished his repast he would leave.

Then he saw him again — the beautiful shepherd boy. He was standing in the center of the stage holding bagpipes, an instrument that the Romans legionnaires had brought back from Egypt and bequeathed to Italy and later to the British Isles. At least that was what the Jesuit had learned in his wide reading of history. The boy had placed on the ground a straw basket to receive tips from tourists after he played. Father Weiss had once spent Christmas in the Apennines of Abruzzo not far from Rome and witnessed something similar, local mountaineers playing the pipes before magnificent outdoor creches to celebrate the birth of Christ. He thought to himself how fitting it was that shepherd boys, so central to the nativity story, upheld the tradition by caroling the Christ child with homespun music made from the belly of a ram and the wood of the acacia tree.

Now the boy, costumed in fleece and wool and tasseled hat, placed the pipe to his lips, fingered the holes and produced the haunting notes of the Christmas song renowned in all of Italy: "You Descend From the Stars, O King of Heaven…" The priest was transfixed by the beauty of the music, the magic of the moment and the grace of the boy. As he played with deep concentration the ribbons on the pipe fluttered with the flow and ebb of the musician's breath, the beating of the priest's troubled heart obligato to the notes. And soon a fountain of involuntary tears welled in Father Weiss's eyes, rising up from the past to besiege him now after a lifetime spent defending them behind a barricade of prayer and sophistry and struggles between concupiscence and conscience. He again sensed the presence of the evil one, crouching and ready to pounce.

The song ended. The olio of emotion, sacred and profane, had left the elderly observer breathless. Slowly, he regained his composure, wiped his eyelids on the back of his hand and rose to his feet. He gathered up his belongings and made his way to the stage where a few tourists sent coins jingling into the shepherd's basket. Father Weiss's offering was soundless — a ten-lira note. The boy remarked the largess with a sharp "Oh," and locked eyes with his admirer. His gaze conveyed not merely gratitude but a hint of interest.

The old priest turned on his heel before he could receive thanks and as quickly as his shaky old legs could manage, left the arena.

He soon was sitting down in an outdoor cafe of the main square where he ordered a whiskey to calm his nerves. As he waited for the drink, he of course lit another cigarette, craving narcosis in two forms. He was at odds with himself. Did he ache to remember or long to forget? There was no doubt in his mind that he had a malaise of the heart. But it was his body that cried out for fulfillment. And he felt that this faun of a boy was not flesh and blood but a visitation from archaic times, a phantasm that would dissolve at his touch.

The whiskey came; he drank it down and ordered another. He smoked and coughed. He ran his hand through his thick silver hair. He felt a tap at his shoulder.

"Signor?"

The priest in mufti inhaled sharply. It was he, the shepherd boy.

"You left this in the Greek theater," the boy said, holding out the beechwood cane.

Father Weiss then realized that in his haste to leave he had forgotten about the newly purchased article. He felt dizzy; the apparition from the past had come to life, fully formed with warm breath like a sirocco and the earthy odor of animal skin. He stammered a thank you. He took the cane.

"No, sir," the boy said, "I should thank you. The generous gratuity."

The old priest was captivated by the glow in the shepherd's steel-gray eyes and the unnerving beauty of his red mouth as it formed his words. "Please," he said. "Your playing was lovely. You are skillful for one so young."

The boy lowered his thick eyelashes. "I started playing when I was ten."

"And — may I ask — how old are you now?"

"Sixteen."

"Sixteen," the priest repeated. "Just sixteen, my, my."

"That's old enough in these parts," the boy said. "In Sicily we grow up quickly." He paused and added, "And die young."

Father Weiss was taken aback by the child's fatalism. And, despite scruples, he was decoding the statement about growing up quickly. Impulsively, he blurted, "Would you join me for a coffee or something?" As soon as he said it, he felt a pang of guilty pleasure.

The boy did not hesitate to accept the offer, sitting down. "Yes, thank you."

"What is your name?" the priest asked.

"Ambrosio."

"Ambrosio," he echoed, thinking the name fitted such a lad who wanted only a wreath of laurel to resemble a demi god. "What will you drink?"

"A glass of Lambrusco, thank you. I'm parched."

"Yes, the day started cool but grew warm," the priest said. "What is your village?"

He pointed to the northeast and said, "*Castigghiuni*, we say in Sicilian. In Italian it is Castiglione. Castle of the Lion. It was built by the Normans hundreds of years ago. My people have a house and farm in the valley near the river Alcantara. That's an Arabic name. The town is very old." He shrugged. "And we are poor." He smiled slyly. "We pray to the Madonna of the Chain for good harvest." He hunched his shoulders again. "Sometimes the Madonna hears the prayers. Sometimes no. I come to Taormina and also Messina to play the pipes at Christmastime to earn money for the family. The farm does not always produce enough to feed the family"

The wine came and he took a sip. "You are a foreigner," he said.

"Yes."

"English or American?"

"German."

"Ah! You speak Italian well."

"I have lived in Italy for many years."

"Ah!" He took another sip. "We are all foreigners in Sicily, one way or another. We are Italians and Greeks. We are Moors and Normans. We are Lombards and Spaniards."

The priest marveled at the shepherd boy's apparent erudition. "Where did you learn such history?" he asked. "What school did you attend?"

He drained the glass for he was thirsty and said, "School? No school. I have to work all the time. But we live in history around here. We don't have to go to school. Listen to the names: Castiglione is Italian; Alcantara is Arabic; Naxos is Greek. I could go on and on." He rose. "I must go play the pipes in Naxos and be home by nightfall. How long you stay?"

"I'm not sure," the old man said.

"I see you again? You very handsome."

Father Weiss blushed down to his breastbone. "Perhaps," he struggled to say.

"I hope so. I come here often." He tipped his tasseled cap and went away.

The German priest was left with a dry throat and quickened pulse. He ordered a third whiskey and sat there for several minutes, unaware that he had been under keen observation since his arrival in the piazza by a dandified Englishman sitting at a neighboring cafe. The observer was Reginald Bliss, who wore a smug and knowing smile.

SIX

At dusk Father Weiss sat in the garden of Father Attilio's house, bewitched by the blinking fireflies and the serenity of the hour. The yellow cliffs in the distance, visible through the garden foliage, were slowly turning orange in the alchemy of the setting sun.

He also was bewitched by the magic of certain written words.

He had spent much of the afternoon reading in translation "*The Great Weaver from Kashmir,*" an early work of the Icelandic writer Haldor Laxness. He was drawn to the book at first because he discovered from a guidebook that the author had written the novel while staying in Taormina and he found a volume in Italian at a bookstore near the Catania Gate. He was eager to read things composed here. He thought perhaps he might delve the wellsprings of genius for inspiration in his own modest attempt to reach some reckoning by scribbling words on paper in this place of pastoral and savage beauty.

Laxness's tale of an Icelandic poet's search for truth did not disappoint the reader. Father Weiss was astounded by the parallels with his own struggles that he unearthed in the prose of Laxness, a former convert to Catholicism and one-time Dominican monk. He reread one passage over and over:

"I have vowed to leave no further room in my soul for anything other than the celebration of the spiritual beauty of creation. No soulless wish or physical longing, No fleshy desire or pleasure. I am betrothed to the beauty on the face of things. I intend to travel back and forth through existence like a jubilant monk of the world who beholds the smile of the Holy Mother in everything that exists. My bread and wine will be the glory of God on the face of the creation, the image of the Lord on the Lord's coins. I am the son of the Tao in China, the perfect Yogi of India, the Great Weaver from Kashmir, the snake charmer in the Himalayan valleys, the saint of Christ in Rome..."

The voice of the Icelandic character spoke to his heart. But weren't such aspirations doomed from the start? And indeed as the story unfolds the poet Steinn's ethereal vows crumble to dust; he fails in the quest for perfection, as all humans must, and loses his boxing match with the Devil. Of course, the author's skills are elliptical, not prone to such easy conclusions, the priest thought, as he fingered the dusty, dog-eared pages of the book. He might draw another lesson: that God loves sinners, too, and the well of redemption is bottomless.

Father Weiss considered that the novel, written after the Great War when Laxness was only 23, might also have something to say about the Devil's work in fomenting deadly strife among nations, food for thought after the recent enormities committed under the fasces and swastika. The former writer for Vatican Radio in the war years, though personally shielded by treaty, had firsthand knowledge of the depredations of Hitler's henchmen in Italy and elsewhere. He had to confess that he often wondered where God hid His face as the Satanic atrocities of those days unfolded. The eternal question posed by Job and every theologist, amateur or professional, down through the ages. He had no answer that would not shake the foundations of his faith.

With a clap of hard binding he closed the book, having decided to take dinner in town. The day had been fraught with emotion and he wanted to relax and view the passing scene.

He headed for a trattoria he had passed near the Duomo on the Vico Ebrei, guessing from the name of the location, Hebrew Alley, that he might find Jewish food there. In his years at Rome, he was an habitué of the Jewish Ghetto by the banks of the Tiber, which boasted some of the best inexpensive restaurants in the capital city. As he tapped the stones of old Taormina with his cane, he recalled how his gustatory delights came to an end, shadowed by the events of October 16, 1943, when the jackboots of the occupier tramped through Venice Square in a violent mustering of some one thousand Jews, compatriots of Jesus who had been residents of the Eternal City for nearly two thousand years and inhabitants of the Jewish quarter for forty decades. The memory made Father Weiss, as a German and a priest of God, burn with shame. The Nazi thugs wrested these loyal Roman citizens, given full rights by the Italian Republic, seventy-three years earlier, from their homes and shops, herded them on cattle cars and sent them to join their fellow European Jews and other people despised by the maniacs of Aryanism in the ovens of Auschwitz, burnt offerings to the fallen idols of hate, prejudice and pseudo-science. Did we do enough to save them? the priest asked himself. Did Pius XII do enough? Bah, he thought, the historians will make their judgments sooner or later and probably get the facts wrong. He knew from personal experience that the Jesuits who ran Marquis Marconi's enterprise in Vatican Radio did their best to shield their independence from the Fascists and Nazis and alert the world that Jews and other pariahs were being corralled into walled ghettos, auguring even worse fates.

Father Weiss himself was among those who helped the pope craft his Christmas radio address of 1942, bewailing the plight of the the victims of "the hurricane of war." As the old Jesuit continued walking to the restaurant he tried to recall the exact words. "Let me see, let me see," he murmured. "It went something like this: 'Mankind owes a vow to the exiles'...No, the 'numberless exiles whom the war has torn from their native land and scattered in the land of the stranger.' Yes, yes, how could I ever forget? 'Who can make their own the lament of the Prophet, Our inheritance is turned to aliens;

our house to strangers.' I remember finding the citation in Lamentations 5:2, I think it was."

A villager smoking a corncob pipe turned to look at the stranger muttering to himself. He spat tobacco and shook his head dismissively.

The wanderer kept remembering and muttering: "Then the radio address went on, let me see, 'Mankind,' yes, 'mankind owes that vow to the hundreds of thousands of persons who, without any fault on their part, sometimes only because of their nationality or race, have been consigned to death or slow extermination.' " Father Weiss's gaze fastened on the cracks in the weathered cobblestones as he neared the Duomo. A dog in a doorway started barking at him.

"You see," he told himself, " we did what we could under desperate circumstances. Did we not? Did we not?" But of course he knew that one never could have done enough to counter these epic acts of cruelty, acts of which the world was still mostly ignorant. Such monumental questions should have eclipsed Father Weiss's personal crisis but no such luck. He still was obsessed with the question of why the Lord had shaped him from such contaminated clay. Had he himself to blame or God Almighty? He would have to work out the answer to this question before long. Time was running out.

He came to the Piazza Duomo and soon found the alley where he had seen the restaurant. Pointing to the street sign, Alley of the Hebrews, he asked a passerby if it was a Jewish restaurant.

The villager removed his yellow beret, scratched his

head and regarded the visitor in a manner that suggested that he had lost his marbles. Then he laughed aloud. "No, *Signor*," he said. "There is no Jew food around here." Then the villager added in what was clearly hyperbole, "There are no Jews in all of Sicily. We kicked them out in 1492." He laughed again as he drifted away.

Father Weiss frowned and his eyes followed the man with a look of disgust. He found a nearby restaurant where the tablecloths were decorated with branches of the wild olive tree and canisters of breadsticks. When the waiter came the diner ordered spaghetti with mullet roe and artichokes. As he recalled, it was a kosher dish. And very delicious.

After dinner the Jesuit sat in an outdoor cafe in the Piazza Duomo and ordered a grappa nightcap. This was getting to be a habit. There was a chill in the air and he turned up the collar of his gaberdine jacket. He would have to buy a topcoat, he figured, for when the weather turned cold in earnest. He could use a hat too. He sipped the golden brandy and as usual thought of the past. Always the past. The future was too dark to see clearly.

The square was thronged with the customary *passegiatori*, the promenaders who filled the squares of Italy after the evening meal to see and be seen, drink digestifs and eat ice cream. The men, arm in arm, led the parade and the women lagged behind, gossiping and giggling. The kids chased each other around the fountains. The men strutted like roosters and the women let them strut. They knew who the real bosses were; on the hearth the positions were reversed. The men, the women realized, were too weak in the head, too fragile of ego not to stage a burlesque, to make the *bella figura*. So the women humored the poor simpletons.

And Father Weiss watched the eternal show, sipping the strong pomace drink.

"So, Padre, we meet again," a syrupy voice said. It was the Englishman. This time his older companion was with him.

"Hello," said Father Weiss, without flavor.

The Englishman said, "May I introduce my companion, George?" He turned to the older man and added, "George, this is the nice priest I was telling you about: Father Weiss."

The priest tried to avoid frowning. He was not happy to have been a topic of their conversations.

"Charmed," said George with a curt nod.

"How do you do," said the priest, mimicking the English expression. He always wondered how such an incomplete expression evolved, and when posed with it himself was often tempted to rejoin, "How do I do what?" Still, he had used it out of habit.

George appeared tired. He wore a gray fedora at a jaunty angle and a tan tweed suit. His face was cross-hatched with wrinkles and the stub of a gray mustache clumsily colored brown grew over his thin upper lip.

Reginald Bliss said, "We just enjoyed a splendid meal at the Excelsior Hotel. Rather pricey but the grilled lamb was worth every lira. May we sit down?"

George looked pained. "Reggie, don't you think we should call it a night?"

"Stop being an old fuddy-duddy," said the younger partner. "It's the shank of the night." He peered at the priest. "Isn't it, Anton? May I call you Anton?"

"Of course," said the priest without enthusiasm, to both questions.

Reginald Bliss took a seat, followed with obvious reluctance by his partner. The younger man raised his hand, "Oh, waiter!"

The server arrived, his hands tented in front of his apron.

"Three champagne cocktails," Bliss said, holding up three fingers.

"*Si, signor.*"

"Not for me, thanks," said the priest, raising his glass. "I already have a drink."

Bliss shrugged and dropped one finger in his sign to the waiter. "Do you always deny yourself?" he asked airily.

"I have moderate habits."

"I've known many clergymen with habits of self-indulgence, if you catch my drift."

"I'm not sure I do."

The Englishman let the subject drop — for the moment. He measured the priest with a crafty smile. He took another tack: "Have you been absorbing the beauties of Taormina? It has many delights, as I'm sure you have noticed."

"I've seen some fine churches. I've spent some time in the Greco-Roman theater."

"That's all well and good but surely you don't prefer stones to — shall we say — natural objects."

"Yes, there is much natural beauty hereabouts," Father Weiss conceded. He realized the Englishman was playing a game of cat and mouse but he hardly knew how to extricate himself.

"And the people?" the interrogator said slyly. "Don't you find them rather beautiful? Or are you too chaste to think of them that way?"

The priest had had enough of the game and the appearance of the waiter with the drinks provided an opening to divert the course of things. The priest said, "You know Taormina well, Mr. Bliss. Do you have some sightseeing suggestions?"

Bliss stroked his chin. "Matter of fact, I do. I would visit the Old Fountain where my countryman D.H. Lawrence took up residence. You've heard of this writer?"

"Yes, but I haven't read any of his works. I'm told his novels were somewhat risqué."

"I'll say!" replied Bliss with a chuckle. "I'm certain all his books are condemned by your church. They seem all to have the word 'love' in their titles: *Sons and Lovers, Women in Love, Lady Chatterley's Lover*. That one was banned in half the Western World. You don't know what you're missing, Padre. I'm told he modeled Lady Chatterley after an Englishwoman who settled here in Taormina. And the lover was modeled after a Sicilian gardener that she took up with. It's all so delicious."

George, drowsy-eyed, interjected, "I met the chap once or twice in the London clubs. Handsome fellow, I thought, in a rustic way. He died about twenty years ago." George then shielded his mouth and said in a whisper, "He was a bit of a Nancy, I thought."

Bliss laughed.

The German priest didn't understand the sobriquet and anyhow didn't care to know the meaning. Though, he had a notion.

"I'm told the house at the Old Fountain now is being rented by another writer, an American boy. I forget his name."

"Truman Capote," George said helpfully. "I read his book, *John Fury*. Didn't like it." His frown deepened the ruts on his face.

Bliss said, "I saw him once at the hotel bar with the friend he rents the house with. He seems to drink a lot."

"He's very little and blond, like a cherub," said George. "And his eyes are always following the young Sicilian barmen and waiters."

"Birds of a feather...," said Bliss.

The old priest pretended not to follow the drift of the conversation. He started to shiver as the evening grew colder. "I think I'll call it a day," he announced as he tossed off the grappa.

"If you must," Bliss said under hooded eyelids. "But before you go I have another sightseeing suggestion for you."

"All right," said the priest, rising from the chair. "What

is it?"

"I suggest you visit the Public Gardens. The place is quite popular and the foliage and flowers are lovely. It is not far from IX Aprile. It's very charming and I'm sure you will find pleasure there. It's very nice at night too."

"At night?"

"Yes. There are lamps here and there. It's romantic."

Father Weiss had no reaction to this description. "I bid you both good-night," he said. Then he noticed that George was dozing, his chin on his breastbone and drool issuing from his mouth.

On the way back to his apartment the old priest happened to glance up a flight of stone steps and caught sight at the pinnacle of the tour guide dressed all in white, his costume luminous in the dark alley. His ashen hair was swept back and brilliantined. The man bowed to him; the priest continued on his way but the sight of the tour guide remained emblazoned in his mind.

The priest readied himself for bed. A brisk wind rattled the shutters as he searched for the wool nightshirt he had bought years ago while vacationing in Bavaria. It was plaid and ratty at the edges but he took an infantile comfort from wearing it though the weather had been too warm for its use so far. As he searched his luggage he noticed that the night was filled with an unusual chorus of animal noises in the valley: dogs howling, donkeys braying, cats mewling, sheep baaing. What on heaven and earth was going on?

This was Sicily, he concluded, and dismissed the question from his mind. He soon found the frayed nightshirt, put it on and went to sleep, serenaded by an orchestra of animals.

SEVEN

Concetta laid breakfast before the old priest, poured his coffee and asked, "Did you sleep well?"

He looked up at her from the newspaper. She appeared haggard; a stray ringlet of black hair curled over her forehead. "Like a baby," he said, sipping coffee.

"And the noises didn't bother you?"

"Noises?" Then he remembered, "Oh, the animals. No, they didn't disturb my sleep. What was that all about?" He quashed the cigarette under his heel.

Concetta fixed him with her black onyx eyes. "You should leave Taormina," she said ominously.

He formed a puzzled smile. "Leave? Why on earth ...?"

The clatter of a squadron of sparrows taking flight from the trees cut off the conversation.

"Hear that?" she said, "Even the birds know."

"I don't follow."

"We think we are so smart. But the earth, the plants and the animals, they know much more than we do."

"But God placed these things here to serve us." He glanced down again at the newspaper.

"Maybe. But in my experience the servant is often smarter than the master. And a flea can be smarter than a man. You should leave as soon as possible."

"May I finish my breakfast first?" he drawled.

"This is no joke."

He was chastened by her words. "I'm sorry," he said. "But I still don't understand."

She placed her palms on the table and leaned close to his face. "Look here, you know what all that rumpus was in the night?" she asked in a dark sibylline voice. "The animals were fleeing the mountains for the valley. And the valley animals were flocking to the coast. Some even broke through their pens."

"I see. They feel some disaster is coming. Sixth sense, so to speak."

She placed her hands on her hips, signaling a small triumph. "At last you're as smart as a flea."

"A nice compliment." He went back to reading about the United Nations peace plan sponsored by the U.S. and Britain.

"Again you joke but I am serious. For your own good, leave. The animals, they feel tremors that we can't feel. They hear voices that we can't hear."

His smile was condescending. "Now you go too far, Concetta. What voices?"

"Yes, the mountain speaks. If you ascend to the fumaroles you will hear them too."

He drank coffee. "You're saying Mount Etna will erupt. When?"

She shrugged. "I don't know. Soon. You must leave."

"But why? Taormina is not on the slopes. We're too far away to face danger."

"For an intelligent and educated person, you know little of this matter. The volcano spits poison gas and ashes into the air and the wind carries them all over. You'd be foolish to stay, Padre."

"Then why in heaven do you and the others stay here."

Her gaze lingered on the snow-capped mountain, blue in the haze of morning, this megalith that was always with them like an unruly kinsman.

"We belong to the volcano and she belongs to us. She has two faces, like Janus.

She kills and she gives life. If she sometimes acts wildly and wickedly, that is her nature. We are tied to this place. You are not."

He pondered her words. The garden had a view of the sea where the priest saw fishermen casting their nets under a turquoise sky and a gang of circling terns. Church bells pealed in town. The sun climbed the eastern sky to reign over the long aqua line of the Ionian Sea and the blue hills of Calabria behind. He looked up at this village soothsayer. "Life seems to be going on normally," he said.

"I told you, people are foolish." She paused.

Father Weiss finally said, "I will consider your advice."

She gave a grunt of resignation. Then she said, "You don't look well, you know? Wait here, I will give you a dose of fish liver oil."

He grimaced but did as he was told.

He made his way to town, intending to climb up to the house called the Old Fountain about fifteen minutes above the village center. The place where D. H. Lawrence lived for five years required a steep ascent. He passed streets named for sojourners and foreigners like Wilhelm Von Gloeden, who photographed Sicilian boys in erotic poses, and landscape painter Otto Geleng. Both were Germans whose works circulated throughout Europe, causing a wave of tourism to this once obscure Sicilian outpost by wayfarers seeking natural beauty and otherwise unmentionable pleasures. On his ascent over ivy-clothed stone staircases often scarred by the wounds of wartime rubble, the old priest saw many tangible proofs of such attractions, both beautiful vistas and the often-dizzying beauty of the local inhabitants. What a comely race of people, he reflected, had this cauldron of humanity produced with God's help over the millennia! What a lovely fusion arose here from the mingled bloodlines of Sicels, Sicans, Phoenicians, Greeks, Byzantines, Arabs, Romans, Normans and others!

He stopped to rest as he reached the Street of the Capuchins, rewarded by another grand view of the sea. He assumed that there was nothing much to see of an old house that the guidebooks said was of no particular architectural interest, owned by a peasant who returned from working in America with a few coins to rub together, unlike most of his compatriots. The old priest leaned his cane against a balustrade, sat on the rail and lit a cigarette. He let his eyes sweep over the splendid scene before him, the steep cliffs with their plunging gardens, rich with cacti and carob and citrus trees and flowers of every description, all crowned by the reflecting blue mirror of Mare Ionia crowned it all, ready to conjure the Fata Morgana. He even could catch a glimpse of the faraway coastal railroad depot surrounded by a rose garden that the station master carefully tended. Distances evaporated in this hilly place, he thought. And everybody nurtured growing things. He blew tobacco smoke into the air and coughed. The wind was brisk in this altitude and he felt cold. This reminded him that he was going to buy a coat.

He resumed his journey and found the house, a building of stone and stucco barely distinguishable from the neighboring buildings. There was a large garden where he wickedly could imagine the English lady dallying with the man with the hoe. He banished the impious thought by making the sign of the cross.

He finished the cigarette and took the Ring Road toward the Corso, where he recalled having seen a tailor shop marked by a swatch of cloth tacked to the crosspiece of the door just above the amulet against the Evil Eye. Even heading down hill he felt winded and congested. On the way, he mulled over Concetta's admonition and persuaded himself that her fears were unjustified. He chuckled at the idea that he, a Jesuit, a reasonable acolyte of Saint Thomas Aquinas almost had fallen under the spell of a superstitious Sicilian folk magician. She meant well, he thought. But he would leave Taormina when he was good and ready.

He found the tailor shop and a short while later emerged with two new articles of clothing that would fortify him against the chilly nights: a black woolen cape lined in yellow silk and a black beret. These rakish garments were chosen deliberately — with the encouragement of the tailor — to set him apart from his vocation and add spice to his waning years on earth. A small dose of vanity, after all, was permitted to a man who had sacrificed so much for Holy Mother Church. He put them on immediately.

The tailor, an androgynous-appearing young man with sunken cheeks and ginger hair, on learning that his customer was eager to see the sights, suggested he visit *La Villa*, a local name for the Public Gardens. The man eulogized the destination with typical local hyperbole: "as beautiful as The Garden of Eden before the fall." The priest remembered that Bliss also had praised the gardens and so he decided to see the place for himself.

The gardens lay a short distance from the main square, the southern boundary marked by a long stone wall at the edge of the cliff upon which Taormina stands. Father Weiss approached the destination by the Via Roma. In a village full of splendid vantages this spot served as the jewel in the crown, with panoramic views encompassing the countryside, volcano and sea, with a flock of fleecy clouds grazing above. Even in late autumn the place trilled with avian, plant and insect life. The sounds of splashing fountains and caviling parrots provided natural background music to the pageant. Varieties of trees and wildflowers added color and shade to the scene. The old priest descended a stone staircase that led to one of several strange edifices of stone, wood and brick in a mishmash of styles that he assumed would serve as gazebos or pagodas where the visitor could rest and drink in the sensual pleasures of the place. He meandered along the gravel paths amid the odors of exotic plants, the sight of goldfish sashaying in the central fountain and the many other natural marvels at hand. These sights and sounds might have been an occasion for the retired cleric to bear silent witness to God's bounty, to become "betrothed to the beauty on the face of things," as Laxness put it. But instead he felt himself gripped by baser feelings more rooted in the earth than in the airy places of the spirit. He knew this, whether he could admit it to himself: A serpent slithered in the gardens of Taormina.

The old priest sat on a stone bench to catch his breath. He took from his pocket his breviary and as an antidote to poisonous notions started to read the midmorning prayers;

> Come, Holy Ghost, who ever one
> Art with the Father and the Son;
> Come, Holy Ghost, our souls possess
> With thy full flood of holiness.

> In will and deed, in heart and tongue

With all the powers, thy praise be sung;

And love light up our mortal frame

Till others catch the living flame.

The Jesuit heard the sound of voices on the path. He looked up and saw approaching him the honeymoon couple he had met on the car trip to town. They were accompanied by a lame guide in a grey cap who dragged his left foot behind him like a sack of stones. He wore a florid mustache in the manner of King Umberto and an expression of pseudo-sophistication. The young couple noticed Father Weiss sitting on the bench and at first seemed not to recognize him in his new flashy clothes but soon nodded in recognition. The priest responded with a slight bow.

Then the halt-foot man with the gaudy mustache began his practiced soliloquy about the gardens and Father Weiss stopped reading the breviary to eavesdrop. Thus he learned that the park was the brainchild of Florence Trevelyan, an Englishwoman who lived in Taormina in the 19th Century and bought the former farmland to create a bucolic adjunct to her villa in the manner of the great landowners of the British Isles. She also owned the rocky outcropping on the coast called *Isola Bella* and married a local doctor who was also town mayor. She designed the park's idiosyncratic style. His auditors made the grunts of appreciation that seemed warranted but it was clear to the old priest that they were going through the motions, so to speak, to hoodwink the people back home in America into thinking that they were not so rapt by the exploration of each other's bodies that they had no time for Italy's cultural wonders to seduce them.

The German Jesuit then scolded himself for his cynicism. And this led to even deeper regret. To whom could he confess his evil thoughts and desires? Certainly not to Father Attilio. Only to the Living God Who for some ungodly reason fashioned him with a reasoning mind and a concupiscence for unholy things. Why was he chosen to arm-wrestle with the Devil? Why he? As always, the answer eluded the old priest.

The trio of two honeymooners and one mangle-foot guide moved down the path and Father Weiss continued reading his breviary to a chorus of birdsong. After a while he rose to continue exploring the place. The sun, now at the apex of its ascent, sketched dappled shadows slanting through the olive trees onto the stone walkway. Then the sunlight blinked as an airplane passed overhead. The voice of the tour guide slowly faded and Father Weiss felt himself alone in this wretched Eden. He found a remarkable stone garden where five dolmens were erected to mark the tombs of the Englishwoman's five dead dogs. The site reminded the priest of a miniature Stonehenge, with prehistoric monuments he had seen in a picture book in the Vatican Library. How odd, he thought. Next he came upon plaques fixed to the trees with the names of local combatants who gave their lives for *La Patria* in the Great War. Many were beardless striplings who had traded their tasseled caps for the plumed headgear of the *Bersaglieri* and the hardships of famine and malaria for a glorious death in the trenches of Europe and the deserts of Palestine. There was a Devil's bargain for you, the old priest thought.

He continued touring the park and soon passed a beautifully formed young lad who seemed to be wandering aimlessly along the path. He was olive-skinned and slight and wore a gold earring and rustic clothing. As they crossed paths the youngster turned back toward the old man and gave him a honeyed smile.

Father Weiss hesitated and quickly realizing what was up, recited under his breath instead of a traditional prayer a remembered quotation from Flaubert's *Temptation of Saint Anthony:* "Shake the vermin from thy rags! Rise up from thy filth! Thy God is not a Moloch who demands human flesh in sacrifice!" Then he hustled down the path without looking back.

He found another bench and sat to regain his composure. He now realized why the Englishman had recommended the park to him and wondered how the man had sensed his twisted nature. Did he emit some secret scent detected only by kindred souls? As he pondered these matters he sank into a pit of despondence.

Meanwhile he lost track of time. He did not notice how clouds were gathering over the seaside horizon or how a rising wind chattered through the oleander leaves or how the sun retreated behind a bank of dark clouds. The pat-pat of large raindrops on the pathways brought him to his senses. In a flash the rain crescendoed to a downpour. "Oh, my," he said aloud. "I will catch my death." Peering into the distance he saw the baroque brickwork of one of the pagoda-like struc tures that dotted the park. He calculated that it was about 30 meters away and would provide shelter till the rain ended. Leaning on his cane he headed there as quickly as possible. The old priest was breathing heavily when he reached the building; the interior seemed about the size of a small room. He entered the brick archway.

As he waited for his eyes to get used to the darkness he heard odd snuffling sounds, prompting him to wonder if there were animals inside. Soon he saw that he was correct: only they were human animals. With a sharp intake of breath he realized that he had interrupted the young boy with the gold earring and an older man engaged in an act of sodomy. He rushed back out into the rain.

The sacristan filled the copper bathtub with what he made sure to inform the old priest was a precious commodity in Sicilian villages — hot water. Meanwhile Father Weiss, teeth chattering like castanets, removed his sodden clothing.

"Thank you, Ignazio," he said as he climbed into the tub and sank into the steamy water.

The sacristan, tongue lolling, shook his head like a disappointed schoolmaster.

"Your Reverence should know enough to come out of the rain," he said.

The old priest looked sheepish. He said nothing in his own defense.

"I bring a bar of soap." said the sacristan.

"Thank you," Father Weiss said again.

When he came back with the soap Ignazio asked, "Where did you go to be caught in the rain?"

The naked old priest began scrubbing himself. "I was visiting the Public Gardens."

"Ah, I see."

"The rain came unexpectedly," he said, mildly annoyed at having to explain himself to this humble man. Behind his annoyance lay the specter of shame.

"I left towels on the counter," said the sacristan. "You need anything else?"

"No, thank you. You've been very helpful."

Ignazio hesitated, appearing on the brink of adding something. He eyed the bather with obvious curiosity. Finally he said, "I must go polish the sacred vessels. My work is never done."

"Yes," said the priest. "But is is holy work."

"Yes," echoed the sacristan. "Father Attilio says that God will reward me." Then he rubbed two fingers together, adding, "But I could use a little more reward in this life." His tongue jutted between his lips as he made a guttural sound to indicate a form of sarcastic laughter.

The sacristan left the priest to soak in the bath and in his thoughts. Despite his attempts to annul it, the scene in the pagoda emerged again and again as an image from the acid bath of his mind. Father Weiss was not naive about sexual matters. He had not been an eremite, after all. And he had not been blind to the blithe breaking of vows by his colleagues in the ministry, in which secret lives blossomed like black roses. Yet he always had tried to take his sacred promise seriously, freely, to break the chains of desire. He was proud of his success in the contest.

Helmut's face now appeared in his mind's eye, that lovely tan face with long lashes over drowsy dark eyes and lips like red fruit. Ah, how that face had set aflame his youthful passion!

Anton Weiss never set eyes on him again after entering the ministry in 1900. But they corresponded for a while and Anton heard tidbits of his history from friends and family as the years passed.

Helmut, always fond of flashy uniforms, joined the Imperial Navy. His parents held a ball in his honor under the gas chandeliers and sconces of the family mansion when he received his commission as Lieutenant in the spring of 1902. Young Anton had read about it in a letter from his mother and that helped him imagine the scene. All the girls in their satin ball gowns and Gibson Girl hairstyles swooning over the dashing naval officer. The rouged matrons focusing their lorgnettes, sizing up the young buck's potential as a son-in-law. They all would be disappointed.

Naval officer Helmut Feld rose in the ranks: Over-lieutenant, Captain-lieutenant, Rod Captain-lieutenant, Corvette Captain, and Frigate Captain. He most likely would have risen to the Admiralty if his further ascension had not been thwarted by fate in the garb of The Great War. At age 36, Captain Helmut Feld, smartly outfitted in his tailored beribboned blue coat joined the clownfish of the deep when his ship was torpedoed in the Battle of Jutland.

He had never married.

The water now was tepid and the old priest rose from the bathtub. After fifty-one years, he thought while drying himself, some essential part of him was mired in the psyche of a love-sick boy. How did he differ from the maidens and matrons of old Lübeck? he wondered. Father Anton Weiss was sixty-nine years old but inside he felt the same as the boy on the banks of the River Trave. Isn't that true of all Adam's seed? The body ripens and withers but the eternal soul is immutable. This fact is both a blessing and a curse.

He looked out the window. The rain had stopped. He heard the three women singing in the garden again. He dressed, lit a cigarette, coughed and went outside

Nothing compares to a Sicilian garden in the wake of rain. The flowers shake off the moisture and come to life again, more fragrant than before. The birds forsake their hiding places and take their customary spots in the orchestra pits beneath the arbors. The trees stand proud, invigorated, wearing cleansed green clothes. The soil sends voluptuous signals into the air.

Father Weiss sat at the wrought iron table with an espresso corrected by anisette. provided by the good witch Concetta, who now handed him a copy of the daily newspaper.

"Here," she said, "read this, since you don't take siesta."

"I'm not sleepy," he replied, scanning the front page:

The communists called a general strike but it was effective only

in the industrial regions of North Italy; the UN General Assembly was in session; Soviet spies were on trial in Yugoslavia; NATO members, including Italy, met in Paris to plan common defense measures; brigandage was on the rise in Sicily.

The old priest laid his cigarette in the groove of a plastic Cinzano ashtray and sipped the espresso. The postwar world was still a mess. Big surprise!

"Next time you go sightseeing," said Concetta, "listen to the radio for the weather."

"Okay," he said with a sheepish grin.

"And take an umbrella."

"Sure, sure," he said, taking a drag on the *Gitanes*.

She glared at him. "You shouldn't smoke."

"I know," he said, taking another puff.

"It makes you sick."

"I know."

"What illness do you have?"

"Asthma. And maybe something else, I'm not sure."

"For a Jesuit priest, you are foolish."

He smiled and said, "You are a keen judge of character."

She sat down across the table from him. "Did you consider my advice?"

He lowered his eyes to the newspaper. "I did," he said in a resigned tone.

"Well?"

"I don't want to leave. I like it here. It is beautiful."

She sighed. "There are beautiful places in the world that lack the treachery of Sicily."

"Treachery?"

"Yes. This land seduces you and then betrays you." She wiped her hands on her apron, emulating, he thought, Pontius Pilate with his ewer of water. "But you can suit yourself."

"I appreciate your concern, Concetta. Can't you say some words over me to protect me from the evil spirits?"

"The priest blasphemes," she drawled.

The comment caused him to laugh and then she joined in the merriment.

Silence reigned between them for a while as he drank his coffee. Then she said, "So, did you enjoy the Public Gardens?"

He blushed at the question before offering a perfunctory answer: "Yes, they are beautiful."

She waited a beat, narrowed her eyes at him and asked, "Did you see the boys?"

He feigned ignorance. "The boys?"

"The country boys."

He lied: "I don't know what you mean."

She looked skeptical but took him at his word. "The local boys go the Gardens regularly to meet tourists. But if you don't know what I mean it is not a fit subject for conversation."

"Now you've piqued my interest,"he said, maintaining the charade.

"Young lads here are more natural. Remember, we descend from the ancient Greeks."

He let the mask fall. "I see what you mean."

"Rich men of a certain stamp come here from the North

of Europe to enjoy practices that are tabu where they come from. Americans come too. A rich American writer now stays at the Old Fountain."

Father Weiss nodded and drew on the cigarette to cover his speechlessness.

"We are more tolerant here," she continued. "And then there is the poverty here in Sicily. This encourages bartering, shall I say? Transactions. You can guess what I mean."

"I can," he admitted. "These are sinful things."

She shrugged. "Many locals, I'm afraid, don't see it that way, Father. They come from the farms and live close to nature."

"But these practices are *unnatural*," he protested, his voice rising.

"Remember the boys are ripe. They have certain desires too. But they cannot touch the girls before marriage without causing dishonor and facing vendetta. So they take another route to find release. It is like an apprenticeship in love."

His voice oozed with disgust. "This is not love," he said. "This is lust."

"Well," she said, hunching her shoulders. "Love, lust? Here, it is not so cut-and-dried. Even some parents turn a blind eye. And they earn money to keep from starving. Later they get married and have children. And things go on as they have for centuries."

"I'm surprised and frankly disappointed that you justify it. Surely the church doesn't approve. And God won't turn a blind eye."

She rose from the table, seeing the futility of pursuing the subject. "*Beh,*" she said, "I have work to do."

And she departed, leaving the old priest to marinate in his thoughts. What if she was right? What if he had wasted a lifetime denying himself the pleasure of physical love, all to no avail if his proclivities were not sinful but natural? Who but the Creator Himself had installed this wolf inside him? What if he were able to see life and love through Grecian eyes rather than through the myopia of the modern puritanical North and the strictures hypocritical churchmen imposed? He was a student of history. He knew that esteemed male figures down through the ages indulged in a passion for beardless youths, especially in manly Sparta, philosophical Athens and warlike Macedon. Was Anton Weiss wiser than Socrates? Braver than Alexander or Lysander?

Get thee behind me, the old priest commanded the tempter. He stubbed out the cigarette and walked over to the church where in the half-light of candles and uncertainty he prayed to Saint Anthony of the Desert, fought the devil.

EIGHT

As the town stirred to life after siesta time, the old priest again made his halting way to the misnamed Piazza IX Aprile to visit the public library. Radios crackled in the oval doorways and the scent of jasmine and the bleats of lambs under the farmer's knife floated up from the valley in the wind. Vendors hawked chestnuts and pistachios as mutilated veterans of the Battle of Sicily held out their gnarled mendicant hands. Somebody somewhere strummed a mandolin. As the retired priest put cane to stone and cane to tile he asked himself how he could leave such a place where the cyclorama of life and death, growth and atrophy so haunted the senses. No, Concetta, the boarder would stay to see the show.

When he arrived at the building the visitor stood under the crenellated bell tower and took a few seconds to consult his guidebook. He learned that the library was housed in a Gothic structure that once served as a church and convent of

Augustinian friars. The villagers built it in 1486 to honor the martyr Saint Sebastian, whose manly figure, tied to a post and pierced by arrows, adorned the canvases of several famous painters. The oils and reproductions depicting this victim of Emperor Diocletian's quest to stamp out Christianity filled churches all over Italy and the ubiquity of the picture, especially in hallowed places, often embarrassed Father Weiss by the near nakedness and masculine beauty of the subject. It was hard for him to avoid the notion that the skill and passion conveyed in the artists' brushstrokes were inspired by motivations other than the urge to give glory to God.

The old priest climbed the steps, passed under the marble lintel and entered a large hall where, sure enough, an altarpiece depicting Saint Sebastian's ordeal was prominently displayed. The visitor did not examine it closely. He asked an attendant for directions to the reading room and soon found himself in another serene space under a wood-beamed ceiling and paneling carved with lions and eagles. He sat down at a long wooden table and drew out his notebook and pen. He had decided to come to the library hoping that for once he could scribble his wayward thoughts and meandering remembrances without distractions.

Where would mistress memory transport him today? There soon came to his mind a palimpsest of his life in the city-state nested on the west bank of the Tiber in the heart of the Eternal City.

It was a fine July morning in 1943 when Father Anton Weiss opted to walk up the hill to the radio station to deliver the script he had finished the night before. He believed that taking the route that passed through the lushly green and manicured Vatican Gardens would lighten his spirits, that its geometric design would create the illusion of order in a world gone insane.

Though Vatican City maintained a stance of neutrality, the world at the Holy See's doorstep wallowed in war. And the German Jesuit day after day felt mortified that the chief agents of barbarity belonged to his native country. A few days earlier the Allies had invaded Sicily. He took this as a hopeful sign of the approaching end of this international dementia.

He stooped to pluck a wildflower from the grass. Just then a summer snowfall of leaflets fell from the sky. He dropped the flower and grabbed a leaflet before it hit the ground. He read:

"Italian friends, Attention! Until now we have sought in every way to avoid the bombardment of Rome. The Axis powers have learned to take advantage of this. But now unfortunately the time has come when we must turn our weapons toward your city. We will make every effort to avoid targeting historic monuments and civilian areas. We are warning you because you still have the chance to save yourselves. Take cover in your homes and avoid potential military targets. Respect this warning. It was made for your advantage. Signed: The Fifth Army."

The Jesuit had read the notice with a grim expression. His

Holiness would be very upset, Father Weiss thought. Pius XII already had pronounced to all nations in his radio speeches — some of which the Jesuit himself had had a hand in composing — that even leaflets straying on Vatican grounds would amount to a violation of the city-state's neutrality. Moreover the pontiff had exerted every fiber of his diplomatic skill to convince the Allies not to bomb Rome; its churches and historic treasures comprised the world's priceless patrimony. The combatants till now had respected the prohibition.

Father Weiss sat on a bench and reached into his briefcase to search among his papers for a telex transcript of the minutes of a British cabinet meeting on this subject, which Vatican secret agents had obtained. He remembered receiving a copy about a month earlier. He might have to write a broadcast on the subject so he wanted to refresh his recollection. Leafing through papers he soon found the transcript and traced the words with his forefinger: "It is agreed that we should on no account molest the Vatican City, but that our action as regards the rest of Rome would depend upon how far the Italian government observed the rules of war."

There it was. What had changed? he asked himself. Would the change in policy cause a breach between the British and their American allies, who strenuously opposed bombing Rome because of the many Roman Catholics in the U.S. armed forces? All these thoughts and others tumbled in his mind. He looked up at the two parabolic radio towers and then turned his gaze on the central dome of St. Peter's Basilica lying on lower ground at eye level to the priest. The products of the geniuses of Michelangelo and Marconi stood face to face. The unthinkable notion of the destruction of, say, the Sistine Chapel or the Pantheon crept into his mind. He arose, feeling shaky. He had better hurry off to the station, he thought, gathering up his things. There would be much work to do today.

And so it happened: In broad daylight on 19 July, 1943 some five-hundred American and British bombers, including the famed Flying Fortresses, armored green birds of prey, left their nests inNorth Africa to soar over the cypresses and hills of Rome, targeting airports, Nazi headquarters and the rail yards in the San Lorenzo district east of the city center, which suffered great devastation. The waves upon waves of steel raiders from the sky tried to rain down their death blows with precision, avoiding the monuments, holy places and artifacts of history. Still, more than 1,600 residents of San Lorenzo would die for Il Duce this day whether they admired the lantern-jawed leader or not. Father Weiss knew for a fact that most residents of the left-wing proletariat neighborhood hated his guts. But the bombs did not know this. They whined and thundered and killed without ideology. More than three thousand died under the bombardment.

The cosseted residents of the neutral city-state heard the pandemonium. The clacking of the radio equipment and chattering of the ticker tape could not block the sound of the explosions from Father Weiss's ears. About three hours later the sirens were stilled as the bombing stopped and Rome began to take stock of the damage.

The German Jesuit was among those chosen to join the pope's entourage as he ventured from the sacred enclave to console the homeless and the bereaved. Amid the rubble of the Basilica of San Lorenzo, Pius, his aquiline features etched with lines of sorrow, sketched his papal blessing over the crowds and doled spiritual loaves and fishes to the war-weary Romans, whose antecedents had seen all this before and who could have made better use of physical food. As his eyes roamed over the debris Father Weiss's mind as usual roved the byways of history, prompting the thought that Pope Leo had convinced Attila to spare Rome but, alas, Pius could not deter Hitler, Mussolini, Churchill and Roosevelt to do the same.

"Ah, well," whispered Enrico Corelli, one of the priest's lay colleagues, "at least some good will come of this."

The priest gave the colleague, a radio journalist, an inquiring look.

"*Il Duce's* days are numbered," Corelli concluded.

Six days later Mussolini was ousted from power and placed under arrest. King Victor Emmanuel then named the weak-kneed popinjay tin soldier Marshal Pietro Badoglio as prime minister. In August the Allied bombers struck again. Though the Wehrmacht showed tenacity in defending the underbelly of Europe it didn't take a Cassandra to predict that the tide of war was turning against the Axis and the days of alliance between Italy and Germany also were numbered. And the Italian people? This life-affirming race for whom eating, drinking and lovemaking were elevated to high art had no stomach for war and starvation.

Ten months later Father Weiss ventured outside Vatican City on a bright June day to take his place among the crowds on the Via Appia to salute the forces of General Mark Clark's Sixth Army as they marched into the city. The citizens of Rome took a page from the annals of their ancestors and exploded with the effervescence of sparkling wine in their jubilance at the liberation from these last barbarian invaders, the modern Germans, ghosts of the Gauls and Goths who pillaged Rome in bygone times. The shameless girls kissed the GIs and rode on the barrels of Sherman tank guns, hitching their skirts to bare their cervine legs. The urchins mobbed the Americans for cigarettes and chocolates. And the oldsters wept with maudlin joy. The priest felt conflicting emotions: happiness for the end of war, sadness for the wasted lives. He heaved a heavy sigh as the people shouted hurrahs.

The priest got off the streetcar at *Ponte Sant'Angelo*, intending to walk the rest of the way to his apartment. The evening was a polished gem of June. The smooth surface of the Tiber mirrored the travertine face and five arches of the bridge surmounted by an indigo sky and the burnished bricks of Hadrian's Tomb in the distance. What loveliness reigns in God's tainted world! The pedestrian now approached the span by a ramp and studied the stucco sculptures of Saint Peter and Saint Paul. As he walked across he stopped here and there to admire the sculpted figures of angels holding the symbols of Christ's passion and death — Veronica's veil,

whips, crown of thorns, garment and dice, sarcastic super-
scription branding Jesus as King of the Jews, lance, vinegar
sponge to cruelly quench the prisoner's thirst, nails, and the
cross itself. How fitting, he thought, that these instruments of
scorn and pain should adorn the bridge, reminding Romans
to revel in suffering for the good of their souls. And that suffering is sometimes salved by the balm of divine intervention
as when an angel, according to legend, appeared on the roof
of the looming Castle of Sant'Angelo to herald the end of the
plague. It also reminded the observer that sanctity could
mean disaster: Dante writes that at the dawn of the fourteenth
century scores of pilgrims to Saint Peter's Basilica drowned
when part of the bridge crumbled under their weight.

As the contemplative young priest approached the other
side of the river he happened to look down at the pedestrian
path on the far bank where he saw something that made him
freeze in astonishment:

He was a mere boy of the Low Saxon physical type.
Perched askew on his blond head was a green campaign cap
bearing the insignia of the Sig runes of his company. A stream
of dry rusty blood ran down from a hole in his unlined forehead to his beardless cheek. He lay spread-eagle on the
stones. The dead German soldier reminded him of one of the
sculpted angels.

How lovely he looked!

Father Weiss surfaced from the depths of his memories
and observed that another person occupied the seat directly

opposite him at the long library table. He was a small sprite of a young man with wispy golden hair and darting blue eyes. He noticed the priest noticing him and smiled. He returned to his reading. Then a somewhat older man emerged from the book stacks and stood before the reader, placing his palms on the table.

"Let's go, Tru," the older man said in American English. He was tall, dark and sullen-looking. His sport shirt was unbuttoned nearly to his midriff. "I need some fresh air."

His companion, the pixieish little man with the bright blue eyes, seemed to pay no attention to the request to leave. "Listen to this, Jack," he said in a lisping voice. "The poetry is mediocre but I adore the sentiment. He recited the words in a voice loud enough for the priest to hear:

'It is not for the love of God
That I have done my soul this wrong;
'Tis not to make my reason strong
Or curb the currents of my blood.
But sloth, and fear of men, and shame
Impose their limit on my bliss:
Else had I laid my lips to his,
And called him by love's dearest name.'"

"Interesting," said the older man. "Who wrote it?"

There was a twinkle in the young man's eyes. "A boy named Symonds in a poem called "In the Key of Blue," written way back in 1893. Ever hear of him?"

"Nope."

"Well, I have. James Addington Symonds. He was a kin

dred soul, if you catch my drift. Lived in Venice, I think, where he had a gay old time, they say. He wrote books about 'Greek feeling' and 'manly love.'"

"And he wasn't arrested?" the companion said.

"No. He was married and had four daughters."

"Well, sloth and fear of men and shame never stopped you, did they?"

The young man heaved a sarcastic sigh. "Nor love of God, I'm afraid."

They both laughed. Then the older man said, "Let's go."

And they left the library, arm in arm.

Father Anton Weiss followed their departure with watchful eyes. How open they were, he marveled to himself. How free. "There," he whispered, *"but for the love of God go I."*

And he too left the library, passing again the altarpiece of Saint Sebastian. This time, he looked long and hard at the painting.

The sun was setting as Father Weiss found himself in the Public Gardens, drawn there almost against his will as if by a magnet. He heard sheep bells echoing in the valley and the beating of his own heart. He wore his black cape and beret and no Roman collar. The palm trees transformed into blue shadows against the pinking sky. The flowers in clay pots nourished the insects, lovingly, it seemed to the priest. He roamed the park with no clear objective, studied for a moment the bronze bust of the English lady who made the garden, observed the movements of the copper-colored fish in the pool. Nobody was around. What was he doing here in this scented place that made his heart trip and his mind reel with taboo thoughts? He felt afraid, excited and guilty, all at the same time, gripped by a fever of emotions. He didn't have to wait long.

A boy appeared on the stone path, hands thrust in his pockets, an unlit cigarette in his mouth. He was burly and walked with a jaunty gait. He looked about seventeen years old, the priest guessed. He wore a soft cap and corduroy clothes. A red bandana was tied around his neck.

The boy approached the priest: "Got a light?" he said in a coarse Italian accent.

Father Weiss fumbled for a match and lit the cigarette, illuminating the boy's rough-hewn features and a sardonic mouth from which he now expelled a gust of tobacco smoke. "You English?" he asked in English.

The old priest's throat was parched. "No, German," he said.

"German, huh?" he said rearing back and smiling. "What you do in Sicily?"

The Jesuit took a couple of deep breaths finding it hard to form words. Sweat beaded his forehead. "You know," he said finally, "seeing the sights, enjoying the sunny climate."

"Sure," said the burly boy, still smiling. "You wanna cigarette?"

"I have my own, thanks." He clumsily lit his own cigarette as he stood there not able to move as if cemented to the stone path. He was wracked by indecision.

"You like Taormina?"

"Yes, I do."

"What you like about it?" he asked in an insolent tone of voice, a tone conveying both jade and seduction.

The old priest blushed to the roots of his hair, searching for words of neutrality, words that would say nothing to discourage or encourage the young man from the all too obvious aim of this undignified standoff at dusk in a secluded garden. "Many things," he finally said. But he might have stammered any inane reply for verbal precision did not matter in this instant. The thing would run its course even if he barked like a dog or crooned like a Fiji Islander.

The boy stamped out his cigarette and cocked his head. He said, "Follow me."

The priest looked here and there. No bystanders. He followed the boy robotically, still not fully admitting to himself that he had reached this moment, the razor's edge of desire long dreamt of and feared. His pulse raced and his heartbeat like a metronome. He felt lost in an unfamiliar rapture. As the shadows lengthened the old priest and the uncouth boy walked side by side toward one of the secluded brick "beehives" that dotted the park. He told himself that he was still unsure whether he would go through with this but simultaneously felt his willpower ebbing away, beaten back by lust.

They stood facing each other in the dimness of the gazebo. The boy was calm; the priest was breathing heavily, leaning on his cane.

"You got money?" the boy asked.

"How much?" the priest croaked. He felt himself inhabited by an alien spirit, disembodied, playing a role on stage or in a dream.

"Twenty dollar," he said.

"I have no dollars. I have lira."

"You have mark?"

"Yes, I have marks."

"Fifty mark, then."

The Rubicon stretched before the old priest and it seemed like an eternity before he reached for his billfold, his hands shaking with expectation and revulsion.

At that moment the beautiful roughneck snatched the billfold from his hand and shoved the handsome old priest to the ground.

"Go fuck yourself, you disgusting old fairy," he spat out in Sicilian before running off into the newborn night.

Father Weiss lay in pain on the rough brick floor of the gazebo, gasping for breath. He lay motionless for some seconds of what seemed like elongated time before making in slow motion the sign of the cross, thanking the Lord Almighty for sending an angel in the guise of a roughneck thief to save him from himself and his lawless vice.

PART TWO — VULCAN

ONE

I am called Vulcan and my spirit lives and works in the belly of the earth. My realm lies close to the nether regions where the fires of Hades rage. Pluto is my next-door neighbor. Unlike my sibling gods and goddesses who enjoy pleasure and power in airy places, I must toil endlessly at the forge and furnace. The thought of this gnaws at me and builds the pressure in my soul. And I explode in anger. I view with pride the havoc wreaked by my sacrificial holocaust. Why do I punish men? Because they stole from me the secrets of fire. But I give life as well as death. My cruelty is regenerative and useful. Crops thrive in the soil of Vulcan. My cooled lava rocks form shelters. I am Vulcan, hear me. I am Vulcan, god of fire.

Eugenio Pappalardo watched the pine trees spark like matchsticks in the woods. There was nothing to do but watch and pray that the boiling rivers of lava would sink into the depression in the Valley of the Oxen and spare the family farm — the vineyards and citrus groves and chestnut trees that have stood for five centuries — from the volcano that never slept but drowsed until it awakened again in full fury to exact its tax. The landowner's neighbors had reported that the prized pistachios of Bronte village northwest of Etna already had fallen victim to one column of the fire-god's wrath and that a second stream a mile wide now threatened the village of Maletto. Pappalardo, the baron of Pedara, had caught the scent of disaster well before dawn as he watched the pine trees tinder. The volcano spoke at low frequency but the hunting dogs had heard its early song and warned their master of the advent. And soon the two main craters were extending claws of fire, smoke, ash and poison gases high into the early morning air. Fumaroles along the slopes sputtered and spit more venom at the sky.

Some villagers fled to the Ionian shore. The citizens of Catania and Messina went about their affairs, carrying umbrellas against the detritus of the eruptions. The denizens of northeastern Sicily were forming their eternal shrugs in the face of calamity. This was both their history and destiny: Earthquakes, tidal waves and volcanic eruptions were written in the geology of the cities and coastal villages in the shadow of Etna, a wild-eyed overlord whose periodic outbursts of temper were unavoidable.

The northerner, sojourner, tourist to cataclysm Father Anton Weiss sat in the courtyard of the baroque limestone mansion that housed the Catania branch of the Bank of Sicily reading the account of yesterday's volcanic eruption in the Paris Herald Tribune. The air even here thirty miles from the craters was thick with Etna's foul breath, the toxic gases and ashes belched into the sky and wind-borne to the lungs of living things. Still, the old priest lit a cigarette as he waited for an appointment with the bank manager to honor a letter of credit to get hard cash to replace the money the ruffian in the Public Gardens had stolen from him. He coughed into his handkerchief and read in English the black ink account of the eruption in the December 3 edition of the newspaper, datelined Palermo, written by a secondhand observer far from the showers of hot rocks and venomous smoke and gas. It was dry reportage. No deaths yet were recorded. Forests were set aflame and solitary farmhouses destroyed but the smithy's anger was appeased and he was napping again. The priest looked up from the newspaper and caught a glimpse through the smoky sky of the 11,000-foot peak of Mount Etna.

And the helpless citizens of Sicilian Ionia supplicated the virgin martyr Saint Agatha — as they have for ages — to lullaby the volcano into a deeper sleep. Catania's workers and tradesmen, led by priests and flanked by vendors of yellow candles, paraded the saint's jewel-encrusted statue containing her relics — lacerated breasts and extremities and her veil — from the cathedral through the winding streets of the seaport, down Via Etnea to the hill called Monte Sangiuliano. They sang and prayed under smoke and ash in what to the Hanseatic Jesuit's eyes appeared like pagan fervor, an emotional relic of centuries past when pre-Christian Catanesi bowed before an effigy of a fertility goddess. Who was he to judge? he asked himself as he smoked and coughed and examined his own conscience, his fragile flesh still hurting from the violent shove to the pavement in the garden.

Concetta had tended the wounds to his shoulder and hip when he returned to his apartment. She asked no questions, passed few judgments. As she cleansed his wounds with herbs, salves and potions of local provenance, unknown to him, the old priest began to regard her as a modern Magdalene for miscreants.

"You're a stubborn old man," she repeated, bandaging his shoulder.

"I know," he said.

"You should go home."

"I have no home." The words had come out like a hollow truth, an echo in a vaulted apse. His older sister Gabi had died in Berlin two years earlier, a widow whose only child, a son, languished in a Russian POW camp. He always thought of Mother Church or the Heart of Jesus as his home. But now he wasn't sure. Four walls and a ceiling with a bed to lay his head. Since boyhood that was the sum and substance of his home.

She fixed him with a knowing stare but said nothing more.

In his imagination he could still see her Delphic expression as he sat in the courtyard waiting to be summoned when his bank draft cleared.

He felt a tap on his shoulder.

"Excuse me, Reverend…"

The speaker was a handsome royal gendarme, a *carabiniere*, wearing a plaintive expression and holding a silver object in his right palm. The young man wore a full-dress uniform, from black bicorne hat with red and blue plume to his high black boots. To the old priest he seemed more beautiful than a sunrise.

"Yes, son? What can I do for you?"

The soldier pointed to the object in his palm, a religious medal. "I just bought this on the Via Etnea. Would Your Reverence be kind enough to bless it for me?"

"Of course, son." He took the medal from the beautiful gendarme.

The soldier said, "It is the medal of Saint Agatha. She protects us from the volcano."

Father Weiss blinked at the sooty sky and said to himself, Ah, my boy, she's not doing a very good job. And might she also protect me from myself in the presence of such as you? The Jesuit signed a cross with his right hand and intoned, "May this Saint Agatha medal and the one who uses it be blessed, in the name of the Father, and of the Son, and of the Holy Spirit. Amen."

"Oh thank you, good Father," said the dark-eyed soldier, receiving the medal and stooping to kiss the priest's veiny hand. Father Weiss's gaze was glued to the departing figure of the golden soldier and the back of his hand burned from the kiss. A bank clerk in a pinstriped frock coat soon came to inform the priest that his money was ready.

Father Anton Weiss folded his bent body into a first-row

kneeler of the Church of Saint Catherine near the Messina Gate and joined his hands in prayer. His eyes swept over the lovely baroque interior of the church. The Jesuit had come to this altar in another feeble attempt to whitewash his soul.

He looked down at the tiled floor, gathering his thoughts. It was noon and he could barely hear the twelve gongs of the single bell in the belfry above the church. They were nearly as faint as the beating of his heart. He raised his eyes to the brass chandelier, then let his gaze fall on the arched niche containing the statue of Christ crucified. The retired priest was alone in the church as the townsfolk were sitting down to the meal before siesta. Even as Vulcan grumbled, the rhythms of village life hummed on. It would take more than fire and brimstone to sidetrack Sicilians from their ancient ways.

His mind raced back to catechism class in Lübeck, a time when his soul was spotless, fertile soil for his black-robed teachers to plant seeds of guilt. His prayer now was not a petition but a question: Why? He spoke aloud to his faceless God in his native tongue: "*Warum?*" A black necklace of whys followed, echoing through the church. Why had a merciful God hatched in him this blackbird of desire? Did not Saint Paul say it was better to marry than to burn? You allow the peregrine falcon and the Bengal tiger to act on their inheritances but forbid men to satisfy the instincts that you bequeathed them at birth. Do you love us less than the beasts? Why? Help me to understand. If you shaped my nature on your unknowable celestial potter's wheel, why do you blame me for your own handiwork and punish me for your distor tions of form? Why, why, why?"

He abruptly grew silent, struggling to keep his emotions in check. He again studied the tiled floor as his knotted hands shook in their posture of prayer. He shut his eyes and shook his head as though to blot out his thoughts. But he could contain himself no longer. He raised his face to the rafters. "I hate you," he blurted out. "I hate you, Father, Son and Holy Ghost...If you exist...I hate you for sentencing me to a lifetime of *warped* feelings." With these words still resounding in the baroque apse of the old church, a bolt of remorse struck the blasphemer and he began to weep. After his shoulders stopped quaking, he said, "Forgive me, Lord," as his egoistic grievance faded. No, he did not fear damnation but he feared losing the opposite. Would he yield the banner on the brink of eternity? he wondered. He had devoted his life to the cause, to warfare between spirit and flesh. Would he surrender now and go to God with a blot on his soul and lose the only thing that really mattered when time expired: membership in the heavenly band of saints? Surely the face of God would outshine his lusts.

The old priest then took a deep breath and fell into a paroxysm of hacking and coughing. He was shaken in body and spirit. When he finally regained equanimity he left the church with slow steps, his cane landing hollowly on the tiles. Once outdoors he spat his bile on the ash-laden stones, mingling it with pigeon excrement and caked sheep droppings.

Hidden from sight in the sacristy, Father Attilio, the pastor of Saint Anthony's, stood as pale and immobile as the sur-

rounding statuary. He was lost in deep thought about everything he had just heard in a tongue he had learned as a school-
boy.

TWO

The old priest awoke from a shallow sleep to the sound coming through the wooden door, three women singing of flowers and faithless men. They crooned, like mourning doves with an auspicious message intelligible only to savants of Siculean lore.

The old priest's nightclothes were bathed in sweat.

He dressed and went outside to seek breakfast in the garden. The skies were clearer this day as Etna snored and smoldered. A breeze blew from the east and the sun tried to recapture his usual starring role in the skies over Sicily. He nodded a curt greeting to the trio of singing weavers who nodded back with an air of inscrutable gravity. A creaking shutter from the second floor, known locally as the *piano nobile,* hinted that Concetta might be spying on him.

He sat down at the garden table and soon *La Strega* appeared with an aromatic breakfast tray. They bid each other good morning and then he said, "The eruptions have stopped, thank the Lord."

Laying the tray on the table, she grunted and said, "Stopped? The beast is merely napping."

He cast her a look that mingled inquiry with admiration. "How do you know?"

Her face told him that the question hardly merited an answer. "I know," she said sharply, handing him a cup of espresso that was as dark as her perennial mood. She troweled his toast with quince made from prickly pear. Meanwhile he sweetened his coffee. He made the sign of the cross and drained the cup, which she refilled. They were silent for a while as the climbing sun burst through the ashen sky, cleared the surrounding foliage and washed over the breakfast table.

"See," the Jesuit said. "It promises to be a fine day."

She didn't speak but her expressive face again told the tale: He was kin to the village idiot. She waited a beat, then asked, "What do you plan to do today?"

"Get drunk," he said in a failed attempt to shock her.

"Why not?" she said with a shrug before sitting down opposite him. She said, "May I pose to you some personal questions?" She had donned her sibylline mask for the interrogation.

He wasn't sure how to answer. He settled on equivocation: "It's up to you, I suppose."

"Why did you become a priest?"

He stammered some before replying. Finally he said, "To

serve God, of course." He noticed how the sun played on her raven hair, revealing fresh highlights as if newly washed. "One may serve God in many ways," she said. "Does a brick-layer not serve God? Or a doctor?" A warbler trilled in a nearby olive tree, prompting her to add, "Even the songbirds serve God, don't they?"

"Yes, but I chose the priesthood to serve God in a special way. To sacrifice myself as Christ did. And to minister to our fellow Catholics." He stared blankly at the smoky volcano and coughed into his handkerchief, then nibbled at the toast.

She eyed him with skepticism. "What about children?" she asked. "Did you not want to have children? A family?"

He waited before replying, mulling the question over. He might have said that the laity were his children and the clergy his family. Or that the human family was his family and other such hollow nonsense. But he knew she would see through his artifices so he told the truth. "No, I never did want those things."

She showed no surprise at the reply. She said, "You de-sire to emulate God? Then why don't you create? That is how we humans approach divinity. We enter the cycle of crea-tion."

The troubled old priest fixed her with an icy stare. "What about you?" he said. "How do you enter the cycle of creation, as you call it?"

She chuckled, as if to say *touché*! "You are correct. I am as delinquent as you are." Then she added a comment that burned him like acid. "But I still have time to change." She noticed his crestfallen expression and felt contrite. "I'm sorry. I shouldn't have said that." She paused, gathering her thoughts. "You still have time."

He shifted his gaze from his coffee cup to her Greek goddess of a face. "Time for what?" he asked.

"To love. It is the most creative and godlike act of all."

The old Jesuit was puzzled by her words. He said nothing more.

Concetta rose from the table, leaving him to chew over their conversation while finishing his breakfast. Meanwhile, an uncommon and unexpected flare of hope rose up in his heart. Maybe he did still have time.

Back in his room he still had to decide what to do with the day that stretched before him while Etna slept. He pored through the guidebooks. On impulse he decided to board a local bus for the coast and breathe the sea air.

The pebbly beach at Naxos fronted a curving bay of blue water cradled by purple hills. The German Jesuit took a seat on a bench facing this picture-postcard scene and drew out his notebook and pen. The place was desolate in December. The surroundings were a far cry from the Baltic but if he closed his eyes and allowed his other senses to hear the griping gulls and the water washing round the piles and smell the scented sea and feel the briny wind on his face, he might transport himself to his birthplace and tap the images that were long lost in the crevices of memory.

Teodor Weiss had features as sour as his world-famous

marzipan was sweet. He was dressed — as was usual most evenings — in a piebald quilted lounging jacket and rust-colored smoking cap with the tassel dangling over his rutted brow. He sat — again as usual, for he was a man of rigid habits — in the leather club chair by the bay window overlooking the gabled street that lined the River Trave. The view was fine but he rarely looked out the window. He was no idle daydreamer, God forbid. His bony right hand leafed through the evening newspaper that lay on his lap while his bony left hand gripped a crystal glass of Madeira. He was forty-five years old and looked fifty-five. In the ash tray near at hand lay the smoldering bent-stem briar pipe that filled the air with the woody scents of Turkish tobacco.

Herr Weiss hurled the pages of *Hamburger Nachrichten* to the carpeted floor and fingered his bristle brush mustache with an air of exasperation. What was Germany and the world coming to? he thought. Horseless carriages and moving pictures? A confounded machine invented by a Prussian chap named Röntgen that can look inside a person's body? A deranged philosopher declaring that God was dead? Women playing competitive tennis? It was all madness!

He took a drink, relit his pipe and puffed ferociously. The mental jeremiad continued: What has happened to our homespun Christian values as we approached the twentieth century? Weren't music recitals, parlor games, church picnics and football games exciting enough activities without our having cabarets where women shamelessly bared their legs? And didn't gas lamps light our streets and homes as well as the confounded arc lamps that cost so much to run? "Confound it all," he said audibly. He fingered his mustache.

"Confound what, Father?" said Anton who had soundlessly entered the room.

Herr Weiss raised his icy blue eyes to the face of his sixteen-year-old son. "Confound the modern world, of course. Confound petticoats, magnetism and tattooing. Confound the automobile and the moving pictures. I'm dizzy with all the changes."

"You can't stand in the way of progress, Father," said the son.

Herr Weiss frowned at the boy. "Says who?" he snapped. "I agree with the English writer — forgot his name — who said something like, 'What we call progress is trading one nuisance for another.'"

"Havelock Ellis," said young Anton.

"Who?"

"The English writer. Havelock Ellis."

"How in damnation do you know?" asked the father, twisting his brush mustache. "Tut-tut, Father. Language."

Herr Weiss suppressed a smile. He admired his young son's erudition though he tried not to let his admiration show. "Isn't he the chap who writes about onanists and sodomites? You shouldn't be reading that filth. Where did you get your hands on his blasted book?"

Young Anton, his face flushed, stammered before answering: "They're passing bootleg copies around at school."

"Well," Herr Weiss added, narrowing his eyes at his son,

"don't let the confounded Jebbies know you read it. The title alone…

"*Sexual Inversion*," said the lad. "By the way, how did you come across his work? The book just came out in German."

"For a candy maker, I keep up with things," he said, his chest expanding like a rooster's. He added on a minor note: "I'll have you know." Pipe smoke wreathed his craggy face.

The sagacious son studied his father carefully, struck by the notion that Teodor Weiss had started life as a Baltic sailor before achieving great success as a manufacturer of marzipan and other confections. The profane thought occurred to Anton that sexual inversion was not an unfamiliar practice to a young seafarer. Then he castigated himself and chalked the idea on the mental blackboard of sins to confess. A war raged in the soul of this rawboned boy, a mortal joust between piety and sexual hunger. He later would call a truce by forming a vocation to the priesthood.

Anton got his hat and coat from the vestibule and said, "I'll see you later, Father."

"Where are you off to?"

"I have a meeting at the chess club."

"The chess club, huh?" the father said in an agreeable tone. "Good, good. Have you studied Steinitz's openings?"

"Yes, father." He reached into his coat pocket. "I have his book right here."

"Excellent. But, see here," Herr Weiss said through the pipe stem clamped between his teeth, "you should not focus merely on intellectual pursuits. You should join the fencing club or the football club or the rowing club. Or all three, confound it. A strong body makes a strong mind, you know."

The boy looked downcast. "I don't believe I'd make the grade.'

"Why? Have you tried?"

The boy hesitated, then said, "No, I was embarrassed to try out." His blue eyes misted over and he fidgeted with his Danish sailor cap.

"Nonsense. You're big and strong."

"But I'm clumsy. Everybody knows that. They laugh behind their hands at me at dance class."

"Dance class, bah!" Herr Weiss's hooded eyes swept over the figure of his lanky son from head to foot. "Take up some manly pursuits, damn it all. Why, when I was your age I was risking my bloody neck rigging and furling sails above a rolling deck. Not mincing around in dance class, by God."

"Yes, Father," the boy replied in a toneless voice.

"Yes, Father," Herr Weiss echoed, with sarcasm. He looked down at his glass of Madeira, then said, "Take the long wool coat. It's wet and windy out there this evening." He picked the newspaper up from the floor and resumed reading.

Young Anton switched to the wool coat and left for the chess club, savoring the brisk evening air with all the sweetness of a discharged prisoner. As he made his way from the brick gabled townhouse where his father still cursed the news of the day the boy heard the ancient bells of St. Mary's Church ring six times. The meeting was scheduled for six-fifteen at the library near the Holsten Gate Tower, some twenty minutes away by foot. He didn't want to be late so he quickened his pace. Helmut would be there.

And there he was sitting at the long walnut table under the leaded glass window of the library, already engrossed in a chess match with Josef Drechsler, the snooty son of the mayor.

Anton reddened with disappointment. He sat down without greeting them for he knew he would be hushed for interrupting the match. He studied his idol's face, the chiseled features, drowsy eyes, sensual full-lipped mouth. His expression was one of confident insouciance in contrast to his opponent's stony concentration. For a moment as Drechsler was contemplating his next move Helmut caught his admirer's eye and gave him a sly smile. It was an ambivalent smile, one that was open to various interpretations, depending on the needs and insecurities of the receiver. As he waited for the game to end to tried to mask his sulky mood with a wan smile.

A quick survey of the chess table showed Anton that Helmut was playing an aggressive King's Gambit, laying a trap for the unsuspecting mayor's son. It gave the observer pleasure to see that Helmut probably would soon crush his opponent with his superior gamesmanship by ensnaring Drechsler's queen. As the observer expected, it took only about five minutes for the end to come.

"Checkmate," Helmut declared. His tone was easy, in no

way triumphant, which, Anton thought, might increase the sting to the opponent. Anton chuckled, consoling himself with the thought that his dandified rival was a well-born dim-wit.

Anton was disappointed to observe that only a fleeting expression of regret passed over Drechsler's handsome angular face. He took defeat like a gentleman, combing his fingers through his thatch of tawny hair and declaring, "I am no match for you, Helmut. Good game." He glanced in Anton's direction. "Hello, Weiss," he said, somehow making a simple greeting sound condescending, Anton thought.

"My turn," said the confectioner's son, rubbing his hands together and starting to take Drechsler's place at the table.

"Not yet," said Helmut, rising from the chair. "We were about to get coffee."

Anton's face darkened but he tried not to show disappointment. He was used to basking in the sunshine of Helmut's friendship without having the rays blocked by a rival. "I'll come with you," he said.

"As you wish," Helmut said in an icy voice.

In a cloud of depression Anton shambled behind the two boys as they walked across the palatial room toward the coffee urn. For weeks now, he had felt a gulf widening between him and his dear friend but had not let himself believe that the relationship was cooling. He was misreading the signs, he told himself hopefully. Some impish agent of insecurity had planted Desdemona's handkerchief in his tortured mind. The tie that had bound Helmut to his gangly friend were mostly intellectual, a shared fondness for fine literature, from Goethe to Shakespeare, and a mutual mastery of brainy pursuits like chess clubs and dialectic societies. Was Anton's rank in his favorite's affections now to be downgraded by his attachment to an effete aristocrat with wavy pomaded hair whose only academic attainments were a second medal in archery and appointment as class beadle due to his father's exalted position in the town? No, Anton could not believe that his friend was as flighty as that.

They reached the table where a rustic maid in apron and bonnet served them coffee and tarts. She had heavy breasts and dimpled cheeks. Helmut and Drechsler paid no attention to the girl or to anyone else, reserving furtive glances for each other and each glance shot an arrow through Anton's heart. If only — the pious Anton had the wicked thought — a sink-hole would open in the floor and swallow his rival up. Then he said a silent act of contrition.

The trio of boys took seats at a nearby table.

Drechsler broke the frigid silence. "Did I tell you I was taking riding lessons?" he said, addressing the question to Helmut. He straightened his four-in-hand cravat with a gesture that reminded Anton of his mother arranging flowers in a vase.

"Capital," said Helmut. "Who is your teacher?"

"Herr Blickstein. He is from Berlin, a disciple of Steinbrecht. I read his book, *The Gymnasium of the Horse*, from cover to cover."

Anton sipped his coffee with the malicious thought: "Ah,

he can read!"

Drechsler resumed speaking in excited cadences. "His motto is, 'Ride your horse forward and straighten him.'"

Anton looked askance at the speaker. "That would seem rather obvious," he said.

But Drechsler paid him no mind, saying, "It's about achieving balance and rhythmic, relaxed paces, what the master called, 'Schwung.'"

"It sounds fine," said Helmut. "Artistic, even."

Drechsler sat up straight in his chair and announced, "When I graduate I'm going to enlist in the Imperial Cavalry."

"Good," said Helmut. "And did you know I plan to apply to the Imperial Marine Academy at Kiel? So we both will serve the Kaiser."

Hearing this out of the blue made Anton's mouth twitch and his eyes prick with the threat of tears. The news that Helmut had devised such a plan without telling him — not to mention the plan itself — plunged his jilted admirer into an abyss of despondency. What about their mutual plans to study classics together at the University of Rostock? His mouth again quivered and he was at a loss for words.

Finally Anton stammered, "When did you decide to do that? You never told me."

Helmut's hooded brown eyes bespoke reproach as he replied, "I don't tell you everything, you know." He shifted his gaze to Drechsler. "My ancestors have been seafarers since the invention of the compass," he said, eyes flashing with pride. "And, besides, I want to contribute to the rise of unified Germany in the coming century. I want to be a part of history as we advance as a colonial power and as a world power." He raised his fist and barked the imperial slogan, "God with Us."

Drechsler smirked and said, "And see some of the world while you're at it, eh?"

"Indeed," said Helmut. "Castles in Spain and all that."

The two boys smiled at each other as if sharing an inside joke while Anton brooded. When and where did his bosom friend adopt this posture of chauvinism, this flag-waving for Kaiser and country? How did the boy who had joined him in rhapsodies over the classic liberalism of Goethe, who had expressed their mutual kinship with Schiller's idea of the beautiful soul, stray to the siren song of strident nationalism? Had the beauty of Helmut's face and form misled his friend into misjudging his character? A nervous tic appeared in Anton's still-downy left cheek. He suspected that Drechsler had a role in the transformation.

The trio of boys finished their coffee in silence. Helmut said, "Let's have that game now, Anton?"

The confectioner's son, feeling more and more like an interloper, snapped out of his reverie. After a pause, he said, "No, I think not."

"What, afraid I'll tan your hide?" Helmut said in a coaxing, jocular tone.

"I'm leaving," Anton said.

Helmut and Drechsler traded puzzled looks. Helmut

said, "You just got here."

Anton made no reply as he headed toward the arched oak door. Helmut looked inquiringly at his companion, who smiled as he reached into his pocket and said, "How about a cigar?"

Young Anton Weiss walked home over the rain-slicked cobbles of Lübeck, the brick and gabled houses looming black against an inky sky. Somewhere on the other side of the river a barn owl screeched. He felt an intolerable loneliness and the pangs that he imagined the Romantic poets suffered when their songs of spring died out. He felt the age-old anguish of first love lost. At this moment, he later would realize, the conviction took final form that he was not fashioned for human love, sacred or profane. He meandered across Holstentorplatz and made his way to the Puppen Bridge where his gaze fastened on the stone statue of the Roman god Mercury. He felt ashamed at the pleasure he took in looking at the effigy's naked form, the slim stone legs rising from the winged boots to the crevice of the boyish buttocks. He averted his gaze from the statue and looked over the stone parapet at the brackish river jeweled with raindrops and the shimmering reflection of the arc lamps. What would become of him? How would he quash these sinful unnatural feelings? Could he just cast them off into the depths of the river where they would die in the mud that spawned them? Slowly there formed in his mind the formula for salvation. He tugged the heavy wool collar of his great coat over his ears. He concluded that his attachment to Helmut represented the first of many hurdles designed by the Lord to test his virtue before calling him to enlist in His ranks.

The disillusioned lad, still gazing at the flowing river, dimly heard strains of music. In an ethereal state induced by the trauma of loss and perhaps the stormy night, he could not distinguish if the sound came from the calliope in the plaza or a celestial orchestra. And so the decision was solidified: Helmut and Drechsler would serve the German Kaiser but Anton Weiss would serve the King of Kings.

The old priest laid down his pen and watched the waves wash over the pebbles of Naxos beach. And he thought: he was now a grizzled veteran of the skirmishes with Satan that had besieged him throughout his priestly life. He had held high the guidon as a novice, regent and scholastic, milestones on the arduous twelve-year road of study and ministry leading to his final ordination as a Jesuit. The intimacy he observed between some of his fellow neophytes who roomed together in the Jesuit houses was not lost on young Anton Weiss. The odor of it filled the atmosphere; but he resisted the diabolic whispers in his ear. The same was true of his assignments to minister in India, New York and Rome where such illicit liaisons and hidden transgressions often were an open secret. No bad examples shook the moorings of his fidelity to his vows. Should he now in the shadow of the volcano, he asked himself, throw down the banner and beat a retreat?

Such thoughts occupied his heart and soul as he walked

from the beach toward the bus station of the seaside village. Car horns blared on the narrow streets. On the way he was confronted by a bootblack who asked him if he wanted a shine. Though such a task was useless in the miasma of ashes lingering from the recent eruption, Father Weiss accepted the offer, persuaded by the plaintive look in the bootblack's eyes. He needed the money, of course, especially as the fire god damaged his business. The old priest stood leaning on his cane as the bootblack, perched on a low stool, buffed the shoes in the posture of a supplicant, reminding the priest of parishioners at the altar rail devoutly waiting to receive the Eucharist. Father Weiss's eyes fell on the bootblack's oiled hair as the man bent over the task with all the concentration of a skilled diamond cutter. First he applied dabs of polish mixed with water, which he then buffed with a tail horsehair brush, removing excess polish and starting to produce a dull shine. Later he brandished a cloth to perform what the priest regarded as a show of legerdemain, using whiplash gestures, flashing hands and flicking wrists, to bring the shine to a pinnacle of brightness.

"There you are, Reverend," the bootblack finally announced.

"Excellent," said Father Weiss, reaching into his pocket for a few liras.

The man raised his hand and said, "Please, Reverend, no charge.'

"But…" The priest was baffled.

"I can't take money. It is a gift to St. Agatha. To appease

the volcano."

"But I insist," said the old priest, his hand stuck in his pocket.

Now the man made a face that mixed sadness with incomprehension. Surely, a priest of God would understand, the expression said. Then he scanned the face of onlookers who had been drawn to the scene, seeking support from his fellows whose eager nods showed that they took his side.

He said to the priest, "Do you wish me years of bad luck?"

The bystanders again nodded sagely.

"Surely not," said Father Weiss with a heavy sigh of resignation. He sketched a blessing over the group and walked away to wave down the bus that appeared in the distance barreling down the coastal road. On the trip back to Taormina he smoked three cigarettes.

THREE

Water danced in the fountain of the chimera in the Piazza Duomo as evening fell on Taormina. The grappa in the priest's glass turned from white to amber in the fading sun. He sat at the cafe table tired and gloomy and hacking from cigarette smoking. Still, the strong pomace wine would improve his mood if not his health. His recent excursions into the past often left him enervated and morose. Finding oblivion at the bottom of a glass, he thought, laid no claim to originality but remained effective. He sipped.

A voice came: "Good evening, Padre."

Somehow, the priest knew that the Englishman would show up like — What's the idiom? — a bad penny. But good manners won the joust with distaste and he said, "Would you sit down, Mr. Bliss, and join me in a drink?"

The English actor closed the parasol he had been carrying against the volcanic debris and parked himself under the cafe umbrella. "Don't mind if I do, Padre, don't mind if I do. I could use some distraction from my troubles. I'll have what you're having."

The priest crooked a finger at the waiter. He asked Bliss, "What's the matter?" He had gotten straight to the point, falling back on his training as a priest hearing confession: *Did you commit adultery? How many times?* And, as in the confession box, he couldn't bring himself to really care about the answer. "Two more grappas," he told the waiter.

Bliss arched an eyebrow. "Oh, just boyfriend trouble. The old man is acting up again. You know how it is."

"No, I don't know," the priest said pointedly. They dropped the subject. The waiter came, deposited the drinks and went away. The Englishman's eyes followed him.The wind rose, causing a vine of bougainvillea climbing the trellis behind them to shower the table with purple petals. Father Weiss eyed the colorful, fragile visitors with pleasure and drank grappa. Also with pleasure. He was of a mind to get drunk this evening. An antic mood had descended over him.

"Ready for the next eruption?" his companion asked.

The priest looked up from his glass. "What do you mean?"

"Etna is rarely sated by one outburst of temper, you see. The beast is merely napping." Bliss produced his cigarette case and lit smokes for both of them. "Brace yourself for another go."

"Yes, so I've heard."

The duo smoked and drank in silence for a while as the

priest dreamily surveyed the twilit diorama in the piazza, the boulevardiers and flirts, the barkers and beggars, promenading to accordion music. Sicilians took heady drafts of life as evening fell. They felt in their bones the ephemeral nature of it all. And the mood was contagious, the clergyman thought to himself.

He asked, "When will the beast come to life again?"

"One never knows for sure. Tonight, tomorrow, next week. But it will be soon — that, I can guarantee. Observe the birds and animals. They'll let us know." He peered at his glass and said, "My, this grappa is strong stuff."

Father Weiss scrutinized his companion. As usual, he was dressed with both care and flair but his grooming was not up to usual standards. His hair looked unkempt under his pearl grey homburg and a day or two of stubble covered his cheeks.

Bliss noticed the priest sizing him up. "I know — I look tired," he said. "Too much revelry but that's what we come here for." He narrowed his eyes. "What about you?"

"What *about* me?" the old priest echoed.

"Why did you come here?"

"I told you — to rest. And write."

"You could do that in other places."

"The climate here is salubrious. And I know the language and find Sicilians charming."

Bliss wore a skeptical look. "I see," he said in a tone that conveyed a lack of credence. "And how is the memoir going?"

The Jesuit did not meet the questioner's eyes but gazed at the stone steps leading to the cathedral doors. "I wouldn't dignify it by calling it that," he replied. "It's just a few random jottings and scribblings. They don't amount to much." He watched the palm trees flanking the piazza sway and chatter in the breezes.

"May I be the judge of that?"

"What do you mean?"

"Would you allow me to read what you have written?"

The old priest did not disguise his horror at the request. "Dear me, no!" he exclaimed.

"Too racy, eh?"

"Indeed not," he answered. "But rather personal."

"Kind of like a diary, you mean."

"Precisely."

"A priest's diary. How intriguing."

"Surely, a man of your worldliness, an actor and all, would be bored by it."

"I doubt that," Bliss said with a roguish look as he sipped his drink.

The priest and the Englishman wound up having a nightcap in the lobby of the hotel where the two vacationers were staying. Exactly how they got there was fogged by the vapors of inebriation after Father Weiss and his cynical companion had lost count of the glasses of grappa they had drunk. The priest's cane had come in handy on the cobbled route. Now they sat in plush chairs shaded by potted palms and drank Scotch whiskey. The clergyman tried to recall the last time he had gone on a bender like this. It must have been some thirty-five years earlier after he marched with students in the St. Patrick's Day parade in New York; his provincial had assigned him there to teach German and Latin at Regis, a newly minted Jesuit high school that had a short supply of qualified teachers. Yes, that was the last time. He still remembered the thunderous hangover he nursed the next morning.

The priest now sipped the Scotch slowly, numbed by earlier drinks to the taste or effect. He drank woodenly, his actions directed by some maleficent puppeteer to whom he had ceded control without knowing it. He eyed the companion, whose face was contorted into a Dionysian comedy mask. Was he the one handling the strings? Or was the priest trying to dodge guilt for his own actions?

"You seem to be taking pleasure in my drunken state," the priest said, removing his clerical collar and stuffing it into his pocket.

"Not at all," said the Englishman. "I'm just happy to see you letting your hair down. It might do you some good."

The priest replied with a shrug and a grunt.

"Drink up," said the Englishman. "I have something better in my suite upstairs."

"What's that?"

"Hah! We call it 'The Green Fairy.' The name is apropos, don't you think?"

"I wouldn't know. What is 'The Green Fairy?'"

"You'll soon find out. Let's catch the lift."

The old priest — no longer in charge of his faculties —

downed the drink, rose slowly and unsteadily to his feet and followed his host to the elevator where the operator whisked them to the fifth floor. They entered the anteroom of the suite, which contained a French provincial two-seat sofa uphol-stered in red velvet, several tufted chairs and an Art Deco-style rolling bar. Bliss put his forefinger to his lips and jerked his head toward a door that, the priest assumed, led to a bed-room. He said, "Let's try not to wake the old man." After in-viting his guest to sit Bliss entered an adjoining room and closed the door behind him. He soon returned with a bottle of green spirits and announced with a curled lip, "Voila, The Green Fairy — absinthe!" He crossed over to the bar and fetched two fluted glasses.

"Absinthe?" the guest echoed dubiously. "Isn't the drink banned?"

"Not in Italy," said Bliss as he poured. "No Puritans in these regions. Besides, it's quite harmless when drunk in moderation and delightful when drunk to excess."

Bliss offered his guest a glass. "I think not," said the old priest, waving it away. "I'm afraid I've already drunk too much."

"Oh, come on," said Bliss. "The drink is highly alcoholic, yes, but it contains fragrant herbs — anise, sweet fennel, and the flowers of grand wormwood. It's very pleasant tasting and relaxing. You've come this far. Who knows? You might have a mystical experience, a religious vision or something of that sort."

Father Weiss found the suggestion distasteful, maybe

even blasphemous but his resistance had reached a low ebb. He accepted the glass and gingerly took a sip. He liked the taste, he had to admit to himself, and he enjoyed its effect on his mood too. He settled back in the chair and took another taste.

His host sat on the red sofa and said, "Aleister Crowley introduced me to absinthe some 20 years ago at his abbey in Cefalù." He cackled. "That's not the only thing he introduced me to but we won't go into all that right now. I don't want to shock you more than I must have already. You know who Crowley was, of course."

"I do not." The drink's fumes reached his nostrils as he waited for the inevitable biographical sketch that Bliss was certain to deliver.

"My, you *have* lived a monastic life," the Englishman said. "Poor chap died a couple of years ago. But while alive, Crowley certainly *lived*! He drained the cup of experience to the dregs. He was a notorious bisexual, a writer, painter, philosopher, mystic, magician and — most definitely — a libertine. Why, he even founded his own religion — Thelema, he called it. The creed was based on magic and sex. I think he believed that Nirvana was achieved through anal intercourse. Do I shock you or may I continue?"

"Oh, I'm not shocked," said the learned Jesuit. "He's not the first apostate I've heard of. Nor the first libertine."

"Well, I used to visit him every year at his temple in Cefalù. I wasn't interested in the religion but I loved the rent boys. Aha!" he added, noting the red tinge on the priest's face.

"See, now I have shocked you."

Father Weiss was noncommittal.

Bliss continued, "That all ended when Mussolini rose to power and kicked the old boy out of the country, undoubtedly prompted to do so by your fellow soutane-wearers. Why do you people like to wear dresses so much? Let's go out on the terrace."

"I don't like wearing dresses," Father Weiss said moodily as he followed Bliss to the terrace. They sat on peppermint-striped deck chairs facing the cascading lights of hilly Taormina and the indigo sea. Bliss poured two more glasses of absinthe. Hints of accordion music rose from the piazza.

"Shall we have a bite to eat?" Bliss said. "I'll summon room service." A blue telephone sat on the occasional table between them. "I'll have sent up some pecorino and salumi."

Father Weiss did not object. He was hungry. He savored a heady second glass of absinthe as his companion placed the phone call.

After ordering the snacks, Bliss cooed into the mouthpiece, "And, oh yes, be sure Ernesto brings the order, will you? Thanks so much."

"Ernesto?"

"A very nice young waiter," Bliss replied, casting what he designed as a meaningful glance at the priest, who found it merely ambiguous. He was growing weary of the stealthy signals and innuendoes peppering the conversation. Yet he had to admit also feeling a frisson of titillation. He drank the pungent Green Fairy and stared out at the velvet night, studded with stars: an old man waiting for his real life to begin? Silence reigned for a time as the priest felt his host's eyes boring into him with what he thought resembled the clinical gaze of an entomologist observing a fly snared in an extrusion of spider silk. Would it be so easy to surrender one's free will?

Soon came a faint knock at the outer door.

Bliss smiled coyly, rose and went over to admit the waiter.

Ernesto was a handsome young Sicilian of the Arabic type with the face of a falcon and the iridescent wavy hair of a raven's coat. He placed the tray of food on the glass-topped wicker table, stood upright and looked expectantly at Bliss; it was a look that seemed to proclaim joint membership in some exclusive secret society. "Will there be anything else, Signor Bliss," he said.

"Not at the moment, my dear," Bliss said as he signed a chit and attached a bank note for a tip. He beamed up at the man and thanked him. When he was gone Bliss waited a second or two and said, "Beautiful boy, don't you think? Or didn't you notice?"

"I suppose he is," the old priest said in a gloomy tone.

"Would you like me to arrange something?"

Father Weiss at first was speechless. Then he said, "Of course not."

"Are you sure? It could happen tonight."

"I am *positively* sure."

"He has a beautiful tool. Like a cobra's head."

Father Weiss used his cane to help him stand up. "I have

to leave," he announced, stammering with confusion and shame. "Thanks for the drinks but I must go."

"You haven't finished enjoying The Green Fairy," Bliss said with a satyr's smile.

"I think I've had enough."

Bliss clucked his tongue. "The sands of the glass are running low, old chap." said the tempter, stroking his fleecy mustache. Father Weiss turned on his heel and stumbled out of the hotel suite.

Outside, he sank wearily upon a bench in the Piazza Del Duomo to catch his breath and corral his emotions. He was grateful that he crowds had thinned, leaving few observers of his sorry state. He tugged the opera cloak tightly around his body. The mandolins and merrymakers had faded away, replaced by the bells of the Cathedral of San Nicolo ominously striking midnight. The priest silently mouthed the words of the poet, "It tolls for thee." And then his chin dropped to his breast as he fell asleep.

"Padre, Padre,"the sacristan murmured some time later as he ever so gently jostled the old priest's shoulder. Dawn peeked over the horizon of the sea. Without uttering a word of reproach or surprise Ignazio helped the groggy Jesuit rise to his feet before taking his arm and leading him down the Corso Umberto to his Spartan room where, reeking of alcoholic fumes, the Jesuit again entered the cave of oblivion on a sheep's wool mattress where he found brief respite from the fray.

In the late morning he awoke to a pounding hangover and an incessant cough that rattled his ribcage. Shafts of daylight knifed through the narrow spaces between the slats of the window shutters. Though sick in body the old man felt hale in soul when he remembered how he had summoned the spiritual agility to avoid the snares set for him by the Englishman, whom he had come to see as the Devil's accomplice. But it wasn't fair, he told himself, to blame Bliss alone. His own concupiscence also played a henchman's role. Still, he took comfort in the thought that he had won at least one round in the contest.

He coughed and coughed and spat into his handkerchief. He rose from the bed and went to the bathroom where he relieved himself and spat up again. No doubt the catarrh had worsened since Vulcan's temper tantrum. From outside his door came the dissonant trumpet of Ignazio's donkey. The old priest craved something to eat. He dressed and went outside where he found Ignazio cleaning the donkey's hoofs with a stiff brush. The small gray-brown animal seemed unperturbed by the grooming as she responded docilely to the sacristan's treatment. Her brays held a note of pleasure rather than complaint.

"What's her name?" the old priest asked after bidding Ignacio good day.

"Filomena," said Ignazio, removing dirt from grooves in her rear right hoof.

"Will she kick?"

"Nah. Sicilian donkeys are a submissive breed. Same as

the Sicilian people." He chuckled at the quip he had made.

"Does she give milk?

Ignazio set the hoof down and unbent his crooked body from the work. "Good milk. Good enough for Cleopatra to bathe in." He laughed and the priest laughed with him.

After a long pause Father Weiss said, "Thank you for your help last night."

"It was nothing, Father," said the sacristan, ducking his head and gently raising Filomena's right rear hoof.

The clergyman approached the man and offered him a twenty lira note but he at first refused to take it. Finally, with a sheepish look, he accepted the money and went back to his task.

"She's a fine looking little animal," the old priest said.

"Look here," said Ignazio, tracing with his calloused hand the dark mane leading to a dark stripe down the back and another across the shoulders. "See, it's a Holy Cross donkey — the same kind that Christ rode into Jerusalem on Palm Sunday. I take good care of her and she takes good care of me. There's an old saying, 'A man without a donkey is himself a donkey.' Hah!"

The priest grunted in appreciation. "She serves you well, eh?" he said, mindful of the donkeys in the life of Christ from the manger to the streets of Jerusalem.

"You see, Padre, without her strong back, we would have little holy water for the church and our fountains would run dry. We go today with the flasks and cans to the mountain springs to fetch a new supply."

The Jesuit's face darkened. "But the volcano…?

Ignazio glanced at the smoldering peak and shrugged. "He is taking his siesta, just like the villagers."

"God bless you, Ignazio," said the old priest, producing an arcane glitter in the sacristan's eyes, as if he were thinking — a blessing as well as twenty liras.

Ignazio said, "Would you bless Filomena?"

"Of course," and he gestured over the animal and recited the formula for blessing creatures. The animal bellowed.

At length Father Attilio appeared on the balcony above them and invited his fellow clergyman to the afternoon meal. "We were just sitting down to table," he said in a friendly tone.

The rustic cleric's table was loaded with the cornucopia of Sicily: cured meats and aged cheeses from a Noah's Ark of animals; the plump offspring of volcanic soil — grapes and fava beans, tomatoes and oranges and many of their cousins; and, of course, those staples of meridional life — bread and wine. Abetted by Concetta's culinary skills, Father Attilio ate well.

"Taste this, my friend," the rotund pastor said, pouring wine from an earthenware flask into his guest's glass. "Tell me that it does not compare favorably with the reds of Ruffino in Tuscany. I dare you."

Father Weiss smiled diffidently. "As a rube from North Germany," he said, "I claim no expertise."

"Ah," said Father Attilio, wagging his finger. "Even a *Plattdeutscher* has taste buds. Go on, drink."

The guest obeyed. "Excellent," he declared, more from courtesy than conviction.

Concetta approached, the personification of Ceres, bearing a steaming bowl of pappardelle with red prawns. She put the dish down on the table; the odor was intoxicating.

As, apparently, was her presence to her employer — if that is a suitable description of his relation to her — whose eyes, riveted on the *housekeeper*, betrayed a mixture of hunger and enslavement. She, as usual, treated him offhandedly with tart words and hooded glances.

"*Salve*, Reverend Father," she greeted the guest. "You honor us with your presence."

The formality of her words had a metallic ring. Or perhaps they were sincerely meant. She had the gift of keeping the Jesuit off balance.

"The honor is mine," he replied, not even trying to match her talent for ambiguity.

She filled their plates and sat down. Silence ruled for a short time except for the clatter of implements as the trio relished the food and drink. Eating was serious business in these parts and talking often was superfluous. Of course, words soon were uttered as the meal progressed — in customary Italian fashion from course to course, from pasta to fish to meat, from vegetables to salads to fruits to nuts, from savories to sweets, from wines to liqueurs to coffee. But the conversation throughout focused on either trivialities or discussions of the merits or shortcomings of the food, which was elevated to a higher art here than disquisitions on world affairs or Greek philosophy. Food talk held second rank only to village gossip, of which there was none at this seating. Still, the old priest sensed hovering in the atmosphere an electric current of unsaid words, of a conversation to come.

Concetta cleared the plates and cleaned up. Her dark eyes looked drowsy. "Siesta time," she said with the languor of a house cat. And she soon left the room as the two priests lingered over glasses of anisette. Father Attilio toyed with the liqueur glass. His demeanor betrayed his seeming mental rehearsal of something he wanted to get off his chest.

He finally said, "May I broach a sensitive subject with you, Padre? More as a friend than a fellow clergyman."

Father Weiss was not aware that they yet were friends. "Yes?" he said in a tentative tone.

"Let me start by saying I heard you in church the other day. I happened to be in the sacristy when you made your *cri de coeur*, shall I call it? The curate of Saint Catherine's had fallen ill and the pastor needed me to fill in."

The host then paused for a reply but the listener merely sat in embarrassed silence.

Father Attilio continued. "It is a crisis of faith, no?"

"I suppose so," Father Weiss said in a subdued tone, wondering why the pastor would interest himself in his troubles. Yes, he was a fellow clergyman but he never had struck the guest as an especially compassionate or sage practitioner of the priestly craft. Perhaps he had underestimated him. The Jesuit fumbled for a cigarette and started to light it, then caught himself.

"Cigarette?" he said to the pastor.

"Don't mind if I do," he replied.

Father Weiss lit both *Gitanes,* took a long drag, then pointed to the cigarette he held and said, "Another of my vices."

A tender expression now animated the pastor's oval features. "Can I be of help?" said Father Attilio. "With your problem, I mean."

"I don't know. It is difficult to explain."

"Of course. It always is. Look, you are not the first nor last priest to experience these doubts, these scruples." He shrugged his round shoulders. "We all have such moments. We are human, after all."

Father Weiss gave the pastor a sidelong glance. The man seemed too pleased with himself, the Jesuit thought. Too cocky in his role of spiritual advisor. But quickly the old priest chastised himself for having uncharitable thoughts. Again, the parry and thrust of a troubled soul with an habitual lack of moral clarity.

Father Weiss reached deep into the marrow of his discontent and found some words: "I am old. I want finally to taste of life."

Father Attilio wore a benign expression. "Then do so," he said. "No better place than here where the Dog Star is brightest in December." He chuckled and added, "Except when obscured by the ashes of Etna. But go on, taste the spiced olives and sweet oranges of our land. They are there for the taking." The pastor exhaled a gust of cigarette smoke and sipped anisette.

Father Weiss was taken aback by his words. But then, he thought, why should this libertine attitude surprise him, coming as it does from a priest who lived openly with a mistress? Still, he protested, "But what about...?"

Father Attilio flashed the palm of his hand like a traffic policeman. "I know," he said, "what about your immortal soul? That's what you are worried about. The English writer Lawrence who often stayed in Taormina has written that Etna is a breaker of souls. But he was a Protestant, what did he know about saving souls? He called us Sicilians sulfurous demons. I say he was right. But we are also saints. The saint and the demon abide together in all of us. I say that in Sicily souls are saved, lost and saved again every day. We see the more merciful face of God. So, go ahead, take a bite of the fruit. Then come and confess to me."

The German priest was astonished by his host's words, by the nakedly transactional nature of the attitude toward sin and forgiveness. Could he, a Jesuit schooled in the snares of sophistry, ever see matters through the same lens, one that neither magnified nor diminished the consequences of Adam's fall but accepted them as a fact of life and circumvented them whenever possible — like the Sicilian tradesman who bribed the notary for his license then walked off to church to pray to his patron saint for the success of his business? Father Weiss was warming to the idea. Then he remembered: the Devil took many forms when tempting Saint Anthony the Abbot in the desert, including lions, swine, snakes and scorpions. Surely he also might assume the form of an erudite Sicilian pastor.

Father Attilio put a finishing touch to his argument: "You recall, of course, Saint Augustine's plea. 'Grant me chastity and continence, but not yet.'"

The old priest slowly shook his head. He did not speak, counting on his body language and facial expression to convey disapproval.

The pastor shrugged and said, "More anisette?"

"No." the guest said, rising from the chair. "Thank you for the meal. I will take siesta now."

Father Attilio nodded approval. "Pleasant dreams."

FOUR

The old priest sat on a bench in the misnamed main piazza of Taormina with his eyes fastened on the crucifix of a church in hilltop Castelmola, high above. Siesta was unpleasant. Indeed, he had not slept at all, disturbed by coughing and restlessness. He had coughed blood again.

The day was cool. He was now feeding pumpkin seeds to the pigeons that swarmed the piazza and thinking hard about his recent conversation with the pastor and the man's captious attitude toward sin and atonement. He reflected that for many Catholics, even priests, the core of the religion resided in ceremony — the incense and bells, the chants and hymns, statues and vestments — rarely going beneath the surface so that the reality beneath the rituals was lost or forgotten. Maybe the Protestants were on to something with their bare bones approach to worship; removing the Papist frippery might make room for a brighter image of the Deity and the mandates for salvation. But what did he really know about such matters? What did anyone know? Theology was the science of the unknowable and thus no science at all.

The wild-eyed pigeons pecked at the seeds that he spread on the tiles. The Jesuit now recalled from his service in Delhi that the pigeon in Hinduism was depicted as a consort of Rati, the goddess of love. He watched the pecking pigeons for a while.

Then he resumed his train of thought: gods and demi-gods were everywhere in Sicily. The sun was a god; the volcano was a god; the sea was peopled by gods and goddesses; the fields of wheat, the groves and vineyards, all were hus-banded by gods and goddesses. Even the Moslem overlords could not cure the inhabitants of this triangular island of their stubborn polytheism. He tried to stop thinking about all this. It merely left him confused. It made him feel as if his faith was slipping through his fingers. Or maybe it was just veering in another direction. Maybe he wanted his religion to worship a goddess of love instead of a virgin. He sat there feeding pi-geons till he ran out of seed. And he felt hollow inside. The pigeons took flight, wheeling over the plaza.

Concetta gave him the name of a doctor in Catania who had treated the pastor once for the gout. The next afternoon Father Weiss decided to pay him a visit. Dr. Diego Finestrella had an office in one of the baroque buildings on the Via Cro-ciferi.

"It is near the Jesuit college," she had told him. "You

should feel right at home."

She accompanied him as he caught the bus at the Catania Gate. He knew that the trip would take over an hour so he brought a newspaper and a book of poems to help pass the time. Concetta saw him off with a sandwich of *prosciutto crudo*, a flask of wine and a warning: "Beware of the horse with no head."

"What?" he said in confusion as he stepped onto the bus.

She smiled and the driver chuckled. It was apparently an inside joke. With a hydraulic hiss the bus started. Father Weiss found a seat near the driver and asked him to explain their amusement.

The driver took the pipe stem from his mouth and maneuvered round the switchbacks with one hand, an obvious veteran of the local roads. "It's an old story," he said. "It goes back centuries."

"I'm all ears," the priest said.

The driver's eyes glittered. Like most Sicilians he was steeped in local lore and eager to convey his expertise. After all, this was the land of seven-headed dragons and singing apples where every man was a folklorist and moral philosopher. The story began, like most local legends, with a calamity: the powerful earthquake of 1693. In its destructive wake the city of Catania was rebuilt in an elegant baroque style and the narrow Via Crociferi evolved into a sanctuary for outlaw nobles at a time when the throne of Sicily was contested by various foreign powers and changed rulers frequently. The street was narrow, compared to wide promenades like Via

Etnea, and had a low profile. It became the secret quarter of this ancient city, a center of trysts and political chicanery.

"A street of intrigue and aristocratic cuckoldry," was the description voiced by the driver as he formed horns with two fingers on his forehead. Father Weiss marveled at the man's command of language.

So the legend of the headless horse haunting Via Crociferi was circulated to scare away snoops and blabbermouths. One night, the story continued, a bumpkin made a bet with his pals that he could go there at midnight and drive a nail under the arch of the Church of Saint Benedict.

"So the idiot does a fine job of banging the nail," the driver said, "but he also catches his cape by mistake." The driver raised his chin in a gesture that somehow conveyed how little he thought of the poor sap in the story. "He goes to leave, the nail holds him back, he thinks it's the headless horse and he dies of fright. Now you know the whole story."

"You tell it well," said the old priest.

"Sure, I'm no peasant. I finished five grades."

"Congratulations."

The driver looked pleased.

The priest lit a cigarette.

The bus reached the coast and went south over the old regional road. Wind from the sea ruffled the leaves of the palm trees, which flew backward as he watched through the window. He read the *Giornale di Sicilia*. His attention was drawn to a story datelined Prague about Catholic bishops defying the Communist regime's order that the church in

Czechoslovakia bow to government control. Such a move, the bishops argued, would foment an uprising of "Holy Martyrs." He admired the cleverness of a quotation from the prelates' statement: "We cannot render unto Caesar that which is God's." A fly alighted on the newspaper. He brushed it away.

He lay the newspaper in his lap and sighed heavily. Religious and racial persecution was a hydra with many heads. Decapitate the Nazi and you were left with the Communist. He stubbed out the cigarette. He sighed again, unwrapped the sandwich, took a bite and swallowed some wine.

The medico Finestrella was old and cranky appearing. But the patient would soon learn that behind the hangdog mien and the *Risorgimento* sartorial touches — starched wing collar, waxed mustache and pince nez — lay an empathetic healer with a lively mind. He was small and dark and his waistcoat bore tomato stains. He was also a freethinker and showed no particular deference to the Roman collar. The examining room on the third floor had a window overlooking the statue of Saint Benedict on the street and exuded the odor of chemicals. A photo of Giuseppe Mazzini in a gilt frame adorned the wall.

Finestrella spoke to his patient in German. "I need the practice," he explained. "In my day all medical students in Italy had to master German."

"I suppose you had plenty of practice in '43," said Father Weiss.

The doctor frowned and shook his head. "When they

were here I feigned ignorance." He looked the German priest in the eye. "I mean no offense." He applied a blood pressure cuff to the priest's arm, read the monitor and removed it.

"None taken. I hated the bastards too." He waited a beat. "Maybe I shouldn't have said that." He made the sign of the cross and looked skyward.

The doctor chuckled at this as he manipulated the patient's stomach.

"How's my blood pressure?" the patient asked.

"A little high. But that's not unusual for a man of your age."

"Father Attilio speaks highly of your skills," the patient said.

"Humph, that old irredentist. What does he know of medicine? I hear you are a Jesuit."

"Guilty as charged."

The doctor used a tongue depressor to look through the pince-nez into the patient's mouth. Then he said, "Your Jesuit colleagues were responsible for much of my education. For better or worse. The Jesuit College is right down the street."

"So I'm told." For some reason he felt obliged to add, "I'm retired."

"Can you ever retire from the priesthood?"

"It's a high church secret but yes."

The doctor walked over to a metal cabinet and fetched a stethoscope. "Once a Jesuit always a Jesuit," the doctor declared. Then he grew solemn as he was applying the magic listening device to the patient's front and back. After a while he removed the earpieces, leaned back against the cabinet and cast the patient a grave look. "You say you cough blood?"

"Yes. But not often."

"And you have lost weight?"

"A few pounds."

"Do you have night sweats?"

"Lately, yes."

Finestrella looked more and more solemn.

"What's the verdict?" the patient said.

The doctor folded his arms. "Well, we won't know for sure till you have an x-ray. The heart is fine but I don't like the sound of the lungs."

"What do you think?"

"Let's not put the donkey before the *carrozza*, eh? Let's get the x-ray." Finestsrella fished in the pocket of his white coat for a pad. "I will write you a prescription. I can't afford an x-ray machine. You will have to go to the hospital. It is not far from here, down the street adjacent to the Benedictine monastery. They will send me the results and I will telephone you."

Father Weiss took the slip of paper, glanced at it briefly and stuffed it into his pocket. "What do I owe you?"

The doctor waved the offer away. "Professional courtesy," he said. "I heal the body. You heal the soul."

Doctor Finestrella said goodbye and clapped the patient on the shoulder. "Don't worry too much," he said. "Whatever you have, modern medicine has miracle cures nowadays. You'll see." He was close enough so the priest could smell his breath, tangy with garlic and red wine.

Father Weiss looked into the doctor's warm dark eyes. "Thank you," he said. "God be with you."

The doctor said nothing to this and Father Weiss wondered if the man was an atheist but he did not pursue the thought. Atheist or not, there was a goodness about him. And that was enough for the old priest. He started off to get the x-ray.

"Oh," said Dr. Finestrella in an afterthought. "And you better quit smoking."

The patient glanced sheepishly at the marble floor.

The old priest exited through the vaulted front portal of the Hospital of Victor Emanuel II, the imposing former monastery where he just had his lungs exposed to that other magic of medicine, the x-ray machine. He chuckled as he recalled how his father had railed against this contraption as an abominable invasion of mankind's right to privacy. He stopped in a courtyard to examine a monument to the king for whom the hospital was named. The bust portrayed him in all his florid glory, grand mustache pointing to the sky, figured atop a regal eagle with wings outspread. All this was mounted upon a fluted column. Vainglory, the priest observed to himself, was, like many things in Italy, elevated to high art. Italian clothiers designed the finest uniforms in military history. War was pageantry — until it reached the serious business of gaping wounds, dismemberment and death. Then, of course, the exercise lost its flavor.

He ambled through the center of this ancient city long ruled by the Crown of Aragon, as he recalled from his history lessons. Might as well sightsee, he thought. He passed moldering houses built of black lava and many baroque churches. He found himself finally in the Piazza del Duomo dominated by a fountain featuring the statue of an elephant made of lava stone that the citizens deemed a talisman against Etna's periodic temper tantrums. Did the locals really believe these legends? He supposed that they willed themselves to believe in order to combat the sense of impotence at living in the eternal shadow of a geologic monster.

He sat down at an outdoor cafe table and ordered coffee. The winter sun was warm and the water murmured musically in the fountain. A young man and a girl seated behind him scooted past on a motor bike called Vespa, meaning wasp in Italian. He reflected that the vehicles were becoming all the rage now — for those who could afford them. They were fine for navigating the narrow streets of the old cities and towns. He sipped coffee and viewed the passing scene. Broad gestures, shouts and laughter. The sensations of a Sicilian plaza in the brief sunlight of winter. He ordered another coffee.

The old priest began to wonder about what the x-ray would show. He did not want to dwell on troubling thoughts so after the waiter brought the coffee and laid another chit on the table he took from his pocket a book of poems and opened it at random to some verses by Schiller. Well, he reflected, perhaps the poet's *storm and stress* would divert his mind from morbid thoughts. Hell, that was a misguided idea, he soon realized as he came upon the last line in Schiller's poem, "Resignation": "What one refuses in a minute No eternity will return." In other words, Gather ye rosebuds...

The old priest noticed that the saltshakers on the table were figured as a peasant girl and boy. He sipped the coffee and toyed with idle notions of how flowers grew and cancers spread. Then he heard the music. The bagpipe was playing Christmas music. The Jesuit's eyes searched the square and there, right by the elephant fountain stood the shepherd boy Ambrosio making the instrument's stomach inflate and the ribbons flutter to the bleats of *O King of Heaven*. The observer's face beamed with unbridled pleasure at the sight of the boy. Why deny it? He was overjoyed to see him. He drained the coffee cup, paid the check, rose from the table and walked over to the fountain.

The old priest melted into the small gathering of people listening to the music. The beautiful boy had melancholy eyes and the cap on the ground held only a few coins. Soon he came to the end of the song and the listeners drifted away, some having dropped a few cents in the cap. But Father Weiss remained riveted to the spot. Ambrosio looked round and caught sight of him. At first he didn't seem to recognize his admirer but soon recognition dawned.

"Oh," the shepherd said. "Good day, Reverend. I did not know you were a priest."

"I'm retired from ministry now. But, yes, I am a priest."

The boy's face registered confusion. He said, "I see" though apparently he did not see.

"No matter. How are you? You look thin and pale."

The shepherd boy looked sad and simply hunched his shoulders in a gesture of resignation.

"What's the trouble, eh?"

At first he did not answer; then he said, "What's the use of complaining?"

"What is it, son?"

He shrugged again and said, "The volcano. It destroyed my father's farm."

"Oh, that's terrible." The old priest peered closely at the boy whose tunic hung loosely from his shoulders like a scarecrow's. The boy smiled wanly, showing two missing teeth. "Was anybody in your family injured?"

"No, we ran from the lava to our house. But two lambs were killed."

Father Weiss clucked his tongue in sympathy. He knew that farmers on the slopes traveled daily to their farms from their houses in the village. "Are you hungry, my boy?"

Ambrosio looked down at the ground. "I will be all right," he said.

"But you *are* hungry." Father Weiss took the boy by the elbow. "Come. Come with me."

They walked to a trattoria in an alley just off the square, by its looks a real family place and not a tourist trap. Ambrosio sat down and inspected the room, eyeing with eagerness the hanging butts of ham and the garlic and salami, the jars of pickled vegetables and baskets of fruit. His appetite overshadowed his shame. The trattoria featured no menu, not even a chalkboard. This was a good sign that they served freshly prepared home cooking. The old priest conferred with the owner about the specialties of the house that evening before joining his young companion at the table.

"We will have a feast," he told Ambrosio.

"Thank you," said the doe-eyed boy in a soft voice. "You are too kind."

"It's impossible to be too kind, my son." He patted the boy's hand on the table.

The owner, who of course was fat, appeared with a tureen of tortellini soup that he ladled into two bowls. The boy's eyes lit up with pleasure as he hung a cloth napkin from the neck of his tunic. As they ate the shepherd told his benefactor some details of his background and troubles. His father was elderly, having married his mother as a widower. She was much younger than he and was the cousin of his deceased first wife. Ambrosio had three adult half-brothers whom he hardly knew since they had left their hardscrabble existences on the black slopes of the volcano when he was only four years old. They also had escaped conscription by Mussolini's generals. They each had emigrated, Eduardo and Mario to America and Carmine to Argentina, and they found jobs and wives. At first they often wrote letters back home describing the hardships and successes of their new lives. But soon the frequency of the letters ebbed from a flood to a trickle and then dried up entirely.

"I don't even know if I am an uncle yet," said Ambrosio, squeezing a wedge of lemon on his plate of shrimp, squid, eggplant, leeks and other ingredients comprising the *frito misto* now set before him. "But I suppose I am."

"Many times over, I suspect," said the old priest, thinking it would be natural for three lusty young men to have re-

produced. He popped a breaded shrimp into his mouth.

The boy resumed the narrative. He told Father Weiss that his mother and father had another son before him, Ernesto, but while tending the flock he was killed in a crossfire between Canadian and German troops in an episode of the Battle of Sicily that the Allies branded Operation Husky.

"I was eleven years old," he said between bites of food and swallows of wine. "He was the age I am now — sixteen."

"That must have been devastating for you."

"Yes. He was my big brother. My hero. When my mother found his body the sheep were licking his blood."

"Terrible, terrible." The old priest gazed at the boy's sad lovely face, a map of suffering that was as exquisite as Tintoretto's martyred slave's. Father Weiss's mind flashed back to Anton's face emerging from the distant past and he could not seem to separate the strands of memory from present reality, the web of sympathy from desire.

"They were awful times," the boy continued. "There was a massacre at my village, Castiglione. It was brutal. I knew many of the victims. Even women, and children. The Germans were cruel."

Father Weiss's weathered face reddened.

The boy suddenly put his hand over his mouth. "My

God, I did not mean to offend you."

The priest's features softened. "No, you are correct. They were very cruel. Especially men like Goering, the leaders. We Germans were not all like that. But too many were. Yes, too many were."

The boy made the sign of the cross. "Lord, forgive me. You are a man of God."

"Nothing to forgive," the priest assured the boy, patting his hand again and admiring his pale alabaster face. Father Weiss had heard of the massacre. The Germans, under assault by the implacable Allied forces, had their backs against the wall and in retreat the troops of the elite Panzer Division clashed with the local farmers. Some said the villagers of Castiglione had stolen food from a German truck. Others accused them of killing several German soldiers. The details were murky. In any case, retaliation was swift and bloody. Sixteen civilians were executed, many others wounded. Hundreds of hostages, including women, children and the elderly were rounded up by the Germans who then vandalized and burned this jewel of a Norman mountaintop village. How had Satan captured the soul of my native land? the old priest wondered.

They ate meat next, veal with lemon, olive oil and parsley. Simple and delicious. The boy had good table manners, the old priest noted, never chewing with his mouth open or making rude noises. Everything about him softened the heart of his benefactor who persuaded himself that his feelings were pure and paternal. He felt stirrings elsewhere in his flesh, he had to admit, but he would stifle them, as God commanded.

The autobiography continued: "I have three sisters too and a younger brother, Giulio. The girls are married off. 'Systematized,' as we say in this country."

The fat proprietor came to the table with a bowl of fresh fruit and dishes of cassata. He wiped his beefy hands on his apron. "*Caffe?*" he asked.

The old priest glanced at the boy who nodded.

"Yes," the old priest said. "And anisette."

"*Subito, Padre,*" said the proprietor, bowing and walking backwards.

The boy was satiated but still looked forlorn.

"You must have courage," Father Weiss said in a reassuring tone.

The shepherd boy cast a quick glance at the priest, then let his eyes fall. "We are cursed in this place," he said as he spooned the ice cream in a desultory way.

"No such thing. You must have courage. God has His reasons for sending us trials."

"I am being punished for my sins."

"Nonsense."

The boy looked up again. His beardless cheek was tinged with red spots. "No. That's what Father Bruno told me in confession." He continued to toy with the ice cream spoon.

"Listen, my son: God does not curse us for our sins. When we atone he sends us the grace to do better. He is all-forgiving. Don't you know that?"

"That's not what Father Bruno says."

"Who is Father Bruno? Your parish priest, I suppose. He is wrong."

The boy appeared confused. "But he is a priest just like you."

"Priests make errors too." He paused before adding, "We are sinners too."

At first the boy did not answer, mulling over the old priest's words. Then he opened his mouth to speak but stopped himself as the proprietor approached the table with coffee and anisette. As the server withdrew he said, "But I have done very bad things." He lowered his voice to a whisper: "Unnatural things."

These words caused the listener a momentary loss of breath. Then he said, "Listen, boy, no sin is too great for God's forgiveness. You must atone and avoid the near occasions of this wrongdoing. St. Ignatius of Antioch has said, 'To all them that repent, the Lord grants forgiveness.'" The words sounded hollow in his own ears. He had caught the thorn of what the boy meant and it stung. When he came to Taormina, he now asked himself, was he avoiding the near occasions of sin? Physician, heal thyself.

The boy looked from side to side. "Can I confess to you now?" he asked. "Even though you are retired?"

Father Weiss rubbed his chin and sipped his coffee in contemplation. He had not brought his stole to drape over his arm; nor was a restaurant table a proper substitute for a confessional in church. Yet he knew these outward signs were not essential for a valid confession. "Why don't you come soon to Saint Anthony's in Taormina? I will hear your confession there, if you like."

"But what if I go outside and get run over by a car? I don't want to die in a state of mortal sin."

The prospect of hearing the boy's confession troubled the old priest. It also ignited a spark in his imagination. He thought of Reginald Bliss wanting to read his memoirs. He said, "The chance of you getting killed by a car is slim."

"But not impossible," the boy said in a minor note of triumph and with a glint in his eye. "Would you want that on your conscience?"

Was he being foxy? the priest thought. He seemed too eager to make this confession. Then he reproved himself for his cynical attitude.

"Well," the priest said, relenting. "Have you deeply examined your conscience?

"Oh yes, father."

"Are you sincerely repentant?"

"I am," he said, fluttering his eyelids and tenting his hands.

In low tones the old priest recited the routine opening prayers and waited rather breathlessly for the boy to begin the confession.

After a silence the penitent said, "I never went to school. I don't know the name for my sins."

"Tell me in your own words."

"There is a man in my village. He is a bachelor and a

painter of pictures. He has befriended me and…"

"Yes, go on."

The rest of the narrative went as the old priest had suspected it would. Some of the details were omitted but easily filled in by one's imagination. The confession seemed to have lifted a burden from the boy's shoulders, as intended by the sacrament. But it left the priest with an olio of strong and disturbing emotions.

"Now son," he said, "do you sincerely resolve to amend your life?"

"I will try."

"You must do more than that. You must resolve never to visit this man again."

"Yes, I know. I will try."

"I repeat, you must do more than say you will try. You must resolve to amend your life."

The boy looked down ruefully at his folded hands on the table. "May I say this?"

"What?"

"Some boys in my village, they commit these acts too. They go to Taormina and other places. They do it for money."

"It is still sinful."

"May I ask, is it more sinful to do such things for money or to do such things as I do — for love?"

The old priest stammered, confounded by the question because it posed a concept that he had never thought of before and that made his worldview totter. "It is not love but something foul," he said. "In any event these are mortal sins."

They heard the patter of rain on the cobbles outside in the alley.

"All right," the boy said. "I am heartily sorry for my sins. And I promise to stay clear of my lover. It will be hard for I often see him in the village. But I will ignore him and his invitations to visit."

The rain crescendoed from a patter to a downpour and the fat proprietor, who had been watching them from a discreet distance, now began to adjust the window shutters.

"For your penance you must make a novena."

"What is a novena?"

"You must say the rosary for nine days in a row for a special intention.'

"All right. What is the special intention?"

"The special intention will be for the salvation of the soul of Anton Weiss."

The boy said nothing but his eyes widened in surprise.

The tainted stand-in for the Lord granted the shepherd boy absolution. Then he paid the bill and escorted the boy outside where they waited under the restaurant awning for the rain to abate. As water flowed through the gutters, no words were uttered between them. The chasm of silence deepened as they waited, submerged in thought.

The boy looked sideways at the old priest, struggling to say something.

Father Weiss noticed his awkward glances. "What is it," he asked.

"You have done so much for me already..."

The old priest put a reassuring hand on his shoulder. "Please. Out with it."

"Well — May I borrow some money? To buy provisions for my family. I will pay you back."

Father Weiss dug into his pocket. "Of course, son. How much?"

The boy appeared pensive. "Say, three-thousand lira?"

The old priest tried not to look stunned by the amount, equal to a week's pay in these parts. "I have not that much on me," he answered. "I can let you have two-thousand."

"Sure, that might be enough. You are so kind. I thank you and my family thanks you, Padre."

"You are welcome."

And soon they went their separate ways.

FIVE

The cobbles were still slick with rain on the Piazza del Duomo when Father Weiss hailed down the bus to Taormina. As luck — or misfortune — would have it, the same driver who brought him to Catania still was working the route.

He smirked at the old priest. "Did you manage to avoid the headless horse, Reverend?"

"With God's help."

He found a seat and peered out the window through the evaporating raindrops. It was siesta time and the streets were mostly vacant and lifeless. A stray mongrel with its tail between its legs scouted an alleyway. He tried reading the newspaper again but found it hard to focus for he could not get Ambrosio out of his mind. The man sitting across the aisle from him was eating a concoction of peppers and salami that reeked of garlic. But nothing distracted Father Weiss from thoughts of the boy and what just had transpired between them. What a singular few hours they had spent together! He had compassion for the boy but this feeling was mixed with a nagging suspicion that he was being decoyed by him in some way. Then he quickly dismissed this idea as the product of cynicism, deviltry disguised as worldliness. And in the background lurked his own struggle against the imps of depraved desires.

The bus wended over the coastal road stopping at every village along the way. Meanwhile the old priest dozed off. Some time later the bus jolted to a sudden stop to avoid hitting a donkey-drawn cart, causing the sleeping passenger to awaken. The bus driver raised his fist and cursed at the peasant leading the donkey. The peasant simply ignored the bus driver and got out of the way. The sign at the side of the road identified the location as Mascali, which Father Weiss knew was a seaside village not far from Taormina. The bus started up again and soon stopped at the town terminal where many passengers disembarked.

The old priest glanced out the window and saw in the plaza an idle carousel. The amusement ride captured the viewer's interest because it had an unusual nautical theme, featuring vibrantly painted marine animals like dolphins and seahorses and decorations picturing Venus in a scallop shell. Father Weiss marveled again at the ingenuity of local craftsmen. Then he saw him, sitting on a motionless shark. It was the platinum-blond tour guide who had given him his business card. He appeared to recognize the priest in the bus and nodded sagely at him. Father Weiss was startled at seeing the man there on a carousel. He did not know why.

The bus started up again heading for Taormina. Father Weiss lit a cigarette and took a few drags. He immediately began to cough. This reminded him of the x-rays.

The bus stopped outside the Porta Catania of Taormina as the village was stirring to life. The activity at this time of day in Italy always struck the old priest as kin to a rhythm of nature like a gust of wind before a rainstorm or a hibiscus closing its petals at nightfall. The passenger used his cane to descend the last step of the vehicle.

Ignazio was waiting for him. "Did you have a meal?"

"Yes," the old priest said. "Don't worry about me."

"Somebody should. Did you drink some wine for your stomach's sake?"

"Yes."

"Good. What did the doctor say?"

He shrugged. "I had to have x-rays at the hospital." The sacristan clucked his tongue. "They are very expensive, yes?"

"Don't worry about me. The Church in Rome will pay the bill."

"That's good, Reverend. Did you sleep?"

"I dozed a little on the bus."

"That's not a real siesta."

"Don't forget, I'm German."

The sacristan made a sour face. "What difference does that make? The siesta is better than medicine." His tongue jutted from his mouth.

The old priest sighed, eager to end the conversation. "I'll try to remember that. Is Concetta around?"

He hunched his shoulders, indicating that he did not know. "I have to go now. I have to wax the floors in the sacristy. Good afternoon, Reverend."

"Good afternoon, Ignazio."

The old priest found the housekeeper ironing liturgical vestments in the laundry room in the rear of the house. He greeted her pleasantly and a conversation followed about the results of the visit to the doctor that echoed the one he had conducted with her brother.

Concetta looked gloomy. She was ironing the lining of a gold chasuble and a filigree of sweat laced her brow. "You must take better care of yourself," she advised him.

He gave a noncommittal nod. Then he said, "Can I ask you a question?"

She continued ironing. "Go ahead."

"You are familiar with almost everyone in town, aren't you?"

She didn't look up from her task as she considered the import of his question. A ringlet of her dark hair fell over her left eye and she brushed it away. "Bah," she said in a prideful tone, "I know practically everyone in the region of Catania."

That had to be an exaggeration, the priest thought. He continued, "Do you know the tour guides?"

"Most of them."

"There is one man who interests me. I've seen him

around a lot. He's hard to miss. He has dazzling blond hair — it is almost white. He has a pale complexion and every time I have seen him he was wearing a white suit."

She stopped ironing and gave the questioner a puzzled look. "Doesn't sound familiar," she said. "Why do you want to know anyhow? Do you want to take a tour?"

"No, but he intrigues me. I am not sure why."

"Do you know his name?"

"As a matter of fact I do. It is Angelo Michele or Michele Angelo. I'm not sure which." He started to reach into his pants pocket. "Here, he gave me his business card." He searched the pocket in vain. He tried the jacket pockets. He frowned. "I must have left it in another article of clothing."

She resumed ironing. "Well, there is a family in Acireale with the surname Angelo. They are shopkeepers. Maybe he's one of them. There is a de Michele clan in Zafferana Etna on the north slopes. They are farmers. But I know nobody who matches your description of this man."

He looked reflectively at the woman, bent over her work. "I suppose it's not important," he said glumly.

Without looking up she said, "You should take care of yourself, old priest. You should take care of yourself."

"Yes, you're right." He went off to his room and soon fell asleep.

In the evening Father Weiss decided to attend a performance of a traditional puppet show the *Opera dei Pupi* of Siracusa staged in an old palace off the Corso. The Sicilians were famous for this folk art form in which beautifully costumed and armored marionettes portrayed swordplay and acts of gallantry by paladins of Charlemagne against Moorish invaders. He made his way down the center aisle of the makeshift theater and found a seat near the front, joining a motley crowd of villagers of all ages and classes in the audience. There was a buzz of anticipation. The puppeteers' visit was a treat for the residents of Taormina. The closest movie theater was in Naxos and they had to go to Catania to attend the opera. Few villagers had television sets, leaving the radio or local music recitals as their main forms of entertainment. The puppeteers, cloaked in black garment and darkness, were very skillful. The crowd followed the action vociferously, cheering when Orlando Furioso lopped off the head of a Saracen or when the Frankish knight Rinaldo disemboweled a dragon. They cooed at the love scenes with damsels in distress and laughed when one of the knights made smart remarks in local dialect, many of which the priest could not follow. In one scene Orlando descended to Hades and fought the devil, a puppet with an evil bearded face, two horns in his head and goatish feet. The knight soon bested the devil on the marionette stage.

Would it were so easy in real life, the old priest thought.

The spectacle ended to loud applause and whistles from the audience and the puppeteers took their bows. The children and adolescents were especially raucous. In Sicily the bambini stayed up quite late, especially when the *pupi* were in town. Father Weiss rose and left the building. He was happy to have had some diversion from his recent worries. He stopped for a gelato and sat on a bench on the Corso to eat it. He as usual watched the passing spectacle of Sicilian life. Some passersby licked ice cream cones, others ate pistachios or chestnuts. Everyone gestured broadly and laughed without restraint as the Puppeteer in the star-spattered heavens manipulated the strings.

He finished the gelato and strolled back toward his apartment. He reached the conclusion that such distractions as the puppet show were good for his mental health and he vowed the next day to take the bus to Naxos to see what was playing at the cinema.

The poster outside the Cinema Nettuno on the Via Schisò trumpeted Walt Disney's *Pinocchio*. It at first struck Father Weiss as quite a coincidence that the subject of puppetry was resumed. But he soon concluded that it was not surprising as he knew that Italians in general and Sicilians in particular were enthralled by this nine-year-old movie about how a puppet made by the wood carver Geppetto magically becomes a real boy by passing tests of virtue. He had never seen the film but knew the reputation was good. He bought a ticket at the kiosk and went inside.

The theater had elegant touches and appeared once to have housed a small opera house or legitimate stage. It had a large orchestra section, a balcony and box seats. It was clear it had seen better days. The plaster arabesques on the ceiling and walls were chipped and the carpet on the staircase leading to the balcony was frayed. He went up to the balcony, steadying himself on the bannister instead of his cane. He sat in the rear right below the projectionist's light cone; he could hear the clatter of the machine. The movie had already started. On the screen — somewhat obscured by tobacco smoke — there appeared the wooden boy in Italian alpine dress dancing on a stage and singing a song dubbed in Italian about having no strings. The old priest soon became lost in the enchantment of the animated story. He was especially charmed by the character of Jiminy Cricket, who serves as the boy's conscience, and the old priest joined the audience in laughter when the cricket said, "What does an actor want with a conscience anyway?" The atmosphere in the theater was boisterous, filled with wisecracking, eating, drinking and smoking. He caught sight of a couple across the aisle engaged in some heavy petting. The ushers, in formal clothes, leaned on walls and did little or nothing to settle things down. The intimacy and darkness of the movie theater provided a breeding ground for bawdy behavior. The old priest turned aside and lit a cigarette. Deep under the carapace of his vocation he didn't really mind thinking about sexual things but he fought hard to repress it. He bought caramels from an usherette in a short skirt. The feature film ended.

The movie was followed by a newsreel. The screen flashed with images of Marshall Tito, Mao Tse-tung and Konrad Adenauer. The narrator uttered stentorian sentences about military parades in Rome, the training of Alpine troops, the midair refueling of a British jet plane and the techniques of the metaphysical painter Giorgio de Chirico. The Jesuit wanted to remain in the theater to see the parts of the film that he missed. He felt the urge to empty his bladder and hoped that there was a toilet on the balcony level so he leaned over to ask the young man seated in front of him if he knew where the toilet was. The man turned round, gave him a dirty look and moved down a few rows to get away from the old priest. The questioner's face reddened with shame and confusion. The man obviously had taken his question the wrong way. Or maybe he was a communist and repelled by the Roman collar. The screen now showed a preview of a film called *Bitter Rice*. He decided to find the toilet on his own. He was glad to find one nearby on the balcony level. The W.C. was dirty and stank to high heaven. Grunting sounds came from one of the commode stalls. Father Weiss relieved himself as quickly as his aged prostate permitted and rushed back to his seat.

On the screen flashed another preview, a Mafia story set in Sicily titled *In the Name of the Law*. It looked melodramatic yet interesting. Maybe he would return in the next week to view it, the old priest thought as he settled into his seat. He unwrapped a candy as the main feature restarted with a tune in English sung over the opening credits, "When You Wish Upon a Star." He soon fell under the spell of this chiffon cinematic dream. For a moment he dwelled in the artists' hand-drawn universe where creatures like Cleo the goldfish, Figaro the cat and a talking cricket trick us into thinking they are real and we accept the illusion with pleasure. His mind wandered over this topic as he surrendered to the charm of the sentimental story of a wooden boy who craved humanity and of his struggles to achieve it. The old priest wondered if the boy realized the consequences of this quest for an immortal soul? But he knew that he was embarking on a sinful train of thought so he focused again on the movie and tried to get lost in it. He unwrapped another caramel.

Then he saw something out of the corner of his eye: it was happening in a curtained box seat slightly lower than his line of vision about twenty feet away. Through a small opening in the curtain he saw in silhouette a person's head bobbing up and down in a man's lap. He turned away from the sight. He was first struck by the contrast between the innocence of the film projected on the screen and the depravity of the atmosphere in the theater. He should have felt revulsion and he did to a certain extent. But — Lord forgive him — he also felt a frisson of excitement. Meanwhile the stringless puppet and the cricket were singing "Give a Little Whistle": "And always let your conscience be your guide."

Father Weiss fixated on the movie screen till the story reached the part he already had seen. He gathered up his things and started to leave when he saw the fellatist rise and leave the box, apparently stuffing paper money into his pocket. The observer froze to the spot but his eyes followed the boy. Was it he? He could not be certain. It was too dark and fleeting a glimpse. But he thought the boy looked a lot like Ambrosio.

SIX

The old priest stared glumly out of the bus window at the passing rosemary hedges, eucalyptus trees and orange groves that lined the Via Pirandello. The hairpins gave him alternate views of the sea and the volcano, eternal presences in a mutable world. The sun was setting and burnishing the greenery with gold. He took out his breviary and began reading the evening prayer: "God, come to my assistance. Lord, make haste to help me." The words rang hollow.

By the time the bus reached the Messina Gate darkness had fallen. Father Weiss disembarked. He had supper with Father Attilio and Concetta. They ate quietly, savoring fried chick peas, caponata, red prawns. Concetta was wearing a floral housedress that complemented her vivid coloring. She eyed the guest warily. She sensed that Father Weiss was preoccupied. Of course he would be, awaiting the results of the x-rays. He wondered why this gifted woman showed such an intense interest in him. He thought of himself as having a dull monochromatic personality that would have little attraction for such a vibrant woman.

The pastor drank too much wine and became tipsy. He skipped coffee and went to bed, leaving him and the house-keeper alone with their demitasses and unspoken thoughts. The rattle of the cups and spoons was deafening.

She finally broke the silence: "Where did you go today?"

He decided to play coy. "Here and there. Why do you want to know?"

She shrugged her shoulders. "I make small talk. You sit there like a mouse."

"You are very forward with me. Don't you respect my holy office?"

"Hah!" Now she chose her words carefully. "I don't be-lieve you respect *yourself* enough. Your humanity is more im-portant than your vows. I know better than most that a cas-sock and a Roman collar are just articles of clothing. But I talk too much."

He grasped the significance of her words. He smiled at her. "No, you often talk sense."

"Thank you."

The coffee smelled good. He sipped some. "I went to the cinema."

"What?"

"I went to the cinema. Does it surprise you? You know, men of the cloth like to be entertained."

She narrowed her eyes at him. "I know all about what

men of the cloth like."

He grunted in appreciation of her meaning and his face reddened a little. He slowly was becoming acclimated to her absolute frankness.

"What did you see?"

"*Pinocchio.*"

"Oh, I saw that picture. I liked it very much. He lies to the Fairy Godmother and his nose grows longer."

"Yes, it was a good picture. It has a lot of moral lessons. About honesty, integrity, bravery and goodness."

Without asking she poured them both second cups of espresso. "It's about evil too," she said. "Stromboli the Gypsy is bad. The fox and the cat are conniving bastards."

"But goodness wins in the end."

"Sure," she said with an impish smile. "It's a fairy tale."

"Yes," he agreed gloomily.

"Did you know that Carlo Lorenzini studied to become a priest?"

"Who is he?"

"That is the real name of Carlo Collodi, the Tuscan who wrote *The Adventures of Pinocchio.*"

"I see. That explains his treatment of the struggle between good and evil. But he never took Holy Orders?"

"He changed his mind." She looked at him and added, "He never married."

His face showed admiration. "You are a wealth of knowledge. How do you know so much?"

She pointed to her temple. "I got a big brain," she replied

without a hint of false modesty. "And I spend a lot of time in the library near the clock tower."

Father Weiss drained his coffee cup. "Well, I think I'll turn in."

She trained her big black smoky eyes on him but said nothing.

"Good night," he said.

She did not say good night. She said nothing in words but her big smoky eyes said something in a universal language.

Father Weiss was dressed in his nightshirt when the rap he half-expected came at the door. The bedside lamp was on. It stood near the glass of Marsala he had been drinking to importune sleep. He opened the door.

She was still clothed in the floral housedress she had worn at the supper table. A curlicue of dark hair strayed over her forehead. He wanted to think that that she was there because he had left something upstairs or that she had forgotten to tell him something important. His suspicion of another motive for the visit was on its face ludicrous in light of his age and infirmities. But then again, his sojourn in Taormina had uncovered a nest of surprises. This was merely the latest one. The moment that now passed between visitor and priest lasted an eternity.

"What do you want?" Father Weiss finally said. The color had drained from his face.

"To give you pleasure." She glanced at the glass of sweet wine. "To help you sleep without Marsala."

"Please don't go on with this," he said, not looking at her. "It is impossible."

She slipped inside the room and unbuttoned the top of her dress. Her naked breasts were large bronze orbs that shone in the lamplight. She cupped them. "Do you like them?"

He looked down at the tiles. "No, stop. Please, it is impossible."

She buttoned up her dress with a knowing smile. "Why is it impossible?" she asked.

"Go now. Please."

"Why?" she repeated.

"You know why. My vows."

She squinted at him in the chiaroscuro light. "Yes, you are a priest. I know. Is that the only reason?"

"Please go."

"Were you tempted, at least."

He merely examined the tile floor.

"I did not think so." She brushed back her hair with an air of acceptance. There was no egotism in her expression. She reached out and caressed his stubbled cheek with tenderness. He could sense the musky odor of her underarms. "I understand," she said. "You poor man."

The next moment she was gone, leaving him to wonder if the whole experience had been an apparition. But he was fooling himself. He knew that it had been among the most tangibly real events of his numinous life. Now he almost wished that he had embraced her, touched her body, and finally plumbed the dark well of physicality. Naturally, he could not have done that successfully so why think about it, oh promiscuous mind?

He took a slug of Marsala and went to sleep.

The next day he took his notebook to the Greco-Roman theater and tried writing again. But the words would not come. Maybe the memories were dammed up too and would not flow. So he daydreamed, following the flight of shore birds over the Ionian Sea, searching the crevices of the ancient columns and stones for runes of classical wisdom. Etna was sending up orange sparks that contrasted with the blue sky. The sleeping monster, the surly leviathan that ruled this place like a benevolent dictator. He wanted a cigarette but suddenly had another bout of coughing, which dissuaded him from lighting one. He stared again at the implacable volcano, the death-spitting life giver that now in his mind stood for all the contradictions and mysteries that drew him in the dusk of his life to this benighted and civilized island. Then he gave up thinking about anything at all. He would seek refuge, as he often did, in the simple unreasoning realm of faith where he sensed presences that he was impotent to explain. He decided to go to church and pray. Faith was his anchor, especially in storms.

The interior of the Church of St. Anthony the Abbot was empty this morning. It was a small and modest place of worship by Italian standards. The old priest thought that the spare decor of variegated stone suited its patron who was a hermit and lived in a cave. He took out his breviary and started to mumble the morning prayers. Sometimes he coughed. Light filtered through the stained glass onto his prayer book. It had the odd effect of highlighting certain passages, in effect emphasizing them:

> *The Lord is God, the mighty God,*
> *the great king over all the gods.*
> *He holds in his hands the depths of the earth*
> *and the highest mountains as well.*
> *He made the sea; it belongs to him,*
> *the dry land, too, for it was formed by his hands.*

The words made him think of Etna, the highest mountain in Sicily, and of the Ionian Sea at the foot of Taormina. They made him think of how He holds in the hands the depths of the earth where the rumblings of volcanic eruptions begin. And these musings set in motion a jumble of hazy ideas about God's will and good and evil and our personal destinies and absolute realities, the catalogue of concerns that have obsessed philosophers and theologians down through the ages. He came to church to pray and find refuge from his doubts and misgivings and his reasoning mind. But they had followed him here. As they had followed St. Anthony in the desert. There appeared to be no exit from the prison of reason. Could that be hell?

The old priest heard footsteps and then a rustle of clothing in the pew behind him. He turned to look. There sat a pretty young woman with soft features and bobbed blonde hair. He didn't recognize her at first. Then it slowly dawned on him that she was the new bride who had shared the motor-car that first brought them to Taormina.

"Hello, Father." A trace of reticence in her voice.

"Hello."

"You speak English?"

"I do."

"May I ask your advice about something? It is important." She looked down at her hands that were folded in her lap.

"Of course, child. Are you Catholic?"

"Yes. But my husband isn't. He is Methodist."

"I see," he said in an encouraging tone of voice. "Might I ask where you are from? I used to live in New York," he added, knowing that small talk often smoothed the path to discussing more serious matters.

"We're from Philadelphia."

"Ah, the Liberty Bell and Independence Hall. I visited once, delightful place. I am a great admirer of American democracy." He studied her with kindly blue eyes. "Tell me, how can I be of service?"

"It's a delicate matter," she said, looking obliquely at the statues of saints.

"Of course, of course." He waited.

"It's my husband," she began to say but just then Ignazio came out of the sacristy to the altar and she clutched her mouth.

"Don't worry," the old priest said. "He can't hear us but I will tell him to go away if he makes you uneasy."

"Please," she said.

Father Weiss went up to Ignazio and whispered in his ear. The assistant nodded and went off to the sacristy. The priest returned to the pew and sat down. "Now," he said. "That's better. Don't be afraid. You can tell me anything in confidence. Would you like me to hear your confession?"

"No, Father. I just want your advice." She hesitated. "It is an intimate matter."

"I understand," he said, despite misgivings about his expertise in intimate matters.

"You see," she began, "this is how it is: my husband doesn't want children right away so..." She paused again.

"Go on, my dear, it's all right."

"So when we...when we...make love..."

"Yes."

"He makes us use certain methods to avoid it."

"I see. And..."

Rosy red tinged her flawless cheeks. "I believe these methods are sinful. I don't want to go to Hell but I don't want to displease my husband either. It has put a wedge in our relationship." Tears began to lather her rosy cheeks. "I don't know what to do."

His tone was soft. "Look, my child, it is not so easy to get into Hell. It is sort of an exclusive club. I doubt that they would allow you in. But tell me, what kind of methods are you using. They are not all considered sinful. For example there are certain times of the month when you cannot conceive but it's still okay to have intercourse."

She was becoming less awkward in discussing the subject. "Yes, I know about that. Father Lawrence back home told me. It is called the rhythm method. But it won't work. You see, my husband wants to have sex every day." She sighed in exasperation. "Sometimes even twice a day. Before we were married I had no idea a wife's duty would be so constant."

Father Weiss stifled a smile. Enjoy it while it lasts, he wanted to advise her. But of course he didn't say it. "Indeed," he said. "Under the circumstances the rhythm method won't work. Then what other forms of contraception does he use? Does he, ahem, pull out?"

She looked grim. "No, he can't manage that. Anyhow I don't like it when he tries. It makes, it makes...I don't know how to explain it."

"It takes the love out of it, doesn't it?"

She jumped to agree with the explanation. "Yes, Father, it makes the whole experience feel somehow incomplete, unsatisfying. And I feel used."

The old priest, who lacked experience in such counseling since he rarely served in a parish, was feeling rather proud of his performance. He said, "So does he use rubbers?"

She looked down at her hands. "That's right. And that's a sin."

"Who says so?"

Her eyes grew wide. "Why, Father Lawrence. The nuns at St. Joseph's. We were always taught that. It's dogma."

"Well, child, I'm not so sure about that. Look here, who used the rubbers, you or he?"

"He, of course."

"Then — the way I look at it — you are not the one committing a sin."

"But I don't want him to go to Hell either."

"But you said he's not a Catholic but a Methodist. And I don't believe the Methodists have the same rules about contraception."

Her eyes became liquid saucers. "They don't?"

"I don't believe they do. And if he was never taught that it was sinful then he can't commit the sin and therefore he can't be condemned to Hell for his ignorance. That is dogma."

He sat back with a satisfied smile.

She bit her lip. "I never thought of it that way." Her face brightened. "Oh Father, thank you ever so much!"

"Not at all, my child. I am merely doing God's work."

"Oh, I think you're a wonderful priest." She rose from the pew, grasped his hand and pumped it vigorously. "Thank you again." She flashed him a big smile, turned and walked out of the church.

The old priest looked skyward sheepishly. He had no idea of the Methodist view of contraception.

SEVEN

At breakfast the next day the nimble-witted Jesuit recalled with satisfaction his spiritual counsel to the young honeymooner. As he ate toast with marmalade and heard the three sisters singing near the fountain he asked himself whether his use of sophistry to balm the sweet girl's conscience was wrong. But he had listened to the voice of his conscience, hadn't he? The priest's own Jiminy Cricket told him it was the right thing to do. And he remembered from his study of theology how Saint Thomas Aquinas wrote that "the conscience binds even in error." Why, the Pope himself could not order him to violate his own conscience. And Pinocchio became a real boy despite having disported on Pleasure Island, growing donkey ears and tail. The spiritual advisor had made a good-natured, devout young girl happy. How could that be wrong? Walt Disney and the Friar from Aquino were on the same page: Always let your conscience be your guide. Father Weiss sipped his coffee contentedly.

"You look pleased with yourself," she said.

He looked up from his cup. He had not noticed Concetta's arrival. "Do I?"

She sat opposite him and poured herself a cup of coffee. "Yes you do. How do you feel today?"

He made the hand gesture that signals so-so. "My cough has been worse. I slept okay."

"Dr. Finestrella has not yet phoned," she informed him.

"I am in no hurry."

"You should be."

She looked weary, puffy-eyed. She drank the coffee in a desultory way. He thought about the almost comical seduction scene of the other night. This led to his thinking about a legend from the life of Sain Thomas about how his brothers had hired a prostitute to seduce him from celibacy. The story went that the future saint used a fire iron to chase her away. A drastic measure, one might say. The old priest had needed no such tools for he had stronger ones at his disposal. No need for weapons against temptations that do not exist. And he was still waiting for two angels to appear to support his struggle with future temptations. "I assumed it was." He finished off his toast, biding his time, sensing that she eventually would confide in him. And the tables would turn. Until now, he realized, the witch had exercised supremacy over the priest. In his dealings with this talented woman he had surrendered to a form of sacerdotal impotence, hadn't he? In his quest to salvage his own soul he had neglected his duty to help save the souls of others. Maybe the tide was turning.

"It's a personal matter," she repeated, at a loss for new words.

"Yes." He waited.

"I no longer believe in the Sacrament of Confession. If I ever did. I am not a child. Anyhow, I have nothing to confess. I have no mortal sins. Of course I am not without fault. Nobody is."

"Correct. Besides, it is not in my nature to cast stones. But I am trained to listen. I venture that even you require a sympathetic ear from time to time." Again he was silent, measuring the pauses like plotting caesuras in a musical composition. Playing her like a violin. It was one of his few real talents, he thought.

She said, "I loved him. Now he is dead. There, I said it."

"Who is dead? Whom did you love?"

She flashed him a fiery look. "I don't want to talk about it."

"Yes you do." Another rest, this time the cyclops' eye, holding the last word for three beats.

"You mind my asking why you look so tired today?" he said.

She toyed with the coffee cup, swirling the accretion of foam on the top of the brew. "I don't want to talk about it." She eyed the eddying foam.

"All right."

"It's a personal matter," she added cryptically.

A solitary tear from her left eye zig-zagged down her

cheek. "Yes I do," she conceded. "His name was Franco. We were childhood sweethearts."

He reached out to pat her hand, feeling a slight tremor there. "What happened?"

"He was *nu cacciator'*, a hunter. The volcano got him. I just heard about it."

"Poor man. How did this happen?"

The current of words now flowed more easily. "Ah, the curse of this volcano, the curse. He was asleep in his cabin on the Piano Provenzana when the lava covered him." Her elbows rested on the table as her hands propped her forehead. Her eyes were closed.

"How terrible."

"He hunted high up where there were lots of deer and wild boar. He was a good hunter but a foolish man. He should have known better. His dog escaped. His widow fainted at his funeral at Linguaglossa. It should have been me."

"So he married someone else."

"Yes, he married someone else. He leaves three children." She wept noiselessly as the tears bathed her face.

He handed her his handkerchief. She looked at it as if it were an alien thing. Then she used it to dry her face, displeased with herself for showing so much emotion.

"Why did you break up?" the old priest asked.

"Can't you guess? As usual around here, my family opposed it. I had no dowry and he was an Esposito."

The old priest nodded knowingly. He had lived in Italy long enough to know what that meant: He was born out of wedlock and adopted. His adoptive parents probably treated him more like a servant than a son. "Still, he managed to get married," he observed.

"Sure. She was older and had been the senator's mistress. Nobody else would have her." She made a rueful face. "But I consider her a lucky woman. She had him for a while and he was a good man. And now she has three kids to help her in her old age. Yes, she was lucky." She brooded silently.

"You were in love with each other.'

She shrugged her shoulders. "We were. But that kind of love counts for nothing in these parts."

He thought for a while, remembering things. Then he said, "Something similar happened to my sister Gabi."

"You have a sister," she said. It was part declaration and part question.

"Yes, she was older than me. She fell in love with a Danish sailor from Jutland. But his parents were poor potato farmers so my parents opposed the match. They arranged for her to marry a rich merchant, an older man.'

He had piqued her interest, a sure bet with a family saga. "What happened to her?"

"The husband had a heart attack and died ten years after they married. She died not long afterward, still young, childless and rich."

"And loveless?"

"Yes, I suppose she died loveless too if you mean romantic love."

She seemed cheered by the sad story. "So love counts for

little up north too, eh?"

"I guess so."

"Except for God's love, wouldn't you say?"

"Of course I would say that."

What she said next had a note of gloating, an air of having cornered his king in the chess match of wits: "Cold comfort when winter comes."

The old priest made no reply to this. But he thought, maybe the tables had not turned after all. She rose, wiping her hands on her apron and clearing up the breakfast things. "I have to get to work," she said.

Later that day the old priest returned to the ruined amphitheater and took up his pen to write. Memories of his sister's unhappy marriage and early death had ignited the spark of composition. He jotted a few random notes about his childhood in Lübeck and tried to put Gabriela in the picture. She was eight years older than he and very lovely. The disparity in their ages made him wonder idly if his parents had used "the rhythm method." He smiled at the thought. Then he tried to picture his sister's face and form. His first memory of Gabriela Weiss went back to when he was about four years old and she was twelve, just reaching puberty, a flower unfolding. She had tawny hair, jade-colored eyes, creamy skin and the shoulders of a Raphael Madonna. He knew her only as a young girl and woman, never as a child. She pampered him, her only sibling, and taught him to play backgammon and ring taw. She invited him to her make-believe tea parties and read him books at bedtime. When she was married at age 19 to Herr Kielmann, the rich dairy merchant, young Anton acted as ring-bearer, clothed in a velvet jacket, a stiff collar and short pants. He was proud to be part of the ceremony but sad to see her yoked to a thirty-two-year-old burgher with a toothbrush mustache and supercilious manner. Though Anton was only eleven years old, he sensed his sister's unhappiness. In the years that followed he saw little of Gabi, who moved with her husband to Hamburg where his main office was situated. She wrote letters to their mother indicating that she was becoming accustomed to her life as the adornment of a prosperous man of business. Her main occupations centered on running the Kielmann mansion on a canal in the Old City and serving as hostess at the many parties and balls they threw for clients, local dignitaries and bankers. Her attempts to bear children were unsuccessful. As the years passed Herr Kielmann drank to excess, ate rich food and suffered a fatal heart attack. Soon, as young Anton could see from her photographs, his sister's once coltish beauty had evolved into the beauty of the pinned corpse of a butterfly.

She died at age forty of a mysterious illness. It is possible to die of disappointment, isn't it? Anton Weiss was a Jesuit scholastic at the time serving in India and was unable to attend the funeral. He learned of her death via cable from their mother. Their father already had died of emphysema three years earlier. It was monsoon season in Bombay and the regenerative rains poured relentlessly on the alluvial soil near Malabar Hill where the Zoroastrian Towers of Silence stood, the place where the Parsi natives brought their dead to be devoured by vultures and excarnated to a higher plane of life. The Jesuit missionary had thought of this as he read the cable while sitting on a rattan chair and listening on the phonograph to a chorale by Palestrina whom Nietzsche credited with composing "timeless, spaceless" music. He could not suppress admiration for this carrion rite of passage of the Zoroastrians, which seemed to the Jesuit missionary a fitting way to be released from the wheel of death and rebirth. And this sparked the hope in his breast that in death his beloved sister somehow finally had found the happiness she once sought with the Danish sailor. And his tears had stained the cablegram in the wooden house in the Ghatkopar Hills so long ago.

Now in the savage splendor of Taormina he wept again at the memory of all this. Was he weeping for his sister or for himself? Probably for both of us, the old priest concluded. The bitter taste of rue lingered over the years and the herb was poisonous taken in large quantities. He had to remember that. It occurred to him that it might be the cause of his chronic catarrh. Would Roentgen's magic machine capture the disease of regret?

The old priest gazed toward grumbling capricious Etna, now set against a scrim of glowering clouds. It looked like rain. He decided to go back to his room. In the courtyard he ran into Father Attilio, sitting at the marble-topped table and sipping red wine. He wore his black biretta at a rakish angle, hinting that he might have drunk more than a glass or two.

"*Salve,*" the younger priest greeted his guest.

"Good afternoon." Father Weiss noticed that Father Attilio had a grim expression on his face. "Is anything the matter?"

"No, " he replied hesitantly. "Dr. Finestrella phoned."

"Ah! And?"

The pastor shrugged his shoulders. "He didn't tell me much. But he wants to see you tomorrow if possible."

"All right. What was his tone of voice?"

The pastor waved this away. "He always sounds the same. Short-tempered and superior." He took a gulp of wine. "Join me?" he said, nodding toward the flask.

"No thanks. I think I'll take a nap."

The pastor consulted his wristwatch. "Kind of late for that."

"What time tomorrow did the medico say?"

"Whenever you show up. That's the way he operates." Then he added, somewhat irrelevantly, "He may be an old atheist but he's an excellent physician."

"I got that impression too."

"I read somewhere that Hippocrates was also an atheist."

"Yes," said Father Weiss, "But I don't believe it is a precondition for becoming a good doctor."

"Indeed, neither do I." The pastor paused to take another drink, then added, "You know, I find out conversations stimulating. We should talk more often."

"I hope to have the opportunity. Good afternoon. I will

take siesta now." The old priest then went inside and went to bed.

.

EIGHT

The next day the old priest sat in Dr. Finestrella's waiting room reading a two-day old copy of *Corriere della Sera*. As usual most of the news was black as the headline ink. The forces of Chiang-Kai-shek and Mao Tse-tung were murdering each other in China. The British governor of Sarawak was stabbed and wounded by a local teenager. The Italian left-wing Socialists and right-wing Socialists were feuding. A group of Ukrainian fascists was captured in the mountains of Austria. Business as usual in human affairs. Did reading the papers, he wondered, distract him from his own troubles or multiply them?

The door to the doctor's office opened and a matron wearing an alpine hat walked out, followed by Finestrella. He bid his patient goodby and added, "*Signora*, don't forget to take the diuretic every day. And eat lots of parsley and drink tea."

She made a sour face and gestured with both hands. "Tea? I'm Sicilian, not English."

"You're a Sicilian with high blood pressure," he retorted. "Drink tea."

She left looking as downcast as a condemned prisoner.

He turned to the old priest. "You're next, Padre. Come in." Father Weiss put the newspaper back on the rack and followed the doctor, who closed the door behind him. He wore a serious expression as he showed his patient to a chair and peered at him over the top of his pince-nez.

"It's bad, isn't it?" the patient said.

The doctor wore a circumspect expression. "Well, as I suspected, you have tuberculosis." He went to his desk, got the x-ray plates and showed them to the old priest. "You see these cavities in the upper right lobe of your lung?" he said using a pencil to indicate the spot on the negative plate.

Father Weiss nodded, though he was unsure of what he saw in the ghostly skeletal image of his thorax and lungs.

"They probably show an infiltration of the bacilli that cause the disease. You follow?"

The patient nodded again.

"By itself the x-ray does not prove the case definitively. But combined with your symptoms . . ." His voice trailed off. Then he added, "I will also have to give you a tuberculin skin test to be positively sure of the diagnosis."

"How did I get it?"

The doctor shrugged. "You might have been infected practically anywhere. The disease is highly contagious. On a bus or train. Why, even in church. I suspect you've had illness for a long time and it's only recently become active."

"I see. Well, I've lived long enough. I will have to prepare myself."

"Don't be foolish, Padre. It's not a death sentence, you know. We have a treatment now: streptomycin. Have you heard of the drug? It's fairly new."

The old priest stroked his chin. "I believe I read something about it in the papers a couple years ago. Is it a certain cure?"

"Nothing is certain but it's highly effective, or so I'm told. I've never used it before." The small dark-eyed physician paced the room with his hands locked behind his back. He stopped near the photo of Mazzini that hung next to a chart depicting the human heart. He turned and faced the patient. "But I don't have the antibiotic here. I will have to order it from Palermo. I will telephone the supplier today. I hope to receive it soon." His tone was tentative.

"Do you anticipate a problem?" the patient asked.

"It is expensive."

"Not to worry. I have money. How much?"

The doctor rolled his eyes. "It depends."

"On what?"

The supplier. You see, the drug supply, like many other things on this island, is controlled by *Il Sindicato*."

The doctor's meaning dawned quickly. "The Mafia," the old priest said.

"I'll mention that you are a priest. It might bring the price down."

Father Weiss chuckled. "Or maybe raise it." He sighed. "No matter. I will try the drug. I am not eager to collect my heavenly reward just yet."

"That's the spirit!" said the doctor.

"How do I avoid infecting others?"

"Ah, you have to be very careful and fairly isolated during treatment. But you don't have to be a hermit if you take precautions. The disease spreads through the air so keep a lot of tissues on hand and always cover your mouth and nose when you cough or sneeze." As he gave the instructions the doctor walked over to the medicine cabinet and fetched an oblong box with the word "Kleenex" on it. "Here," he said, handing the object to the patient. "It's a product that the American soldiers brought over. I have plenty boxes if you need more. You can also buy Italian and German tissues in local stores if you run low. You can even use rags. But you must carefully dispose of the used tissues so that nobody else comes into contact with them."

"How do I do that?"

"Bury them, if possible, or shred them under a faucet."

Father Weiss mulled over the suggestions. Then he said, "I have a brazier in my room. Can I burn them?"

"Good idea."

The doctor then narrated a litany of precautions for his patient, who strove to concentrate on them as his mind made several detours to byways of doubt, self-pity, regret and even relief for having to face this crisis and change habits of a life time. But he knew one thing: He still wanted to live.

"Wait," he said to the doctor. "I have a journal. Might I make notes?"

"Of course."

The old Jesuit nodded and started jotting the instructions: He should wash his hands thoroughly after coughing or sneezing; avoid as much as possible visiting public places or interacting with many people; avoid public transportation.

"I must take the bus to get back to Taormina."

"Take a taxi instead. And try not to cough on the driver."

"Of course."

"If you have the money you might stop off at the department store Rinascente here in Catania and see if they carry electric fans. They have table models now. You can use it to circulate the air where you are staying."

The old priest wrote down this note.

A sly smile now played about the doctor's mouth. "Most of all," he advised, "you should avoid *intimate* contact with another person."

The patient heard this advice with an appearance of equanimity but something inside him churned.

"Oh, another thing," said the doctor.

"Yes?"

"Give me your cigarettes."

The patient paused for a moment, then fished the pack of *Gitanes* from his pocket and handed it over to the doctor who tossed it into a nearby waste basket. "And don't buy any more."

On the taxi ride back to Taormina a clutter of thoughts filled his mind. Was the doctor being sardonic in the comment about intimacy or had he detected some clue in the patient's manner or personality that led him to utter those words? He also worried that he already unknowingly might have infected somebody with the bacillus, which often does not show its grotesque face for many years after contamination. Furthermore he wondered about the reaction of Concetta, the pastor and others to the news of his illness and treatment. His mind meandered.

On the passenger's lap sat the box of tissues, which sat on another box containing a metal fan with four copper blades made in Germany. The old priest was lost in thought but the taxi driver, inspired by the Roman collar or maybe by boredom, wanted to talk. A Saint Christopher medal dangled from the rearview mirror. "So, Padre, where you from, if I may ask?"

"Originally from Germany. But don't hold it against me."

The driver rapidly made the sign of the cross. "Jesus, Joseph and Mary, not at all. Men of God all belong to the same race."

"I'm not so sure of that." The priest gazed out the car window at the passing villas. The fading sun painted them gold.

"God forbid I dishonor a priest in the season of Advent," the driver said, tightening his grip on the steering wheel as he maneuvered a switchback on the Corso Luigi Pirandello. "You know, Padre, I once intended to study for the priesthood."

"Yes? What changed your mind?"

"Ha," he said, making a familiar hand gesture of joining four fingers to his thumb and waving his hand in the air, conveying "Why do *you* think I changed my mind?"

The padre guessed, "You met a girl."

The driver shrugged an "Of course."

"Well, that must mean you didn't have a true vocation."

"Yeah, my blood ran hot. Now we got four kids and another in the stove. But I still love the Church, Padre. I go to Mass every Sunday."

"That's fine."

"And whenever I do something bad, I run straight to Confession. I don't want to be caught with a blot on my soul if I crash on the Corso. Driving a taxi is hellish enough." A cat darted out into the road, causing the driver to swerve the auto. "See what I mean?" Then he cursed and begged pardon for doing so.

"Don't worry," the Jesuit said. "It's a venial sin. Tell me about your children."

"I got three girls and a boy," he said, briefly taking his eyes off the road to look at his passenger. "Stefano is ten, Vittoria is eight, Carolina is five and Bettina is three. The are a bunch of wild animals and the girls are worse than the boy. But my heart belongs to them all."

"Certainly."

"And the Epiphany is close. It's right around the corner. *La Befana* has to bring gifts and sweets for all of them. And who do you think pays for that? I also got to keep the wife happy."

Father Weiss clucked his tongue in sympathy. He was aware of the fairy tale woman's role in Italy as a substitute for Father Christmas. He suspected the driver mentioned it as an inducement to coax a good tip from the passenger. Why not? he thought. In the spirit of the holiday.

Then the driver broke into song:

> "*La Befana vien di notte*
> *con le scarpe tutte rotte*
> *col capella alla Romana*
> *viva viva La Befana.*"

Father Weiss smiled in the back seat as he clutched the boxes in his lap.

The taxi arrived at the town gate and the ailing priest paid the fare and included a good tip. "Happy Christmas," he said, "and God bless your family."

"All the same to you, Reverend," the driver said before driving off.

The old priest stood there thinking, I have no family. Anyway, the man meant well.

He ordered rabbit stew and a flask of local wine in a quiet trattoria near the amphitheater. He chose the place because it was nearly empty and there was less chance of his infecting anyone. He was not coughing much now and he had his tissues with him. He had gone straight from the taxi ride to the trattoria to eat and gather his thoughts before having to go back and inform the Saint Anthony household of his diagnosis. Now and then he looked out the window at the darkening sky. He ate morsels of the tomato-sauced rabbit meat and looked around. The restaurant was a homely place with a crackling fire in the hearth and a polished zinc bar behind which sat an old woman knitting while a young man, presumably her son, tended to the customers. There was only one other customer besides the old priest, a local man whom he had seen once or twice before near the clock tower playing a violin for coins dropped into his felt cap lying on the tiles. The musician drank grappa and chatted with the bartender. As he ate, the old priest had a sense of unaccountable contentment, perhaps caused by the warmth of the atmosphere inside as the wind riffled the palm trees on the piazza. He had tuberculosis. So what? Moments in life when you experienced them deeply and truly could be detached from anticipations and fears. These moments, he felt, had an eternal quality. They were in fact not even "moments" for they existed out of time. He was alive! The man at the bar broke into laughter at something the other man said. And the spell was broken. He finished eating, paid the reckoning, returned to his apartment and went straight to bed. He awoke the next day to the crow of a rooster but strangely no sound of girls singing in the courtyard. After shaking off the cobwebs of sleep he realized that a mere week had passed since he first came to Taormina. It seemed to him much longer. He had slept soundly and unaware that Mount Etna had erupted again.

PART THREE — ASHES

ONE

Ashes fell like black snow on the courtyard behind the Church of Saint Anthony the Abbot. The old priest sat at the marble-top table and watched the cauldron of the volcano in the distance belch tongues of fire and pour undulating streams of lava down the mountainside. He had heard on the radio that the biggest flow was slithering at two miles an hour down the northwest slope threatening again the village of Maletto, the hamlet that at the last eruption was defended by a rocky ridge of cooled lava from ancient eruptions and escaped damage. Would the town's luck hold out this time? The river of lava already had annihilated many farms and groves of fruit trees. And several other vulnerable villages clung to the treacherous slopes. What would become of them? Only God knew.

"Eh Padre, what do you do out here covered with ashes? Go upstairs and I will fix you breakfast."

Concetta had made her usual wraithlike appearance. She

seemed always to move with the stealth of a cat.

He had not told her of his diagnosis yet. Would she ask? "Okay," he said. "But I will go inside the church first to pray."

She wiped her hands on her apron. It was a quirk of hers. "Yes, a priest must pray. It is part of the job. Well, suit yourself. But don't be too long. You need to keep up your strength. You eat like a bird."

"I read somewhere that birds eat ten times their weight."

She frowned at him. "I never heard that. You — how you say it? — You pull my leg."

"No, I truly read it somewhere."

She again wiped her hands on the apron, a white thing trimmed with lace. "*Beh*, come soon to eat. I have sausages today." She peered at him inquisitively for a moment and went away.

It was cold inside the church but free of ashes. He knelt in the front pew, joined his hands and looked at the tabernacle. He began to pray for the peasants and villagers in the shadow of the volcano, beseeching God to spare them to live full and happy lives. He prayed for them to prosper and find joy in their earthly existences. He prayed for them have the chance to savor the fruits of love. He prayed for the soul of Concetta's dead boyfriend.

"If you please, Reverend..." the voice said. He had slipped into the seat beside the old Jesuit. It was Ambrosio.

Father Weiss could not control his instinctive reaction to dart the boy a scornful look. Was it anger that had provoked him to this glower or jealousy? A legion of devils prodded him under the vault of the church. He said nothing.

The shepherd was surprised at the cool reception of the priest who had been so kind to him. "What's wrong?" he asked.

"Nothing, nothing," said the old priest, ashamed of having shown his mixed emotions. "What is it that you want, boy?"

"I am here to make confession. I want you to be my regular confessor."

Color drained from the German priest's ruddy face. "Me? Why me?" he stammered. He quickly realized that it had been a foolish question. He knew why he had chosen him.

"Because you are kind and understanding. Because I know that I can be honest and forthright with you."

The old priest looked around the church to confirm that nobody else was present. Then he said, "Let's go to the confession box."

They went and took the appointed places separated by the wooden lattice in the chestnut wood confessional.

"Bless me Father for I have sinned...

The confessor listened half-heartedly to the penitent's formulaic introduction to the sacrament. He had heard the words countless times before but now they filled him with suspense for what would come afterward. The air in the confessional was stuffy and he tugged at his collar to relieve the sensation of discomfort. But the act was useless because the discomfort sprang from a source other than miasma in the air.

"Yes, go on," the listener said in a gruff voice, omitting the endearments of "my son" or "my boy" that he earlier had used in exchanges with the lad. He was in no mood to soften the edges of the encounter.

The penitent hesitated.

The confessor was haunted by a vision of the boy's bobbing head in the movie theater.

Finally the boy confessed: "I have committed acts of sodomy."

"Again?"

"Yes, again."

"How many times since your last confession?

"Three times."

"Three! It didn't take you long to forget your vow to amend your life. It appears that you did not truly repent the other day."

"I'm sorry."

"Sorrow is not enough. You must make a sincere effort to reform. The sacrament of Confession is not a blackboard where you can wipe the slate clean to allow you to sin again. You must avoid the near occasions of sin."

"But, Father, I stayed away from that man as you advised me to."

"Did you stay away from movie theaters, too?"

There was a moment of silence. The lad said, "How did you know about that?"

"I was there."

More silence as the words sank in. Finally he said in a

chastened tone, "I know it is wrong but what can I do? Our farm is destroyed and the sheep cheese earns us little. Our father is old, at death's door nearly. I must support the family or we will starve. Maybe you want my mother or sister to become whores."

"So you should be a whore?"

"I already was a sinner. I was born a sinner. Look at it this way: I saved them from sin."

"That is sophistry, my son." The old priest's tone was softening. "You cannot justify sin by necessity."

"What does it mean, sophistry?"

"Look, there are other ways to earn money."

"I have no education or special skills. Playing the pipes earns a little but only in the Christmas season. What can I do?"

"Are there no charities hereabouts?"

"This is a poor region still recovering from the war. The governors are corrupt and the Mafia controls most everything. They have headquarters in Palermo but they are like the *polpi* we fish from the sea and put on our dinner tables, if we are lucky enough to eat well. Their tentacles reach far. They give you charity only if you play their game and that would mean committing even worse sins. We are rabbits caught in a trap."

"These mafiosi, they are Christians, aren't they? Have they no God?'

"Money is their god. And power."

The confessor brooded. The lad expressed himself well,

schooled as he was in the institute of suffering. He believed him to be sincere. And he sensed a true tenderness about him. He understood that he could earn a lot committing these acts and also that the boy was not exactly repelled by them. "Well," the old priest said, "the solution is not to continue down the path of sin. Are there no jobs in Catania, for example?"

"Well, a friend of mine in the village," the penitent said, "he got a job as a messenger in the city. He says the company that hired him is looking for more boys. But he had to buy a Vespa, those new motorbikes they make in Milan. They are expensive and my family could never afford one."

"What about a bicycle?"

"They are not fast enough and unsafe in the city."

The Confessor considered this. There was no canon law forbidding his intervening in a material way to help a penitent achieve the state of grace. He said, "Look here, son, you must promise me as I sit here as the intermediary of our Lord Jesus Christ to vow to stop these practices and repent of the sins already committed. And take heart, I may have a solution to your money problem."

"Oh, certainly I repent, Father," he said eagerly. "I sincerely repent. You are so kind. And I should tell you that I am still making the novena."

"Good. Do you know anyone besides your father who is sick in the village?"

The boy thought this over for a moment. "Well, there's the laundress on Via Roma. They say she has the cancer and has taken to her bed. She is a widow and her five children have gone to America."

"All right. Here's what you do for your penance. Gather wildflowers from the slopes. Of course, don't go near the volcano. Take the woman the flowers and try to cheer her up by staying for at least an hour talking to her. Don't discuss her illness so much but speak of pleasant things, like family and beauty and love. Speak to her of bread and wine; dancing and singing. Tell her jokes and remind her of folk tales. Fill her in on the village gossip. Pat her hand for physical comfort. That would be doing the Lord's work, following the example of Jesus. Better than empty prayers."

"Are all prayers empty?"

"No, but they often are. I've found it takes much practice to learn the true art of prayer."

"Can a person pray to acquire the art of prayer?"

The old priest smiled to himself. That was a good question, he thought. It had a metallic ring as it bordered on irony. It signaled a questing mind. "Yes, son," he said. "I suppose you can."

"If I pray hard enough will God change my nature?"

"What do you mean?"

"Will He stop making me seek love in forbidden places and make me desire women. He made me this way, didn't He? Why then can't he unmake me?"

The question rattled the confessor at his core. He too had searched all his life for the answer and could not find it. It lay at the heart of his own suffering.

The penitent had to repeat the question: "Can He?"

The old priest stumbled through locked rooms of his mind for a helpful reply. But this was the best he could do: "You must pray for the wisdom and grace to bear this affliction – for that is what it is, an affliction – as a test of your strength to win salvation."

They then recited the customary formulas and the confession ended.

The boy departed and the confessor sat shaken in the confession box wondering if he had the strength and sagacity to follow his own advice. Or if he truly believed in it.

TWO

Father Weiss sat before two spicy sausages with toast, coffee and an orange at Concetta's breakfast table.

"What took you so long, Father? Everything is cold."

He speared a sausage with his fork and took a bite. "It still tastes good," he said. He was getting used to her treating him like an errant husband rather than a celibate priest. He was tired of the phony reverence and respect he got from others just because he wore a Roman collar. With this woman you had to earn the respect and it was a refreshing challenge.

She poured his coffee. "Here, I reheated it." A pause. "So?"

He looked up from the breakfast with a quizzical expression. "What?"

She put her hands on her fleshy hips. "What took you so long?"

"Oh. In the words of our Savior, don't you know I must

be about my Father's business?" He smiled at her. "That was presumptuous, I know. I was hearing a Confession."

"From whom, a mass murderer? It took a long time."

"You know I can't discuss it."

She smiled in a false way, like a hyena. "*Beh*, I saw him leave the church."

They traded glances that seemed filled with cryptic meaning.

This was an opportune time, Father Weiss decided, to inform his hostess of the medical diagnosis. Anyway, he sensed that she was on pins and needles to know. So he told her the whole story, as related to him by the esteemed Finestrella.

"So don't worry," the old priest said, "I will take pains not to cough in your face."

Her bold brown face was etched with sympathy. She said, "I don't worry. Should I inform the rest of the household."

"Of course. If anyone objects to my staying here under these circumstances, I will find other lodgings."

"No one will object. I will see to that."

"I don't want you to twist arms."

"That's not my style, Padre. My strength lies in my voice not my arms."

He nodded appreciatively. "Yes, I know. In your powers of persuasion."

She nodded back. No words needed uttering.

After breakfast Father Weiss combed his still abundant

silver hair, took up his cane and beret and embarked on his mission. The day was warm for December and a light breeze brushed the fronds of the palm trees lining the Via Garibaldi. The Jesuit glanced skyward and observed that Etna appeared to have eased the temper tantrum, emitting mere sparks from the vents. The sea gulls, quiescent during the latest eruption, were now squabbling like a congress of senators. He wondered if the local populace's propitiations to Saint Agatha had worked their magic and somehow appeased the fire god. For the moment, at least. Faith can move mountains, it is said. So he supposed that it also might have the power to cool the anger of one mountain without changing its location.

He soon arrived at the tailor shop where earlier he had seen the U.S. Army motor scooter for sale. But the vehicle was not parked at the place where he first had seen it some days ago. He peeked over a stone wall to ascertain if it was in the garden. He looked here and there but it was nowhere in sight.

"Can I help you, Padre?"

The question came from the balcony above that featured a cascade of bougainvillea in clay pots. The voice belonged to a scrawny old man of bent posture but lively pale blue eyes.

The old priest removed his beret and, striking the pose of supplicant, said, "Good day, kind sir. Are you the gentleman who had a motor scooter for sale?"

The old man was wearing a white undershirt that exposed his birdlike breast muscles. "I am, Reverend." The narrowing of the sky-blue eyes signaled concern. "Is anything the matter with it? Does Tancredi complain that it doesn't work properly? Did he send you as his emissary? He never had the gumption to fight his own battles. With respect, Padre, remind him, 'Caveat Emptor.' He got the machine for a pittance and I gave no guarantee." His blooming indignation caused a tinge of froth to appear at the corner of his mouth.

The Jesuit at first was puzzled by the man's soliloquy but the last sentence prompted dawn to break. "Ah, you sold it," he said. "You misunderstand, Signor. I wanted to buy it from you."

The old man's face now was contorted into a gargoyle of incredulity. "*You* wanted to buy it? Forgive my asking but what for? Surely not to ride it yourself."

The Jesuit straightened his posture and tried to look insulted. "And why not?"

"I mean no disrespect, Reverend, but well, your age. Look at me. That's why I sold it."

Father Weiss smiled to show that he was not really offended. "No, you are correct. I wanted to buy it as a gift for a young person. May I ask to whom you sold it?"

"That no-account fisherman, Ottavio Tancredi. He said he wanted it to drive to work at the marina from his house in the hills. His jalopy broke down and he couldn't afford a new automobile." The gargoyle face turned into a theatrical mask of mock pity. "He always pleads poverty though the fish jump out of the water begging to be caught while the requests for the fine art of tailoring have gone poof! Since the war all the men buy their suits at the Rinascente department store and they all look like they came off an assembly line. Individual style has gone out the window and craftsmen like me have to beg for bread or sell our belongings to survive."

The man's jeremiad continued for a while as the Jesuit listened with half an ear. Finally, when the old man paused to rasp for breath, Father Weiss asked, "Do you think, sir, this Tancredi person might sell the bike to me?"

"Sure, he would sell his mother for the right price, not to mention his wife." The old man's smile bared a picket fence of missing teeth. He punctuated the statement by spitting a gob of morning mucus into one of the flower pots.

"I see. May I ask what the right price might be?"

"He gave me a paltry fifteen-thousand lira. Use that as a yardstick.

Father Weiss nodded. "Thank you. You are most kind to help me in the negotiation."

"Don't mention it, good Father. Anything to sandbag that cheapskate." The old man's veiny hand leapt to his mouth to indicate shame. "I suppose I am not being charitable. I take that back."

Father Weiss smiled. "Too late for that, I'm afraid. You saw the speck of sawdust in your brother's eye. But the Lord will forgive you, I'm sure."

'That's good to know," the old man said in hushed tones, after looking from side to side conspiratorially. "Especially as it comes from a personage such as your worthy self who has, I presume, influence in such high places." He cast his pale eyes skyward.

Father Weiss smiled again, observing to himself that all

Sicilians from the tailor to the tobacconist to the titled noble are skilled in the sport of rhetorical fencing. "You give me too much credit, but thank you." He made a slight bow. "Now, can you tell me where I might find the esteemed Signor Tancredi?"

"Yes. Take your saintly self to the *comune of* Ramacca about thirty-five kilometers above Catania, ask for the biggest ruffian in town since the days of the Saracens and follow your nose to the smell of bad cheese. That will be him. Oh yes, and don't forget to sample the artichokes. The place is famous for them."

The old priest now bowed more grandiosely. "Thank you. May all your scissors be sharp and your rulers run straight as you continue to practice your fine craft."

The tailor returned the bow. His crooked form had less far to travel in executing the gesture. He pointed a bony finger skyward and said, "Put in a word for me."

Father Weiss arrived at Ramacca via bus and taxi at the noon meal hour when the clangor of church bells filled the noxious air and the storekeepers lowered the metal shades over their shop windows. He often had coughed during the trip but kept the bacilli at bay with Kleenex. The taxi driver had deposited him at the foot of the hilltown and he began walking toward the municipal center with the aid of his cane. After asking many townsmen and townswomen where he might find the man he was looking for and receiving blank stares and philosophic shrugs he felt a tug at the sleeve of his black coat.

"I know where he is, Padre," said the tugger, a boy about eight years old wearing a soft cap and wool knee pants. "Follow me." The seeker was led to a piazza dominated by an imposing winged statue of Italia pointing a sword at the sky and holding an archer's bow in her other hand. The boy indicated a lone man seated under the striped awning of a sidewalk cafe. "That's him," the boy exclaimed, as if he had identified an exotic animal. "That's Signor Tancredi. I know him because he brings my mother fish when my father is working in the wheat fields."

The old priest squinted at the informer in a way that suggested that a secret might have been spilled. He handed the child a couple of coins that caused him to widen his eyes at his glittering good fortune. "Good boy," the priest said. "Do you say your prayers at night?"

The lad looked abashedly down at the cobblestones. "I don't know any," he admitted.

"Well, just speak to God from your heart. That is a prayer."

The boy wagged his head and scurried away, clutching the coins.

The man Father Weiss approached was too engrossed in the plate of pasta and broccoli set before him to to notice a foreign presence until the old priest cleared his throat.

He raised his beetle-browed eyes. "Yes?"

There are two attitudes of Italians toward churchmen: shallow reverence or deep suspicion. Tancredi apparently belonged to the latter caste.

"Signor Tancredi?"

A narrowing of the brow-shaded eyes signaling a boost of suspicion was followed by another monosyllabic "Yes?"

"My name is Father Anton Weiss and I am here on a bit of business."

The eyes of a cornered badger now changed into the eyes of a wary fox. He twirled linguine on his fork and nodded toward the empty chair. The old priest sat.

Tancredi swallowed, took a gulp of wine and asked, "What business?" He wiped his fleshy mouth on a cloth napkin.

The old priest measured the man sitting across from him as a scorner of ceremony. Here was no Bedouin pouring arak in a Saharan tent before trading horses for a Gatling gun. No Red Indian passing the peace pipe before swapping beaver furs for wampum. This fellow was either too guileless or not guileless enough for such behavior. This fellow got down to cases. And the old priest took the cue.

"I want to buy the motor scooter you recently bought from the tailor in Taormina."

The fisherman drummed his work-scratched fingers on the cafe table. "I need it to get to the marina. That's why I bought it in the first place." He waited for a riposte.

"I'll make it worth your while," the old priest parried.

The bargainer had a craggy face of burnished brown leather. It showed no emotion. "How much?" He idly brushed with his scratched hand a dusting of volcano ash from the cloth of the cafe table. Then he winked at the old priest, as if to say, 'The game is on.'

Father Weiss raised ten fingers twice.

Tancredi gestured dismissively.

"Five thousand lira is a good profit."

"So the old fart told you how much I paid. Look here, I had my mechanic put some work into the machine. She used to run like an old donkey. Now she runs like a racehorse."

"All right," conceded the German negotiator, though he was skeptical of the claim, "I'll offer twenty-five thousand."

A waiter brought coffee to the table. Tancredi didn't offer a cup to his table mate. As he poured sugar into the cup, he said, "I like my deals to be sweet."

The old priest surveyed the Piazza Regina Elena's big triangular tiles as he searched his mind for the next gambit. There were two ways to go: up the ante or...He rose from his chair with an eloquent shrug. It worked.

The fisherman stayed the Jesuit's departure by laying a hand on his wrist. "I will take thirty-thousand," he said.

"I will give you twenty-eight."

The fisherman shuttered his eyes and bobbed his head. "Sold."

The old priest resumed his seat. Reaching into his billfold he said, "You drive a hard bargain." He counted out the banknotes on the table under the fisherman's avaricious gaze.

"Aha, look who's talking," the fisherman said. He squinted at his table mate, sizing him up. "I knew that you were a cagey one at first sight. *Vecchio ma furbo.* Old but crafty. And I thought, 'The church has much money but this guy will be a tough pistachio to crack.'" He smiled. "Have a coffee and anisette with me. To seal the bargain."

"It would be my pleasure," said Father Weiss, leaning back in his chair.

After the bargain had been struck the wily fisherman changed his attitude from hostility to friendliness. He even arranged for a fellow townsman to deliver the machine to Taormina with the priest as a passenger as long as he paid the driver's fare back to Ramacca. Father Weiss put a handkerchief round his mouth and knotted it behind his head as he sat behind the driver on the winding roads. Thus he was careful not to contaminate the fellow.

The olive drab motor scooter was parked near the Catania Gate where the old priest now examined it carefully. It had run smoothly on the way to Taormina, purring like a Persian cat. So maybe the fisherman had told the truth about the mechanic's work. He passed his hand over the scooter's step-through frame and leather seat. As he did so he heard Serafina bray.

"Who belongs to this putt-putt, Padre."

Father Weiss looked up from the scooter. He hadn't noticed Ignazio and the donkey approaching. "For the time being, I do," said the old priest.

The sacristan appeared surprised. "Can you ride it?"

"I suppose I could but it's not for me. Let's say it is a Christmas present."

"Oh? For who?"

"A friend of mine."

The old priest stroked the rough carpet of the donkey's back.

Ignazio of the jutting tongue nodded fiercely without knowing why he did so. He was not the type to inquire further of such matters and his gestures somehow emphatically communicated that the book on the subject was closed.

"I know you are sick," the sacristan said.

The old priest nodded.

"We will take care of you."

"Thank you," Father Weiss told him.

The keening gulls wheeled in the blue-black sky above. After Ignazio and the animal departed the old priest coughed into a sheet of Kleenex and stained it with blood.

In the evening the Jesuit visited the library near the Clock Tower to reread the great poem of Dante. And so he killed some time. But that was ill-expressed. Reading such a work, the priest reflected, did not kill time but enlivened it with deathless sentiment. And when he emerged into the wide town square now shrouded in darkness, he felt refreshed and fueled with optimism. Even in *Inferno* the Florentine heard echoes of hope despite the early warning in the text about abandoning this virtue. He recalled Dante saying that he was comforted at the entrance gate of Hell when Virgil "with joyful mien had laid his hand on mine." Filled with these thoughts the old priest moved with his cane across the checkerboard plaza.

It did not take long for these positive feelings to evaporate.

As he passed through the Corso and arrived near the police station he saw a manacled young man being roughed up and shoved into a police car by two carabinieri. He thought he recognized the captive from somewhere. The car drove off.

Father Weiss sidled up to an officer who stood with his hands locked behind his back, watching the vehicle depart. The old priest noted that his uniform bore two stars on the epaulets.

"*Tenente,*" he said, "may I ask what the lad has done?"

The officer regarded the questioner through sunglasses. "Nothing serious," he said with a wry smile. "Just murder."

The old priest looked aghast at both the fact related and the offhand way it was told. The Latin race was known for bravura talk and the British for understatement. But, in truth, the opposite pertained in many cases. "And may I ask who was killed?"

"An Englishman staying at the Excelsior."

This revelation startled the old priest and prompted him to recall where he had seen the suspect before. He was Ernesto, the waiter who was a favorite of Reginald Bliss. He felt a catch in his throat as he stammered the next question, guessing what the answer would be: "Do you know the victim's name, Lieutenant?"

The officer, maintaining a magisterial air, produced a notebook from his pocket and riffled the pages. His index finger found the name: "Bliss, Reginald Bliss."

The Jesuit shook his head dolefully. "How did it happen?

The officer, who stood eye to eye with the tall clergyman, recognized his foreign origins and measured his words. "Well, Padre, the Englishman, he caught the boy stealing money from him in the hotel room. There was a struggle and the boy stabbed him to death with a bread knife. Meanwhile Etna was erupting. Something like this often happens, especially when the volcano is acting up. My Grandma used to say, the door to the Underworld opens and demons come down with the sulfuric ashes."

Father Weiss clucked his tongue.

"Don't waste your sympathy, Padre."

"Why do you say this?"

"The Englishman played with fire. He probably got what he deserved."

The old priest's face reddened. "Good Lord, nobody deserves to be stabbed to death."

The officer spat on the cobbles. "He was one of those perverts. A *finocchio*. One of the host of faggots that invades our land and corrupts our boys."

The old priest's tone of voice dripped with indignation. "Still, he was a child of God."

"A child of the Devil, you mean."

"I will not dispute theology with you."

The officer looked the old priest full in the face. "No, you have the better of me there with your background in the subject," he said. "I have not read the holy books. But I know from my experience the barbarities people suffer in this place. I feel more sorry for the young man. He is the real victim. Like most of them he was lured by the money. There is much poverty here. It's a hardscrabble life. I know."

"If you feel that way why did you arrest the boy?"

The imperious officer grunted, as if to say, where did this yokel come from? "Without such *tourists*," he said with a thick veneer of sarcasm, "Taormina would wither and die. So we have to send a message."

The old priest was silent for a moment. "What will happen to the boy?"

"They take him to the magistrate in Catania. He will stand trial and go to the penitentiary."

The Jesuit said, "If convicted." He was aware that the death penalty in Italy had been banned by the Constitution of 1947 after having been restored by the Fascists.

"He will be convicted," the lieutenant said flatly.

"I will pray for him," the old priest said. "And for the soul of his victim."

"Listen Padre, don't bother about the victim. His soul is already in Hell."

"You can't know that, son. God's mercy is limitless."

"If Sodomites enter heaven I don't want to step foot there."

Father Weiss wagged his head in sadness. "I will pray for you too."

The old priest walked off, his eyes cast down. He just then hungered for a cigarette. But he resisted the temptation.

THREE

Father Weiss set out the next morning to perform what the catechism books called a corporal work of mercy. He entered the revolving door of the gilded Hotel Excelsior and approached the front desk. "Ahem, young man," he said to the clerk. "You have a guest here, an Englishman. His first name is George. He was the friend of the man who, ahem, shall we say, met his Maker under unfortunate circumstances recently."

The falcon-faced clerk looked over his rimless eyeglasses at the visitor. "I believe you mean Mr. Penwood, yes?"

"I didn't know his last name. Is he still domiciled here?"

"He will check out today, Padre." The clerk, one of those paper pushers who adopted an air of dignity far above one's station in life, still regarded the old priest over his rimless glasses as he picked up the house phone. "Who shall I say is calling?"

"Bishop Anton Weiss," the visitor replied, elevating his own rank just to take the man down a peg.

"Certainly, Your Excellency," the chastened clerk said, hastily dialing the number.

The old priest exited the lift and walked down the lushly carpeted corridor to the room he recalled having visited on a recent night and the memory sparked a flashback to the hangover he had suffered from the bitter wormwood of the Green Fairy. He used the lion's-head brass knocker.

The door opened to the diminutive elderly form of George Penwood garbed in a Madras dressing gown. His red-rimmed eyes looked his visitor up and down. He had a grey stubble of beard and a cigarette dangled from his lips.

"Come in."

"Thank you." The visitor stepped inside the room, holding his beret and cane in two hands as his eyes swept over the untidy suite, bearing signs of packing for departure.

Penwood narrowed his gaze. "I didn't realize you were a bishop."

"I'm not," he admitted a trifle sheepishly. "I was just having a bit of fun with the hotel clerk."

"Yes," Penwood said, taking the visitor's beret and cane and placing them on a console table. "The man could use a dose of humbling." He nodded toward an armchair. "Please, have a seat."

Father Weiss sat down and his host sat on the couch facing him.

"So the priest lies," Penwood said.

"I confess."

Penwood waved his hand dismissively and said, "A peccadillo. Now, what can I do for you, Your Excellency?" He said the grandiose title with a sardonic drawl.

"I came to offer my sincere condolences. What a horrible thing to happen!"

The Englishman studied the flowers tufted into the Deco carpet. "Yes, it was horrible. Horrible, indeed." He shook his head. "But, you know, Reggie liked to play with fire."

The old priest observed to himself that the Carabiniere lieutenant had said much the same thing.

Penwood continued, "He was always taking risks." He looked contemplatively into the distance, reliving his grief. "He liked the danger. I am convinced of this. It added a *frisson* to his exploits." He squashed out his *Gauloises* and took a cigarette case from his pocket to light another one. He held the case out to the visitor. "Cigarette?"

Father Weiss shook his head, resisting temptation.

Penwood lit the cigarette and expelled a gust of smoke.

The old priest coughed into a Kleenex. Then he stuffed the tissue into his pocket and turned to gaze at the old *Florenzer*, excavating this word from the memory lode of his childhood. It was the German term his father and chums always had used, while snickering, to describe homosexuals. It was derived from the idea that *Florentines* epitomized the dandified ways of such men. The old priest now remarked to his surprise that in the present context the word echoed in his thoughts with tones of affection rather than disparagement.

Is that what I am? he wondered: an old Florenzer. The idea did not repel him.

He said, "Is there anything I can do to help you deal with your grief?"

Penwood played with the quilted lapels of his dressing gown. "We can talk," he said. "Can I offer you a drink of something?"

The old priest shook his head. "No, thank you." He searched his mind for a gambit to spur conversation. As a spiritual counselor he had learned it always was more effective to ask questions than to answer them. "Where will you go now?"

Penwood inspected his fingernails. "Back to Bath, of course."

"Is that where you live?"

"Yes."

"May I ask how you make a living?"

"I import wine."

"Ah, I see."

The Englishman had a ruminative tone. "Claret from France, Port from Portugal, Sherry from Spain, Chianti from Italy. Only the best, of course. The English are a race of wine snobs."

"How did you meet Reginald?"

Penwood had a faraway look. "I first saw him on stage. At the Theater Royal on Old Orchard Street. He was playing Lord Darlington in Lady Windermere's Fan. Typecasting, I should say. He was wickedly handsome in those days,"

The old priest nodded. "I can believe it."

"I was smitten. I showed up at the stage door with flowers and my calling card. A mutual lady friend made the introductions." He sniffled at the memory.

"You fell in love with him."

"Oh, yes. At first, I must admit, it was mainly physical. He dazzled me with his good looks, his youth and his glamorous profession. I was twenty years his senior. What he saw in me I'll never know."

"You do yourself an injustice."

These words caused the Englishman to widen his eyes in pleasure and wonderment that any man might compliment him in such a fashion in the sunset of his life. Particularly a clergyman.

"You are kind. Anyway, as the physical side of the relationship ebbed away we became kind of old shoe with each other. You know how it is." He stopped himself. "Well maybe you don't. But it happens to couples. Naturally he, ahem, *went astray* now and again." He sighed deeply and corrected himself. "More than now and again. But listen, I didn't blame him. Not in the least. He was always full of vinegar so I put up with it, As long as he came home to me. And he did. He always did."

The old priest was becoming emboldened to ask more intimate questions, out of fascination as well as the desire to play the role of a good listener. He asked, "Did you *stray* too?

"Never," he said with ironclad conviction. "Not my style. I play for keeps."

"That's admirable, I suppose."

"Besides, the flame on my candle burned lower, if you catch my meaning."

"I do."

Penwood took a deep drag on the cigarette, then asked, "Did you consider our relationship sinful?"

The old priest paused before answering. He said, "My church considers it so. I would not usurp God's position as the ultimate judge."

"A canny answer," the Englishman said. "Did you know that Pope Paul II was in the habit of committing sodomy with his pages?"

Father Weiss blushed. "I did not."

Penwood flourished the cigarette. "Of course I can't swear to this. I read it somewhere."

"All men are sinners," the old priest said flatly.

The roles of questioner and answerer now had been reversed. "Where are you from, Padre?"

"Germany."

"Where in Germany?"

"Lübeck."

"Well, what do you know! Your city was in a way responsible for damage to my house in Queens Square in 1942."

The old priest knitted his brow. "I don't understand."

"In the Baedeker Blitz. The Luftwaffe bombed us in retaliation for RAF raids on Lübeck and Rostock. We have a common bond. Isn't that nice!"

"I wish it weren't that kind of bond."

"I am sure we could find others," he replied with an impish smile. "If we looked hard enough." He rose and stubbed out his cigarette. "Well, I'm afraid I must finish packing. I have a train to catch."

"Of course," said Father Weiss, who also rose to his feet.

The Englishman stuck out his hand. "Thank you for coming."

The old priest gripped the offered hand. "Don't mention it."

As he turned to leave the Englishman touched him on the shoulder and said, "I wish I had what you have."

"What is that?"

"Faith. Faith that our lives are not hollow. Faith that the earth spins for a reason. Faith in the power of love. Faith, I suppose, in God."

"Yes. I believe I do have faith, though sometimes I am not so sure. It does not come easily. One has to fight for it every day. Like a soldier constantly at war against a powerful enemy."

"What enemy?"

The old priest rubbed his stubbled chin as if he were thinking along these lines for the first time. "I think the enemy is Reason. We are plagued with it. Faith lies outside the realm of Reason. It is a gift gained through prayer and grace."

Penwood looked baffled as he wearily shook his head. "Is that the best you can do, Padre?"

The old priest put a comradely hand on the seeker's shoulder. "Yes, it's the best I can do. Except to repeat what

Thomas Aquinas has said. Let's see if I remember the words: *To one who has faith, no explanation is necessary. To one without faith, no explanation is possible."*

The old priest exited the hotel and walked slowly back to his room. In the courtyard the three sisters were weaving and singing.

> *"Buona sera cari amici tutte quante le cristiane*
> *questa sera v'aggiu a dice della festa de rimane*
> *che dimane è Sant'Antonio lu nemice de lu dominait*
> *Sant'Antonio Sant'Antonio lu nemice de lu dimonio.*
> *Li parenti e Sant'Antonio una moglie gli vogliono dare*
> *ma lui non ne vuol sapere, nel diserte si fa mandare*
> *pe n'avé la siccatura de sta a fà una creatura*
> *Sant'Antonio Sant'Antonio lu nemice de lu dimonie."*

The old priest smiled paternally at the girls as he passed the fountain. He understood the gist of the song. It was about Saint Anthony in the desert outwitting the Devil and his blandishments. He entered his room to wash up before lunch.

FOUR

Concetta brought to the table a plate of pappardelle with sardines. Steam rose from the food, wafting odors of the sea and wheat fields to the old priest's nose. His appetite sparked. He had chosen to eat alone since the diagnosis to avoid any chance of infecting the others. Etna was dozing again so he ate outdoors, the sun peeking from the clouds. A honeybee droned over the fragrant plate.

The housekeeper wiped her hands on her apron and sat at the marble-topped table. She was careless of catching the illness, feeling armored by her wizardry. Her lively brown eyes flamed like a torch. "Eat," she ordered him. "You grow thinner every day."

He twirled a ribboned noodle on his fork and ate. "I'm hungry today," he said.

The woman wore a satisfied look. "Good. How is the cough?"

He gave an eloquent shrug.

"Much blood?"

"Some." The fresh sardines tasted delicious to him. "Not much." He took a piece of bread and soaked it in the sauce.

"You must keep up your strength."

He looked up from the food and smiled at her, showing gleaming dentures. "You are like the daughter I never had."

"*Pah!* And never will have." She poured red wine into a tumbler and shoved it across the table to him. "Drink up. It will improve your health and your mood." The noon bells pealed as she watched with narrowed eyes the old priest drinking the wine and eating the pasta and sardines musky with the mingled scents of olives from the oil and salt from the sea, embroidered with flakes of pepper green and pink and black. The sounds of brass horns from a religious procession somewhere in the distance melted into the wind. Another funeral? Another petition to the saints of Ionia? Another day in immutable Sicily.

He lay down his fork and looked at her. He said, "I expect the good doctor has not phoned yet?"

She shook her head. "It takes time. The request for medicine has to pass through many hands."

"Yes. So I understand. Including God's hands, I suppose."

She frowned. "That would put God in some bad company."

"Ha-ha. You have a quick wit."

"I inherit it from my mother and grandmother."

"Not your father and grandfather?"

She waved this idea away. "I don't know if you've noticed but the men around here are slow."

He laughed. "Yes, the goddesses of Greece often held the upper hand over the gods. Zeus was outwitted at every turn by his wife Hera."

"You know the old stories, eh?"

"I do. I am a Jesuit after all. We study the classic books."

"We here know them not from books. They populate the very air we breathe."

His handsome old face grew somber. "I have a question, Concetta. Do the people here believe not in a pantheon of gods and goddesses but in the one true God?"

The woman hesitated to answer. Then she said, "I will put it this way: many fear God so they must believe in Him. But they are considered benighted by the freethinkers and their sort. Since the end of the war, we have many Communists in Sicily who profess to be atheists. But they still cross themselves when they pass the church. So you tell me if Sicilians believe in God."

"Okay. Do *you* believe in God?"

"Hah! I knew you would get to this question. Here's my answer: It depends on how you define God."

The old priest nodded appreciatively. "I define him as indefinable."

"Good," she said, nodding in turn. "Then we believe in the same God." She rose, wiped her hands on her apron and left.

He continued eating.

After siesta the old priest dressed, checked his image in the bathroom mirror and decided he needed a haircut. He was about to head to the barber shop on the Corso where he often had observed juveniles loitering on the threshold smoking cigarettes and ogling passing girls. But then he remembered his illness and decided it would be wrong to subject the barber or other customers to the danger of infection. So he searched the bath cabinet and found a scissor that he used to trim the white straggles of hair at his sideburns and nape. Afterward he inspected his handiwork and decided it was good enough. Then he went outside to the garden where he hoped to sit for a time and distill energy from the glimpses of sunlight. On the way he passed Concetta, who was hanging laundry to dry.

"What happened to your hair?" she said with a sour face after removing a clothespin from her mouth.

He stopped in his tracks with a baffled look and touched the side of his head. "I gave myself a trim," he said.

"Jesus, Joseph and Mary," she declared. "As a barber you make a good shoemaker. You should stick to your paternosters." She pointed to a lawn chair. "Sit down there; I'll be right back."

The old priest meekly sat down.

She soon returned with a worn striped apron and a sharp pair of scissors. She tied the apron round his neck like a barber's smock. "*Madonna*," she said. "What a haircut! You look like Ignazio's donkey. Raise your chin."

The scissor began to snip first at the left side of his head, moving expertly as if it had a life of its own. Snip, snip, snip. Tufts of white hair floated to the earth, attracting yellow-breasted tits and other garden birds gathering nesting material. The barber's hands moved nimbly over the old priest's cranium, much like a subtle caress. He allowed himself to luxuriate in this rare sybaritic moment. Snip, snip, snip. And soon he was dozing again in the lawn chair. Concetta finished the haircut and left him there to return to her chores.

He awoke some time later when a horsefly hummed round his head and landed on his nose. He swatted the creature away. He had forgotten where he was but quickly reoriented himself. He had no idea how long he had slept. The air was chilly and the sun was low in the sky. He felt his newly cropped head of hair, rose and went inside to look in the mirror. He turned his head from side to side, admiring the housekeeper's handiwork. He knew she had many talents but hardly expected an expertise in barbering. The proof stood before his eyes. He smiled at his image, yielding to a moment of vanity. Though he had been told now and again throughout his life that he was handsome he never could see it with his own eyes. Maybe he was too habituated to the sight of his own face. Or maybe some inner feeling of unworthiness blinded him to the reality of his physical beauty. Now he could not help thinking, would Ambrosio admire his appearance? He donned his cloak and beret and ventured out to meet him.

As he walked down the Corso toward the main square

he looked toward Etna. The volcano now grumbled but did not spit. More villagers walked the streets than in the past few days. Life seemed to be returning to normality. In the square he came upon a vendor of roasted chestnuts and he bought a bag. He sat on a bench by a tree under the Clock Tower — the prearranged rendezvous point — and began cracking the nuts open and eating them. The air was cool. The chestnut shells attracted regiments of pigeons who marched around and pecked at them.

The old priest snacked on chestnuts and waited. The day before he had sent a message to the lad via the taxi driver whom he had come to know from his various trips to Catania and elsewhere. A current of anticipation electrified his senses as he waited. It was, he told himself, a feeling derived from the knowledge that he was on the brink of performing a paternalistic act of charity. He recently had taken pride in his priestly acts of comfort and counsel given to the Englishman and the American honeymooner. His gift to Ambrosio would fall into the same category, wouldn't it? He was doing God's work. Yes. He scattered bits of chestnut meat before the parading pigeons. The square was still dusty with volcanic ash. A fountain babbled across the way. And the old priest waited and ate chestnuts.

He finally saw the boy walking with an odd mixture of jauntiness and unease under the arched portal on the south side of the square. He looked here and there till he spotted the priest waving to him. He smiled and crossed the square with long strides toward Father Weiss. As he neared the bench under the big tree where his benefactor sat the smile grew broader and broader.

"Good evening, Padre."

The old priest nodded and stuck out the paper bag. "Have a chestnut," he said by way of greeting.

"Thank you." His hand dipped into the bag.

Father Weiss let his eyes sweep over the young figure before him. The sandy curls of his hair fell carelessly over his white onyx brow. One might imagine a a laurel wreath encircling his head, now hatless in the brisk December air. His light eyes conveyed a mixture of fire and ice and his delicately sculpted face radiated with the illusion of innocence. The septum of his nose curved pleasingly and his manly chin was cleft. He was dressed as usual in farm clothes that on his slender form appeared to his observer as the raiment of a prince.

"How are you?" the old priest asked.

"All right," the boy said half-heartedly. "But times are still hard."

"Have you been good?"

The lad raised his right hand. "I swear I have," he said after swallowing a morsel of chestnut. "And I have visited the widow with cancer, which made her very pleased. I too took pleasure in the visit. To help others boosts one'a own spirit. This I learned."

"A worthy lesson," the old priest said.

The shepherd sat on the bench next to the old priest and looked down at the flagstones. "Why did you want to see me?"

"All in good time. Let's have a coffee." Father Weiss rose, scattered the rest of the chestnuts to the squabbling birds and led his companion to a nearby cafe. They ordered two espressos and biscotti and were quiet for a while but the boy seemed fidgety.

"You didn't bring your pipes," the old priest observed. "Why not?"

"I had to let the bag and the pipes dry out. Too much moisture ruins them, you see."

The old priest nodded.

"Anyhow," the boy said ruefully, "my mood is too low to play music now. I cannot put my heart and soul into the playing."

"Ah, yes. I understand. A good performance requires a certain brio, doesn't it?"

"Yes, Padre. Do you play music?"

"I had piano lessons as a boy. But I wasn't very adept."

Ambrosio looked sharply at his benefactor. "Tell me about your boyhood," he said.

The old priest's cheeks reddened. "There's not much to tell," he replied, fiddling with the coffee cup.

"I don't believe that. Was your family rich or poor?"

The old priest hesitated, slightly taken aback by the frankness of the question. Then he said, "I suppose you would say we were rich by comparison to your condition. My father owned a candy company. He made marzipan."

"Oh. Many Sicilians make marzipan, too. It's a specialty here. I have an uncle in Siracusa who owns a marzipan store.

He fashions his own figures. But he is not rich."

"I guess he does it on a small scale. My father sold his goods all over Europe and even in America. But you are right — the Sicilians are the best designers of marzipan in the world. And they make the tastiest. The fruits and vegetables are astoundingly lifelike. And other figures. Why, I even saw a marzipan sheep in a store window off the Corso. Amazing."

"Yes, and they are handmade from almonds grown locally. As a people we have talent for many things. Except maybe keeping body and soul together." The boy looked sullen. Then his mood brightened and he said, "Tell me more. Where were you born in Germany? What is it like in the North? Does it snow even in the lowlands?"

The questions came like machine gun fire. And the old priest did his best to sketch the broad outlines of his early life and lineage. The diffident clergyman began even to enjoy the retrospection of his background and became flattered by the lively interest that the boy took in it.

Especially this boy for whom he had such strong and confused feelings. He did not want to admit to himself that he was in love with him.

"And did you have many friends?" the boy at one point asked.

At the question the old priest's face hardened into granite. "No, " he said haltingly. "Not many at all."

"I'm surprised by that. "You're so good-looking and kind."

"Well, I was quite shy." He sipped coffee and nibbled at

a biscotto. He seemed eager to change the subject. To dwell on such things had no good purpose and it clearly blocked the path to salvation. No, we should avoid such detours of the mind and memory. One must stay on the path of right-eousness and — what? — sanity!

"Surely you must have had one or two friends."

"My sister was my friend."

He waved this idea away. "Sisters don't count."

The old priest's throat grew tight with emotion at the memory of Helmut Feld in youth.

The boy noticed the gravity of his benefactor's demeanor and prosecuted his inquiry. "So you had a special friend," he said. "I can see it in your face."

"Yes."

"And you were betrayed."

Anton Weiss looked up in a startled way and said, "How do you know thus, my boy? Your intuitions are strong."

"Tell me more, Padre. It helps to unburden yourself, I'm told."

The old priest formed a sardonic smile. "Who's the Con-fessor now?" He paused before continuing. "He was a school-mate of mine in the Jesuit academy in Lübeck." The narrator gazed at Ambrosio. "You remind me of him. He is dead now. Killed in battle in the First War, before you were born."

Ambrosio chuckled at a thought: "Maybe I am his rein-carnation."

"Do not blaspheme." The old priest looked down at his big awkward hands, gnarled with arthritic tendons and ligaments.

"You loved him," the boy said point-blank, flashing a knowing smile.

The old priest looked up, startled, and he frowned. What did this whippersnapper know of love? he thought. Wet behind the ears, stinking still of mother's milk. And yet...

"I believe you are right," he finally said. "I loved him in a way."

"Were you *in* love with him."

Father Weiss showed his interrogator a flushed face but did not reply. He did not need to.

The boy nodded and asked, "What was his name?"

"Helmut. Helmut Feld," he said as if in a trance.

"Helmut," the boy echoed and laughed. "The Germans have such funny names. They don't sing like our names. They stab like a knife."

"Yes, you're right. They stab like a knife." And his facial expression showed the pain of a stab. Then he looked at the boy with an admiration that he could not suppress for his sensitivity and his beauty. What must it be like, he wondered, to spend day after day in the presence of such a perfect artifact of nature? What must it feel like to take him in one's arms? Of course, his conscience rebelled against these thoughts and he sought to banish them. It was terribly difficult when the evil spirit whispered in your ear. He finished his coffee, took up his cane and slowly rose to his feet, the apparition of Helmut and the fleshly presence of Ambrosio merging before his eyes to form a single identity.

"Let's go," the old priest said.

"Where?" said the boy, also rising.

"*La Befana* comes early. I have a present for you."

Ambrosio's eyes widened and glittered with expectancy and he followed obediently.

They walked south along the Corso and went through the Catania Gate to the parking place overlooking the hills and the sea. The old priest leaned on his cane. "There she is," he said, nodding in the direction of the olive-green motor bike.

The boy looked confused at first, his eyes scanning the vehicles parked there. "Where? What?" he said.

"The motor bike." He paused to collect his words. "It is my gift to you in the name of the Three Kings who paid homage to the infant Jesus," he added, lacquering his words with a veneer of sanctity, helping persuade himself that his motives were pure, rising above any desire to reap garlands of gratitude or affection. But the pleasure that shone from the lad's enchanting face was a reward from which he could not avert his eyes.

"Oh, holy Jesus," the boy said, rubbing his hands together, "how can I ever thank you? You are much too generous."

"Well, you can thank me by obtaining the job as a messenger and working to help your family. You can thank me by attending church regularly and leading a virtuous life. You can thank me by accepting with an open heart all the blessings of life that come to you and sharing your good fortune with others." As he recited these words the old priest felt a river of emotions babbling over him, feelings he could not control or even name. His voice cracked as he finally said," I want you, my son, to be happy." He reached into his pocket and produced a piece of paper with formal writing and stamps on it. "Here is the title to the vehicle. It is yours free and clear."

The boy's eyes were misty. He took the title and said, "It must have cost a lot of money. I can't pay you back."

"Did baby Jesus pay back the Magi? There is no need. Do you know how to drive that thing?"

"Oh yes," he said. "I have driven my friend's once or twice."

"Be off with you then. And God be with you."

"Does it have a full tank of petrol?"

"I'm not sure. Here," the benefactor said reaching into his pocket for a thousand lira note, which he handed to the boy.

Ambrosio gave his benefactor a penetrating lingering look. Then without warning he took the old priest's face in his hands and kissed him long and full on the mouth. A second later he slid on to the seat, started the motor and drove away.

The old priest was frozen where he stood, like Lot's wife. He gingerly touched the flame on his lips.

Concetta the housekeeper had observed the scene from the second-floor window.

FIVE

Later, lying abed in his room, Father Weiss relived the moment of ecstasy. He could not help it. He fingered his rosary beads and tried to pray but his ravenous mind could not be controlled. In his memory he drank and drank the nectar of the kiss. How could he avoid it? He had been in the desert for so long.

There was no denying that the act had caused the blood to flow from the caverns of desire to his crotch. Lord, this too was not his fault. He was reminded of something Leonardo da Vinci had said: "A penis sometimes displays an intellect of its own, moving without the permission of its owner." Leonardo was a genius, wasn't he? This was a biological fact and therefore no sin, the old priest thought. And the great painter also shared a passion for youths.

Father Weiss tried again to pray and erase the matter from his mind. He said all the prayers he had ever learned from the Our Father to the Hail Mary to the Glory Be to The Apostles' Creed to the Nicene Creed to the Prayer to St. Michael . . . And gradually he fell asleep. And he dreamt of a trio of angels speaking to him in Italian as they all waited interminably at a train station where the ticket office was closed and the dreamer fretted that he would not be allowed to board the train. Worse yet, he searched his pockets and found no money to buy a ticket. Then one of the angels gave him money. This angel had the face of Ambrosio.

The old priest's sleep was long and he might have slept even longer had he not a coughing fit forced him awake. The spasms rippled up from his ribcage to his throat. He made his way to the bathroom where he disgorged a rank stew of sputum and mucus and God knows what other liquids worthy of a witch's cauldron. Then he opened the taps and washed the red and green and yellow gallimaufry down the drain. He returned to sit on the edge of his bed and wipe his mouth with a tissue. He had almost forgotten how ill he was. He resolved to use the pastor's telephone as soon as possible to call the doctor to inquire about the arrival of the antibiotic through the various arcane channels dictated by the Byzantine local customs. He dressed and went outdoors. The day was grey and cool. The sisters did not weave and sing by the fountain. A lizard darted over the flagstones and up the side of the tufa wall that fronted the olive grove. It was too late for breakfast. He decided to walk to the cafe on the Piazza San Domenico for a cappuccino and toast. He bought a newspaper on the way.

He sat at an outdoor table rather than indoors to gain the fresh air that scattered the airborne imps of his illness. The cafe seemed empty of customers and a waiter soon approached the table. He was a lanky young man with fair hair and an obsequious smile. The old priest placed his order and sat back and began thumbing through the gazette. He tried to read the paper but could not focus beyond the headlines. Unbidden his thoughts fled to Ambrosio. And the kiss.

The kiss!

He cursed his own imbecility. The realization struck him like a hammer on an anvil: the boy was in great danger of getting his disease from the kiss. He left money on the cafe table and hurried off to find a way to warn him.

The taxi driver's name was Matteo. He wore a pencil-thin mustache and had a lazy right eye. But he was an excellent driver who knew every millimeter of the region's mountain roads like the furry back of his hands. And he did not charge an old maid's dowry for his services. Best of all, unlike most locals, he was not garrulous, providing the space for peaceful reflection.

As the old priest climbed into the back seat of the Lancia sedan Concetta stood watching him with her hands on her hips. She looked him keenly in the face.

"Where are you off to now, Padre?" she said in a gruff tone of voice that failed to disguise her concern. Having witnessed the kiss gave her extra cause to worry. Most Italian men were accustomed to kissing each other on both cheeks but not full on the mouth in a passionate way, not in public at least. And certainly not clergymen.

"I have an urgent mission," he replied. "I will tell you about it later."

Matteo gunned the motor and headed down Via Crocifisso, flanked by lemon groves and stately villas. The driver had been instructed to drive to Castiglione where the priest recalled that the lad lived. They would have to take a route down Mount Tauro to the state road overlooking Naxos, then climb again through foothill and mountain towns that lay in the shadow of the angry volcano. Matteo estimated the journey would take about an hour.

As he steered the vehicle the taciturn Matteo turned to his passenger and pointing to his AM car radio said, "May I?"

His passenger nodded.

He switched the instrument on. The driver was proud of the radio, a sign of his prosperity that few of his colleagues could afford in their autos. Soon the tenor voice of Francesco Albanese as Rodolfo in *La Bohème* flew over the air waves to resonate in the sedan as it curled its way to Castiglione, an aerie village overlooking the Alcantara valley.

Now, as the fictional poet of the opera marveled at the iciness of his lover's little hand the old priest's heart grew icy with the fear that he had played a role in endangering a young shepherd's life. And it struck him now that he did not even know Ambrosio's surname. But certainly it would be easy to trace the whereabouts of a young villager with such an uncommon first name, he thought. It was unlikely that there were even two persons bearing that name in a small mountain village unless they were related. He was determined to find the lad and warn him to consult Dr. Finestrella or another physician and immediately get tested for the disease. He also considered the possibility that Ambrosio was already in Catania at the messenger job but then he might find a friend or relative to get word to him. Or he might get the name of the company he worked for and drive to the city to tell him in person.

These plans and others rattled in the old priest's brain as he watched the back of the driver's gray head sway in rhythm to Puccini's music. He looked out the window and saw a signpost for the town of Fiumefreddo, the birthplace of Ignazio and Concetta. Then he said to Matteo, "It's a lovely opera, isn't it?"

"Si, Padre," said the driver, who rarely spoke unless spoken to and even then was a man of few words. "It is very romantic." Then Matteo fell silent again and listened to the music.

Romantic, the old priest considered. Yes, he supposed the opera was romantic in the Italian sense of love and death as two sides of the same coin. In the eyes of the church Giacomo Puccini was a sinner, having fled his birthplace of Lucca with a married woman and sired a son with her in open defiance of contemporary mores. Anton Weiss recalled as a young man reading accounts of the composer's escapades in the gazettes of North Germany. Indeed tales of the Tuscan musical genius's scandalous behavior reached far and wide. Since divorce was impossible in Italy in those days Puccini married the woman only after her husband died. But, the old priest reflected sardonically, the composer's disreputable behavior did not end there. His roving eye and infidelities fed fires of jealous rage in the wife, who suspected her husband of seducing their servant girl whom she threatened to kill and then booted from the household. As a result the girl poisoned herself, and her family had the corpse examined by a doctor who declared her to have been a virgin. This spurred the family to bring charges against Puccini's wife, who was tried and found guilty of slander and other crimes. The composer paid off the family and they dropped the charges.

My heavens! the old priest thought. Puccini's life itself was a grand opera composed by the Fates. He then was startled to recall a line from another Puccini opera, the somber *Il Tabarro:* "He who has lived for love has died for love." That was it in a nutshell. The dark romance of the Italian character. He shook his head in wonderment. The axiom made him think of the shepherd boy. Why?

The next signpost read: Piedimonte Etneo. The foot of the mountain of Etna. Much of the countryside here bore signs of the volcano's destruction — downed trees and ravaged wheat fields and vineyards under seething rivers of cooling lava flows. Father Weiss frowned and he cranked shut the car windows as Musetta tantalized Marcello with *Quando m'en vo,* the mocking Musetta's Waltz.

Now the Lancia sedan coughed and climbed toward, the

next town on the corkscrew route. The passenger, noting the Linguaglossa name, turned to the driver. "Matteo," he said, "I know what lingua means." He pointed to his tongue. "But what does *linguaglossa* mean?"

Matteo's eyes were riveted on the winding road. He shrugged and said, "We Sicilians call it LinguaRossa — Red Tongue." Then he pointed to the volcano. "A metaphor, Padre, for the tongues of lava that has plagued the village over centuries."

"I see," said the old priest, reflecting that the locals indeed had the gift of poetry and used it to salve their wounds.

The usually reticent philosopher behind the steering wheel broke character to add, "History tells us it was built by the Greek settlers upon a lava flow." Then he shrugged again and tuned his ears to the final act of the opera.

Ah, thought the old priest, the Sicilian talent for turning stones into bread.

At last the sedan reached the town of Castiglione. At nine-hundred meters above sea level it bestowed on the visitors grand views of the valley below. Etna lay to the southwest, smoking like a furnace. Matteo parked the auto on the Via Edoardo Pantano in front of the Basilica of San Giacomo. Father Weiss noted that the style of architecture was baroque, reminding him of Lübeck's churches except they were made mostly of brick, not stone and certainly not lava stone.

The old priest climbed out of the car, leaving Matteo behind the steering wheel. The first thing he noticed was how cold it was at this altitude. He shivered and clasped his cloak at the neck. He leaned in to the driver and said, "Be good enough to wait here while I explore."

The driver nodded and left the motor running so he could continue listening to the music.

Father Weiss looked from side to side, then up at the Norman castle towering over the town. There were as usual men in soft caps, smoking cigarettes and pipes and cheroots, seated at the various cafes that dotted the neighborhood. He assumed they engaged in debates not about the prospects of the next wheat harvest but on how the government in Rome was stealing them blind. He decided first to enter the basilica to ask God's help in his enterprise. He climbed the wide stone staircase and entered the church, which was dedicated also to the Madonna of the Chain ,whose statue adorned the main altar. The interior sparkled with white and gold decorations under ornate chandeliers. He knelt in the first pew and began to pray, looking up at the gaudy effigy who was revered as the patroness of the enslaved and imprisoned and of the community of Castiglione.

"Hear me, Queen of Heaven," he prayed in silence. "And entreat your Son to free me from the chains of my sinful passions. I too am enslaved in a way and imprisoned in a dark cell of carnal weakness. So help me please, I beseech you. I also ask that you help me undo an evil caused by my careless adventures with a young boy, adventures camouflaged by the pursuit of my priestly duty. Help me to find him and persuade him to get the help he needs to perhaps save his life. In the name of the Father, the Son and the Holy Ghost, Amen"

The old priest's knee creaked as he regained his feet.

He returned to the sunlit street and headed toward a cafe on the Piazza Sammartino where pensioners and idlers gathered. His inquiries about where he might find a lad named Ambrosio were met with blank stares and shrugs. The same reactions came from the men playing bowls in another nearby square. He was puzzled by his lack of success. This was not a large village and Italian townspeople were as gregarious as birds. Then it occurred to him to start asking women instead of men, who tended to be more suspicious of strangers, even clergymen, and more tight-lipped than the women. Women were naturally talkative and in any case had their ears cupped more closely to the ground. These were admirable qualities, Father Weiss thought.

The inquirer then approached a group of women washing clothes in a melodic fountain and doffed his beret like a gallant.

"Good day, ladies," he said.

The five women at first glanced at each other in wonderment, then looked at the suppliant with wide eyes.

"Good day, Father," they chorused in a tone more respectful than the one used by the menfolk. The sounds of scrubbing ceased, giving more play to the babble of the fountain. They waited expectantly for the clergyman to continue, their movements as stone-still as the lion carved into the fountain.

"May the blessings of God lighten your work," he said diplomatically, knowing that the daughters of Greeks, Arabs and Normans expected a certain politesse in such encounters. A ceremony of sorts. It was considered impolite to come straight to the point.

"Thank you, Father," they said in unison, and they glanced again at each other.

"It is a fine day," he said as a mountain wind whipped the hem of his cloak. He coughed and added, "Though a bit brisk."

They all nodded their heads.

"Perhaps you can help me find somebody," he finally said.

They traded curious looks and nodded again.

"I am looking for a young shepherd boy, a native of Castiglione. It is most urgent that I find him. I know only his first name: Ambrosio. Are you acquainted with him?

All the women shrugged as only Sicilian women can shrug. They shrugged not only with their shoulders but also with their elbows, hands, necks, chins and, yes Lord, even their eyes.

"Never heard of him," said their spokeswoman, who appeared older than the others.

The puzzle deepened for the old priest.

"Maybe he's from Linguaglossa," said another woman, who had sturdy arms and frizzy red hair.

"No," said the spokeswoman. "I know everybody there."

Father Weiss had an idea. He asked, "Is there a widow in town with incurable cancer?"

They traded looks again and shook their heads. A flurry

of comments came from different mouths: "Who's that?" "Not that I know of." "Poor soul, whoever she might be."

"You can ask at the hospital," said a round-faced young woman who wore a red kerchief on her head.

"Better still," said the spokeswoman, pointing down the street, "ask Lorenzo the postmaster. That snoop knows everything and everybody. It' a well-known fact that he reads all the mail."

"That sounds like a good idea," said the black-robed sleuth, returning the beret to his head. "Thank you and God bless you, ladies." He turned and left them chorusing thank-you's and returning to their laundry. He walked up a path edged by steep cliffs that fell to the valley below where the Alcantara River flowed. Flocks of sheep embroidered the hillsides.

Lorenzo the postmaster sat on a high chair behind a desk littered with bags of mail and rubber stamps. He wore a braided kepi affixed with a brass badge. He happened to be a dwarf. He raised curious eyes to the old priest as he entered the office.

"Sir Reverend," he said. "How may I be of service?"

"Good day, Mr. Postmaster," the old priest said. "May God be with you." He then had a small fit of coughing and Lorenzo gave him a worried look.

"Are you all right?" the postmaster asked.

"Yes," he said, wiping his mouth with a tissue. "Just a slight catarrh."

"How may I be of service?" he repeated.

Father Weiss told him briefly about his search.

The postmaster firmly shook his head. "No such boy lives here. Nor anywhere around here."

"You're sure?"

"I have been in the postal service for sixteen years. I know practically everyone in the province. You must be mistaken about the name. Maybe he goes by a false name. Some of the boys do that."

The old priest looked desolate. "Why? Why would they do that?"

The little man returned the question with a question of his own: "Where are you from, Father? If I may ask."

"Rome. And before that Germany."

"Where do you stay in Sicily."

"At San Antonio Abbate in Taormina."

"I see," he said, though the old priest had no idea what he saw. Then he explained: "Here's the thing. The better looking boys from the small mountain towns go to Taormina and Catania to meet the tourists and be free. The Sicilian girls are off limits but, ah, the tourists — women and girls, men and boys — they have looser attitudes and they look for adventure. Our boys take advantage of this. I hope, Reverend Father, you catch my meaning without taking offense. Speaking the truth can never be sinful, don't you agree?"

Father Weiss nodded, recalling how Concetta had told him a similar thing.

The dwarf postmaster continued the explanation. "Now, I could not follow their example." He threw his arms out wide. "Look at me. Nobody would find me handsome. In any case, the boys invent false names to protect from scandal and avoid dishonor to their families. So maybe your Ambrosio is really called Stefano or Marco." His big shrug added an exclamation point to the explanation.

The old priest hung his head, wondering how he would proceed. Imposter or not, the boy must be warned.

The little man then added, "I know what you might do. Consult the schoolmaster, Enzo Polizzi. He has class photos. Maybe you can recognize the boy who styled himself 'the food of the gods.' Come, I will direct you to the schoolhouse." He glanced at the wall clock. "They will just be closing for the midday meal." An orchestra of church bells tolled.

The postmaster locked the office doors and led the searcher up a steep side street that came out on the Piazza Lauria. The school was there, housed in a fine old stone and stucco palace painted matte yellow and festooned on the second floor balcony with an array of regional and national flags. Lorenzo the postmaster left the old priest at the wooden doorway arched with white limestone. He doffed his cap and bid the visitor good luck. Then he waddled on bowed legs over the cobbles, undoubtedly toward his own midday meal, which no self-respecting Sicilian would forego. As the old priest watched him fading into the distance he could not help wondering if he had a wife and family. He had been too reticent to ask. The door to the school was ajar and the visitor entered unannounced. Making sure that the top of his cloak was unclasped to show his clerical collar, he approached the receptionist's desk and announced himself to the person sitting behind it, a thin and sallow-faced woman of uncertain years whose upper lip was shadowed by a distinct mustache.

She showed no deference to his collar as she picked up on the desk an old-fashioned candlestick telephone and dialed an interior number. She whispered into the mouthpiece, nodded her head and replaced the receiver on the hook. She pointed to the main staircase and said, "He will see you. One floor up and turn right. The maestro's name is on the door."

The old priest bowed curtly. "Thank you."

Enzo Polizzi had the owlish face of a scholar and the corpulent body of an epicurean. He looked to be about fifty years old. He sat behind a desk cluttered with academic paraphernalia — books and papers, a small brass bust of the blind poet, a black telephone and a miniature version of the Italian tricolor on a balsa flagpole stuck into a marble stand. At the approach of the Jesuit, he beamed, rose from his seat and stuck out his hand. "Come in, come in, Reverend. I am honored to meet you."

Father Weiss did not grasp his hand. "You will forgive me, Maestro, if I do not shake your hand. It is for your protection, I assure you. You see, I have an illness and I would not want to take the chance of infecting you. But I am equally honored and I thank you for agreeing to see me on short notice."

The teacher's large dark eyes narrowed a little behind round rimless eyeglasses. "I understand," he said and pointed to a chestnut swivel chair.

The old priest sat.

"So now, how do you like the rumpus Hephaestus has been making lately?" Polizzi said, using the Greek work for Vulcan in the certain belief that a learned Jesuit would understand the reference

"Ah yes," said the visitor. "I guess he's up to his old tricks. But it's no joking matter, is it? These antics have tragic results."

The teacher wore a sober look. "Indeed. " He sighed. "I suppose you would call it the wages of sin." He idly rearranged papers on the desk. "Now, how can I help you?"

Again the old priest summarized his quest as the teacher sat back in the swivel chair and listened intently as he fiddled with a pencil. The narrator included the news he had just learned that the boy probably used an alias. When the recitation ended Polizzi said, "May I ask: why the urgency to find him?"

Father Weiss looked down forlornly at the mosaic floor. He said, "It is a private matter."

Polizzi fiddled with the pencil. "All right," he said. "I should not assume the role of Father Confessor. I transgress the boundaries."

This comment caused the blood to rise to the old priest's face.

The schoolmaster said. "I beg your forgiveness. I have a tendency to be an old snoop. I am by nature curious. It is sometimes a failing but it led me to become a scholar. Like most things — including the forge of Etna — it is a double-edged sword."

Father Weiss noticed the speaker's soft manicured hands manipulating the pencil. He wore no wedding band.

Polizzi looked at his wristwatch. "Look here," he said. "Let's discuss this further over a plate of pasta with fennel and anchovies. There's a good *casalinga* place right around the corner. What do you say?"

"O.K., but I must pay."

"Not on your life. You are my guest."

The steam rising from their plates wafted odors of the sea and garden and wheat fields to the diners' nostrils. The trattoria was rustic-looking with ceramic plates on the great stone walls and a blazing fireplace to fend off the chill mountain air. The brass andirons were polished to the gleam of the southern sun. The head of a wild boar surmounted the fireplace.

Polizzi ate daintily. His serviette was tucked into his collar, covering his paisley tie and blue wool vest. His table manners were impeccable. He wiped his mouth after every sip of wine. He twirled the spaghetti on his fork with scientific precision.

The old priest picked at his food; he lacked appetite.

"Come, eat," Polizzi urged his guest. "Since you are ill you should eat. May I ask the nature of your illness? I don't mean to pry but, as I said, I am a curious person."

"I have TB," he blurted. "Don't worry, though. I know how to protect people with me." He showed the schoolmaster his wad of tissues. "I make sure the little airborne devils don't escape when I cough."

"Are you being treated?"

"I am seeing Dr. Diego Finestrella in Catania. Have you heard of him? We soon expect a shipment of a new serum from Palermo."

"Yes, I know of Finestrella. He has a good reputation so I suppose you are in capable hands. But surely eating well will make you better able to resist the disease."

Father Weiss made an effort to eat more and silence reigned for a while.

The schoolmaster cleared his throat, then asked, "How did you meet this boy?"

"I met him in the Greek theater at Taormina where he came to earn money by playing the pipes."

"Ah, like the goat god Pan."

"No, the bagpipes, not the flute."

"Of course. The shepherd's instrument, brought here from the Orient by the Roman legions. Many of our boys play the bagpipes." He paused to eat. "What does he look like."

Father Weiss tried to describe Ambrosio's angelic appearance. Wait, he was not called Ambrosio, was he? The old priest still felt a stab of betrayal from the boy's deceit.

The listener took a slug of wine and said, "Many of our boys look like that too." He paused with a sly smile. "We have beautiful boys in these mountains."

The old priest looked down at his plate where he fiddled with his fork. He said, "You say 'our boys' in a paternal way. Do you have children of your own?"

The schoolmaster dabbed at his lips with the napkin. "No, I am a bachelor." He paused for effect before adding, "Just like you."

"I see."

The schoolmaster laid down his utensils and leaned back in the chair. He inspected his fingernails in a manner that suggested that he was carefully composing his next conversational gambit. Then he looked up. "I sense, Reverend, that we are kindred souls."

Father Weiss pondered this, then asked, "In what way?"

"In many ways, I believe."

"Such as?"

"Well, for one thing we are both steeped in the knowledge of Greek culture."

"We Jesuits are avid students of the great civilizations of Greece and Rome and many other classical studies," replied the old priest, refusing to take the bait.

"Yes, yes, of course but you seem to have a special affinity for the Greeks. As I do."

"I don't know what makes you say that."

"Pure instinct. People like us have a knack for recognizing our fellows."

"Do we?" The Jesuit had drawled the words that cloyed his mouth.

Polizzi narrowed his eyes at the old priest. "This boy," he said, "was he not your Hyacinthus?"

The Jesuit scholar grasped the mythological reference to the male idol of Thamyris and Apollo. "He most assuredly was not," he said sternly.

"Perhaps not in deed but in desire."

"You are impertinent." He began to rise. "I thank you for the meal"...

Polizzi reached out his hand and placed it on the old priest's arm. "I beg your forgiveness. I am too blunt. I did not mean to offend you. Look, I'm sure you are chaste. You cannot help your proclivities. I do not blame you."

Father Weiss was frozen to the spot. "Perhaps I blame myself, " he croaked.

"You must know that it is wrong to do so. You are as God made you."

The old priest wearily sat down. "I don't know what to do. I am afraid that, like Apollo, I may have accidentally delivered the fatal discus to the boy."

Polizzi raised his hand, calling for the check. "All right," he said, "let's find out who your Hyacinthus really is."

SIX

On the way back to the schoolhouse the old priest and his companion made a detour to bring cheese and wine to Matteo, the driver, who now hummed to the music of Verdi. Then they scaled the weathered cobbles of Castiglione, adding the latest scuffs to centuries of wayfaring sandals and shoes and boots. The thinness of the mountain air caused the diseased visitor to breathe heavily on the climb. But this did not override his eagerness to learn the identity of the lad whom he felt compelled to help despite his trickery. Etna sputtered and glowered in the distance.

The schoolmaster nodded to the mustached receptionist and led the way as he ponderously climbed the baroque marble staircase to the second-floor office where he offered his guest a seat as he rummaged through metal file cabinets. He soon produced a sheaf of photos that he carried to his desk. He sat heavily down opposite the priest and shoved the photos toward him.

"Here are group photos of students in your friend's probable age group," Polizzi said. "Look through them. See if you recognize him."

Father Weiss's hand quivered a little as he handled the black-and-white photos. The kids were dressed in uniform, girls seated in the first two rows and boys standing in the last two rows. Smiles were non-existent on such a formal and serious occasion, creating the record of a family milestone in a semi-literate community. The results were destined for prominent places on the pitted walls of peasants and marble mantels of the bourgeoisie.

He had to examine only three photos before he found the face of his young Judas.

"Here's the rascal," the old priest said, pointing to the figure of a boy in the middle of the back row. He wore a tweed coat and knee britches. Polizzi nodded sagely. "So. This is your shepherd kid? Hah!"

"Yes, that's him," Father Weiss said expectantly.

"Well, well, well. Rascal is the right word for him. He bamboozled you from start to finish."

"Tell me."

"His name is Giuseppe Monte. To begin with, he is not sixteen but eighteen. He passes for younger." He sat back expansively in the swivel chair, straining the buttons of his waistcoat. "And he is far from a poor shepherd boy. That is all pantomime. His maternal grandfather owned a large vineyard in Randazzo and the family was well off. When his father abandoned the family before the war, taking up with a

French lady tourist and heading north, the mother had a nervous breakdown. The grandfather helped financially but he was an aloof and reserved man who hardly served as an adequate father figure for young Giuseppe. And, naturally, he made no secret of his disapproval of his grandson's effeminate leanings."

The old priest interjected, "A perfect formula for rebellion." His heart again was softening toward the boy.

"Indeed," said Polizzi. "The boy grew sullen and withdrawn. Though obviously intelligent, he failed his studies. Six years ago, when he was only twelve, he began to run errands for the Germans. Of course this ostracized him in the community. But he seemed to relish the role of outsider. He was like a proud leper who displayed his wounds in the public square."

The old priest clucked his tongue. "Poor boy," he said.

"More recently he began hanging around with the village Bohemian, a self-styled modernist who slapped paint on canvas and camouflaged a lack of talent behind the facade of abstract art. You know the type. His name is Pietro Scotto and he lives in a garret near the Norman castle. His sexual orientation is obvious to all with eyes to see and ears to hear."

"So he abused the child, took advantage of his degraded mental state."

Polizzi wore the omniscient smile of Buddha when he said, "If you ask me, it was a two-way street."

The sound of clambering feet and excited chatter came from the staircase as the students were returning from the midday meal. Polizzi looked at his wristwatch but made no move to dismiss the visitor.

Father Weiss, however, took the cue. "Well then," he said. "Where can I find the boy?"

The schoolmaster looked gloomy. "That would be a problem."

"How so?"

"Well the village gossips are buzzing like crazy. They say that Giuseppe and the painter left town yesterday for the mainland. Went to make their fortunes in Rome, they say. Left on a green scooter that the boy somehow had got ahold of." He hunched his shoulders. "I don't think we'll be seeing them for a while."

The old priest's handsome weathered face was etched with lines of despondency. What could he do? he thought. Could he chase a couple of wild hares to Rome?

Polizzi patted his visitor's arm. "Listen," he said. "You have to give up trying to find this boy. It's no use."

"I suppose you're right," the old priest said in a low voice. He rose from the chair, holding his cane and beret in his left hand. "I give you my sincere thanks. And my blessing."

The schoolmaster rose too. "Don't mention it," he said, shaking the old priest's gnarled hand. "May I turn the tables, so to speak, and give you a bit of advice? Spiritual advice, if you will?"

Father Weiss nodded. "Go ahead."

"Stop flaying yourself like Saint Dominic. Don't leave

your bloody footsteps in the snow."

The old priest climbed into the back seat of the taxi and Matteo started the motor. The driver caught sight in the rearview mirror of the dejected expression on the passenger's face but said nothing, waiting for instructions.

"Let us return to Taormina," the old priest finally said.

"Yes, Father."

The radio was silent now, befitting the gloom. The winter sun on its western path was faintly visible in a minacious sky. And Etna reigned on the throne of earth. Unknown to novices like Father Weiss, Typhon the snake-footed monster strained against his chains in Tartarus, creating a tinderbox in the bowels of the earth. Matteo, who was of primeval lineage here, sensed the danger. "Reverend," he said, "I will take a different route back to town. The volcano is angry."

Father Weiss, looking puzzled, said, "How do you know?"

"There are tremors under the road."

"I don't feel them."

"I do,' Matteo said as he maneuvered the car down the steep winding road from Castiglione to the sea.

"How do you know where to go?"

The laconic driver merely touched the side of his nose.

Soon Matteo's prophecies were taking visible form. A burst of steam and ash shot from the vents of the geologic beast and darkened the sky.

"Roll up the windows," the driver commanded and the passenger quickly obeyed.

On the road trip the canny taxi driver made a dizzying number of detours and backtracks as the passenger, who could hardly see his own hand in front of him, sat back and mumbled prayers. Though the windows were shut Father Weiss could sense the noxious air and he covered his mouth and nose with several tissues and stifled his coughs. He blamed himself for endangering the boy and did not want to compound the error by placing Matteo in peril too. Now he could see some brightness in the sky ahead through the front windshield.

"The olive groves are on fire," the driver announced as he made another sharp turn onto a dirt road. The curtain of night fell fully on the countryside and the headlamps of Matteo's car spotlit a rutted road that seemed in the old priest's eyes to lead to nowhere. Still Matteo drove through fields and shuttered villages, past farmhouses and roadside shrines dedicated to the Virgin Mary and Saint Agatha and Saint Anthony and all the reborn demigods of the pre-Christian pantheon, none of which, the old priest thought, could stop now the onslaught of lava and steam and ash. And the old priest coughed into the tissues and prayed. Meanwhile Matteo with almost mystical reserves of confidence drove and drove, somehow avoiding the spitting wrath of Etna.

At last Father Weiss could see the lamps of the coastal road and the sign for Taormina. Matteo turned to look at him with a reassuring smile. The taxi entered the road where a few other autos were heading for Naxos and Messina and other places where they might seek refuge from the eruption. Here and there the old priest saw knots of villagers walking by the side of the road also seeking safety. Matteo began to whistle the "Brindisi" from *La Traviata* as he turned the car off the main road to make the ascent to Taormina. The effervescent song marked what seemed a triumphal moment.

SEVEN

Father Weiss used his cane and Matteo's hand under the crook of his arm to assist his climb out of the back seat. He was breathless and tired. He reached into his pocket and found some banknotes that he stuffed into the driver's hand.

Matteo looked at the bills. "This is too much, Padre," he said.

The old priest frowned at the suggestion. "No, it is not too much. Take it with my blessing and thanks. You are a wonderful driver and a man of fine instinct."

"All right, Padre. I thank you for your kindness."

The old priest sketched a blessing over the driver's head. "Have a holy and happy Christmas," he added.

Matteo then climbed into his car and drove past the Catania Gate into the night. Father Weiss watched him go. Then he turned toward the house and saw Concetta standing on the balcony, one arm akimbo at her waist. She narrowed her eyes at him disapprovingly.

She said, "Here you are at last. I was worried about you."

He coughed into the tissue, then said in a faint voice, "I'm all right. "

She looked skeptical. "You don't appear so good. Come, have supper with us."

"I'm not hungry."

"You must eat to keep up your strength."

"I cannot eat tonight." He did not say what he thought: that he had not the strength to eat or to talk or to climb the stairs to the dining place. Not now. Not tonight. The events of the day had drained him of energy. "I thank you for the invitation. But no." He started heading for the door to his apartment.

"I have good news for you," she said.

He stopped in his tracks. "Yes?"

"Dr. Finestrella phoned. Your serum has arrived from Palermo."

Was this good news? He supposed so. Of course it was! But somehow it did not lift his spirits, dissolve the cloud that hung over him in the wake of the boy's betrayal and his own sense of guilt over having possibly infected him and his impotence to do anything about it.

"That's fine," he said to Concetta with little enthusiasm. "That's very fine."

"You must go to Catania first thing tomorrow," she urged.

"Yes, first thing tomorrow," he agreed, failing to moderate his apathetic tone of voice. "I am bone tired. I must sleep now. Good night."

"Yes, good night," she replied, concern stealing into her voice.

He shut the door behind him.

He drank his usual glass of Marsala to help quiet the cough and made ready for bed. He was content to lie down but tossed and turned on the pillow. Despite his weariness sleep evaded him as kaleidoscopic bursts of color appeared behind his eyelids and a torrent of disconnected thoughts flooded his mind. Oh, he wondered, how will I ever warn the wayward boy about the danger? He was so lovely and yet so deceitful. So lovely. And then a vision came into his mind of mighty Etna, implacable Etna, beneficent Etna bellowing over Sicilian Ionia with breath aflame, spitting cinders on the land and spreading ashes over the ancient stones. Ashes, the detritus of fire. Ashes, symbols of regret. Ashes…

He finally fell asleep.

There are many kinds of sleep. There is the sleep that resembles a cruise over water where the sleeper rocks and sways on the surface of slumber; there is the trance-like sleep where reveries dance in the depths of the dreamscape; there is the syncopic sleep when the brain appears to shut down and blackness descends. This last was the kind of sleep that fell on Father Anton Weiss on that chilly night in December 1949 in Taormina, Sicily.

He awoke to find himself fully dressed in pristine new clothes. Somehow, the fact did not surprise him. He rose from the bed. He felt light, almost weightless. It was as though the sackcloth of advanced age had been lifted from his shoulders. Oblique rays of dawning light filtered between the slats of the window shutters. He went outside and soon reached the Piazza IX Aprile, the misnamed main square of town. No-one was about. No shopkeepers swept the stones in front of their stores, no old women in black clothing with downcast eyes and tented hands headed to mass. The hands of the clock in the ancient tower were immobile.

Then he saw him.

It was Angelo Michele standing at the foot of the double staircase leading to the doors of the Church of Saint Joseph. Or was he Michele Angelo? As usual the tour guide presented a dazzling picture in his white clothes and platinum hair. He smiled at Anton Weiss and walked toward him.

"Come with me," the tour guide said.

Anton Weiss followed him, caught in his magnetic field. He was led to the north end of the plaza where stood an ornate two-wheeled traditional Sicilian cart yoked to a white horse. The wooden cart was decorated on every inch of its length and breadth with colorful tableaus of local history and artful geometric designs. The horse's tack, bridle and mask were also brilliantly adorned. The viewer admired the carvings and paintings even for the craftsman's lack of restraint; the excess itself enhanced the artistry, he thought.

The guide climbed on the cart and took the reins. He offered his hand to Anton Weiss who clambered aboard. "Where are we going?" he asked.

"We are going sightseeing," the guide replied with a be-atific smile.

"What is the fee?" the passenger asked.

The guide chuckled. "Don't worry about that." Then he clucked his tongue and flicked the reins.

"But where exactly are we going?"

The guide gave him a sidelong glance. "To the Alcantara Gorge," he said.

Anton Weiss nodded and leaned back in the seat as he listened to the clop of the handsome horse's hoofs on the paving stones. He knew of the Gorge, the geologic wonder carved by the Alcantara River that flowed in both directions from Mount Nebrodi past the slopes of Mount Etna and to the sea. The basalt columns of the Gorge were sculpted by nature's hand over many millennia into monuments of stone. The passenger was eager to finally see this beautiful place. Somehow he knew: There would be nothing but beautiful places from now on.

They reached the Gorge, a Gothic cathedral fashioned by the Deity whom Anton Weiss would soon meet face to face. Angel and man climbed down from the painted cart and waded hand in hand through the shallow foaming waters of the river, surrounded by the ribbed vaults of solidified lava, the pointed spires and flying buttresses of igneous rock and the stained glass of vitrified cascades. The place was perfumed by citrus groves and filled with the melodies of falling water. The guide cast his beneficent smile on his companion, a smile that bore the message that he knew what Anton Weiss now also knew.

A grotto lay ahead. The wayfarers looked at each other and headed toward it. Anton Weiss's soul brimmed with joy and perfect happiness. He apprehended the secret now. This was real. This was real! And all else had been illusion.

And Anton Weiss — infant, boy and man — walked through the grotto and into the light.

THE END

ABOUT THE AUTHOR

Anthony Mancini, former director of the journalism program of the English Department of Brooklyn College, is the author of seven novels, many of which have been reprinted in international editions in Japan, Finland, Romania, Spain, France, Germany and Holland.

Mancini spent his early career as an award-winning reporter and editor for 20 years at the New York Post, covering a wide range of subjects, from crime to politics to the arts.

He contributed articles to many national and local newspapers and magazines, including the New York Times, Washington Post, New York Magazine, Cosmopolitan, Travel & Leisure, Self, Penthouse, Gentlemen's Quarterly, New York Daily News.

A native New Yorker, Mancini was born an identical twin to Italian immigrants. His father was a carpenter, mother a housewife. He worked his way through high school and college as a delivery boy, golf caddy, bus boy, dishwasher, short-order cook and in many other odd jobs.

Mancini's first novel, Minnie Santangelo's Mortal Sin, was a Reader's Digest condensed book selection. Another novel, Talons (1991, was a Literary Guild selection. He also has published: Minnie Santangelo & the Evil Eye; The Miracle of Pelham Bay Park 1982; Menage; The Yellow Gardenia and Godmother.

Tolmitch is proud to offer Mancini's latest novel, Ashes, the story of a retired Jesuit priest who sojourns in volcanic Taormina in 1949 where he confronts the ghosts of his past and the shades of his foreshortened future.

Professional Societies: *Society of the Silurians, Authors Guild, Authors League of America, Professional Staff Congress.*
Awards: *2017 Peter Khiss Award for Excellence in Journalism given by the Society of the Silurians; 1976 First Prize in Feature Writing by the Uniformed Firefighters Association.*

**Read more Anthony Mancini stories at
Tolmitchebooks.com**

CPSIA information can be obtained
at www.ICGtesting.com
Printed in the USA
JSHW061019030423
39804JS00003B/22

9 781637 605257